THEY LOOKED LIKE HUMANS, JUST SMALLER...

Lon Howel's spaceship crashed out of overdrive into a star system he was unfamiliar with. It was a last, desperate attempt to elude an alien spacecraft that was chasing him. The alien ship had come from a saffron-colored star near the Crab Nebula; and though the ship was much smaller than Howel's, it had attacked with weapons far in advance of anything known to Terrans. Lon knew that he and his three-man crew would have to sacrifice their lives before they could allow the aliens to trail them back to mother Earth. So Howel and his people headed toward a nearby green planet that circled a ringed yellow sun in the distance. But when they landed on this unknown world they found a race of people more unique than anyone could have imagined—a people that seemed both hyper-intelligent and primitive at the same time. Unfortunately, they also seemed to have a very casual attitude toward impending danger, an attitude that could prove disastrous since a massive alien fleet was bearing down on their world.

FOR A COMPLETE SECOND NOVEL, TURN TO PAGE 81

ABOUT MURRAY LEINSTER:

Murray Leinster…was born William F. Jenkins on June 16th, 1896 in Norfolk, Va. His writing career began in 1916 with the publishing of his first story, "The Foreigner" in *The Smart Set* magazine. Although he is considered one of the great writers of the science fiction genre, in his early years Leinster wrote many tales in other genres: jungle, mystery, horror, and western. Leinster broke into the science fiction field with his story, "The Runaway Skyscraper," which appeared in a 1919 issue of *Argosy* magazine. During the '30s, '40s, '50s, and '60s Leinster was a regular contributor to well-known pulp and digest magazines such as *Astounding Stories, Amazing Stories,* and *Weird Tales*. Leinster is considered the father of "parallel universe" stories with the publication of his 1934 story, "Sidewise in Time." During his long career Leinster was nominated for many writing awards, including the coveted Hugo Award, which he won in 1956 for his novelette, "Exploration Team." During his science fiction career, Leinster published over 30 novels and over 170 short stories. He passed away on June 8th, 1975.

PLANET OF THE SMALL MEN

By
MURRAY LEINSTER

ARMCHAIR FICTION
PO Box 4369, Medford, Oregon 97504

For more information about Armchair Books and products, visit our website at…

www.armchairfiction.com

Or email us at…

armchairfiction@yahoo.com

CHAPTER ONE
Attack from Nowhere

STARS exploded into being on every hand with all the suddenness and violence of catastrophe. The *Marintha,* battered and scarred, came out of overdrive into normal space with the frantic speed of a bat just streaking out of hell.

A lifeboat blister was gone. There was a swollen streak all along her plating on one side as if something improbable had played upon her briefly and softened the metal so that it bulged from the air-pressure within. One of her atmosphere-fins had been blown jaggedly off and there was a gaping hole in an after-compartment.

Lon Howel saw the great ringed sun off to one side, swimming grandly in space with its attendant family of planets. It was a yellow sun, sol-type except for the ring telling of some ancient satellite which had blundered inside Roche's Limit and splintered into dust.

THERE was a green planet not far from the *Marintha.* But somewhere there was that slug-shaped other ship—smaller even than the *Marintha*—which against all reason and probability and even possibility had attacked the Earth ship with insensate ferocity near a yellow planet many, many light years back toward the Crab Nebula. The attack was preposterous, because the evidence had been overwhelming that there could not be another race in all the Galaxy that human beings needed to fear.

But there was another race. The bulbous ship—rather like a loathsome slug in outline—had not only attacked the

Marintha without warning but its first fire had hulled the exploring-yacht and shattered an atmospheric-fin. Worse, when Lon threw an overdrive in absolutely automatic response to danger, the bulbous ship had been able to follow.

It went into overdrive too, and for the first time in all history meteor-detectors rang a strident, continuous alarm signal while a human ship sped through emptiness at two hundred times the speed of light. Which meant that another solid object was within detector range and stayed there.

The slug-ship had a matching course and velocity. It was capable of pursuit even in overdrive. To remain within a quarter-million miles of a ship at nearly two billion miles per second could not possibly be an accident. It was pursuit.

Lon Howel didn't believe it at first. Then he tried evasive tactics—in overdrive! They didn't work. And he tried to outdistance the ferocious pursuer by overloading his drive, adding forty more light speeds to the safe maximum. The pursuer matched it—which was something to make Lon's face turn slowly gray as he realized its implications.

Travel in overdrive is trying at best. Even a week in overdrive with the knowledge that an enemy trails one—an enemy one cannot battle—is worse. But a seeming unending flight during which it becomes apparent that one's pursuer mockingly refrains from annihilating you merely because he wants to be led to your home planet, which will be practically defenseless against him—that is far worse.

So Lon Howel cut his overdrive and the stars exploded into being all about him. He counted two seconds while abstractedly noting the ringed sun and the nearby green planet. Then he stabbed home the overdrive button again.

And there was the snapping rasp of an arc somewhere, a shout from the engine-room—and nothing happened. The arc died and the smell of scorched insulation was in the air for an instant before the air-changer cleared it. The *Marintha* was still in normal space, a ringed yellow sun in the distance, and there were the two—no, three—no, four planets circling it.

Caryl came quickly through the door into the control room. She said quietly, "The overdrive's gone, Lon. The energy surge when you cut it out wrecked the very heart of it."

Lon said heavily, "There's a good trick gone. We might have gotten away. I don't know how good the slug-ship detectors are." They had spoken of the enemy ship by its shape, lacking any other information save of its enmity and its power to destroy. "But if there was any delay at all it got out of detector range before its pilot could come out of overdrive too. And I figured I'd be off on a new course before he could pick us up."

Caryl nodded. Once they had decided that their pursuer was waiting to be led to the planet from which the *Marintha* had come, they had taken time to plan every maneuver carefully. Even the two-second pause in normal space had its reason.

"We should have destroyed our star maps before now," said Lon coldly. "We should have bombs on hand to blow the *Marintha* to atoms. Since we've stopped leading the way home they'll stop playing and take us. Of course we must die so we can't be drained of any information.

"Get busy destroying all our navigation stuff, will you? Set everybody at it. I'm going to head for that planet yonder. If we can land on it we may have time to duck before they can find us. By the color and sun it should be an oxygen planet."

The *Marintha* was plunging toward the green world on interplanetary drive as he spoke. Caryl nodded and went back out of sight. There was no time for sentiment now. The *Marintha* was one of literally hundreds of exploring craft out in space from Earth.

Humanity was expanding with splendid confidence. The days of romantic exploration had returned. The cracking of the problem of speed-faster-than-light had set men free from their own solar system. The Mathewson discoveries of the basis of pathogenicity had wiped out all fear of plagues from alien micro-organisms.

The solution of the mystery of the Lost Race had seemed to ensure that humanity could have no enemies—because the race that had been mankind's forerunner had apparently been a galaxy-wide culture, which had perished by its own act and had left no potential enemies of its descendants alive. So it had seemed.

Humanity had been sallying forth to occupy and populate a galaxy with an estimated three to four hundred million habitable planets awaiting its coming. Anybody could take a yacht or a colony ship and go out and find a planet that was his for the taking. But the *Marintha* had found an enemy. And any race that could trail in overdrive had humanity at its mercy.

There was the smell of scorched cellulose—a heat ray on star maps and navigation records. The air-changer battled valiantly with the smell. It strengthened and weakened as new batches of paper and records were thrown into the cone of intolerable heat. The *Marintha,* though, was unarmed.

The heat ray was designed only to clear away vegetation around a landing place on a strange world. Hand-weapons had seemed all that any ship needed to carry. An antiquated gun, shooting explosive bullets the size of one's little finger, was the most dangerous device on the ship. Superson pistols were adequate protection against any form of wild life smaller than an elephant.

The *Marintha* was doomed. Only if she could get down somewhere on the planet below would there be even a faint possibility of a lease on life for the four humans on board. And they had an obligation greater than self-preservation.

To be captured alive or even in dying to furnish information by which an enemy race could learn of the whereabouts of humanity would be a form of treason so monstrous as to have no name. Lon did not even think of seeking to save his own life or Caryl's or either of the others. It did not occur to him to try to compromise with the stark necessity of dying.

AN unwarned Earth might be subject to attack. The slug-ship had weapons humanity had not dreamed of. The beam that made one whole side of the Earth ship's beryllium-steel hull bulge out like wet paper—the fraction of a second delay in getting into overdrive would have drained her of air and left everything intact for an enemy's inspection—that beam was not only unknown but unimagined by men.

The weapon that had blown off the atmosphere-fin and holed the hull and sent the lifeboat spouting off in flaming fragments had never been conceived. It was not a matter of material missiles. It was something else. Humanity, warned, might turn its thoughts to warfare and arm itself. But humanity now was defenseless.

So Lon sent the *Marintha* plunging toward the green planet. He tried not to hope, but it was hard to refrain. In a fiftieth of a second the slug-ship should have overshot the place where the *Marintha* had cut her overdrive field.

It should be seconds before the fact could be noted and interpreted and it was possible that, with haste to introduce errors, the slug-ship might be trivially off-course and actually out of detector-range when it got back.

If it hadn't stopped and turned about in less than five seconds it would be ten thousand million miles away.

To be within a quarter-million miles of the exact line—meteor-detector range—and a quarter-million miles of the correct distance would be superhuman.

Lon found himself casting his mind ahead feverishly. If he could get to ground. If he could conceal the ship under water or in towering vegetation! If he could somehow hide on a planet from pursuit he could not evade in space, then the crew of the *Marintha* might contrive something either to defeat and destroy the slug-ship—or to escape with the news of its existence and, inevitably, that of the alien race that had made it.

The disk of the green planet grew and grew. Lon piled on every ounce of acceleration he dared. He saw a blue sea and polar ice-caps. He saw a cloud-mass looking like a blob of white, overlaying green land and blue sea alike. The round face of the world almost filled the forward screen and his speed was so great that he could not possibly stop short in time to land on the near side; he must circle and ground on the farther hemisphere.

He swung the battered little explorer yacht back on its course and began to apply deceleration. Careful math was needed for such a task but he did not intend to ground gently at a predetermined spaceport. Anywhere on the far side of a ten-thousand mile disk would do. The deceleration built up and in spite of himself he hoped.

Then the alarm rang stridently.

He set his lips and abandoned all flimsy and now impractical plans for continuing to live. He flung the *Marintha* about again, end-for-end. He plunged for the planet's face once more, crushing acceleration pushing him hard against the pilot's seat. He changed course a little.

There the sea looked deep—very deep. He had hit atmosphere at full interplanetary speed. If the *Marintha* didn't break up and reach ground only as a shower of incandescent metal droplets, at least she'd plunge down to the very greatest depth of this unknown sea and the slug-ship would never be able to locate or recover her.

Caryl climbed through the door and struggled to his side. "No chance, Lon?" she asked quietly, panting a little with the strain of fighting such acceleration.

"Not a prayer," he said briefly. "Sorry," Then he added steadily, "I wish you were back on Earth, though."

Something flamed past the *Marintha's* hull. It was a near miss—a miss by feet only. A second and third and fourth followed—all near misses and all on one side.

"Trying to make us sheer off," said Lon evenly. "We could go around the limb of the planet and they know it. They don't want to riddle our hull for fear of losing useful data. But they've got to. We'll hit that deep now, I think, even if they smash us first."

He switched on a stern visiplate.

The slug-ship was still so far away that it was invisible. But its location was in no doubt. As he looked a thin pencil of ravening flame sprang into existence, seemingly reaching from infinity to the hull of the fleeing space-yacht. The *Marintha* reeled.

Another and another and another of the instantaneous bolts winked into being and each time the *Marintha* shuddered under the impact. Her drive went and her gyros. She hurtled on toward the planet, turning slowly now and quite helpless to avoid a crash. Acceleration ceased. Lon reached out his arm and put it around Caryl.

"Tough luck," he said wryly. "Nice to have known you, Caryl. Look me up on the other side, will you?"

She kissed him, very white. There was a rending crash as another bolt struck. The slowly tumbling little ship was near indeed to the green world. A rotating port showed it, so near and so huge that they could only see a part of its surface. It was so near that it was suddenly down. They fell and the details of its surface grew more distinct.

"I guess eight hundred miles," said Lon, "and before the instruments went we were hitting a hundred and twelve miles a second." He held her fast. "Be seeing you."

The surface of the planet toward which they fell was abruptly blotted out by a flaring incandescence. That was the air, compressed by their fall, heated by compression to a blue-white.

CHAPTER TWO
Death from the Sky

THEY felt nothing. They waited for the ports to break through and all the interior of the ship to fill with the incandescence that would snuff out life before they had time to know death as it took them.

But nothing happened—nothing. The incandescence died away. They felt all the sensations of free fall—absolute weightlessness, unreasonable giddiness. The inherited panic that has come down to men from the ancestors of the Lost Race itself.

But the vanishing of the incandescence hinted that their fall was being checked—which was impossible. Nothing external could have slowed the fall of the yacht without shattering its hull and crushing the life out of its occupants.

Air screamed past the wrecked *Marintha*. From the thinnest of whistlings at the upper limit of audibility it became a high-pitched shriek, then a squeal, then a moan, which went down and down the scale. And Lon Howel looked sick with dread as it appeared that something was acting to break their fall without any sensation to tell of it.

He watched the screen. Revolving, it showed the thickly green-clad planetary surface below, the distant, curving horizons, then a sudden glimpse of a sky already glowing blue between the fading stars. In that path of sky there were futile flashing lightnings, stabbing at the *Marintha* but stopped at the ring of the atmosphere.

The features of the planet's surface swelled before their eyes. They would not hit the deep part of the sea. They would strike the shallows near a continental shoreline. Lon clenched his fists. No—they would strike on land itself. It was outside of all reason or credibility, but they were not plummeting downward any longer. They were descending swiftly but that was all.

When mountains were discernible as separate swellings of the ground they were merely in a dive beyond that of an atmosphere-flier. When a mountain crest reared up level with them they were descending not much faster than a parachute. But they felt no braking. Their sensations were still those of free fall.

Then there were trees rising to meet them and the *Marintha* crashed into a monster pile of interlaced branches and foliage, caromed off and splintered a group of slender stalks, growing straight and tall—and suddenly reached solidity with a bone-shaking crash, tumbled over and was still.

When the final crash came Lon was holding Caryl close, trying to use his body as a cushion. He succeeded. His head rang from a knock that came of the final turnover but Caryl was unharmed.

He got dizzily to his feet. "Everybody out—fast! If the slug-ship put some sort of tractor on us to keep us from smashing we've got to get away before they start fishing it back up out of atmosphere! *Outside!*"

He shouted it through the door from the control room. He helped Caryl, ignoring a trickle of red down his cheek. The four who made up the crew of the *Marintha* ran for the exit-port.

Caryl was first out the side-port—now on top of the hull with the ship lying on her side. She jumped to the ground, followed by the others. There was Burton, big-game hunter extraordinary and engineer for the private expedition. There was her father, a biologist of note on Earth but on this yachting cruise through light-centuries of space a zestful ship's cook.

They were bruised and battered by their landing. Without exception, they still did not quite believe that they were alive. But they went swarming out of the wrecked space-yacht and Lon snatched up what hand-weapons he could and joined them in scuttling off into the jungle, which almost hid the ship.

Again nothing happened. They ran and panted and scrambled until they were a mile away. There they stopped, gasping for breath. Lon passed out Superson pistols. He gave the antique firearm to Burton. There was a heat ray with which they could build fires. That was all their equipment.

They had abandoned the *Marintha* because they certainly had not checked her headlong drop to destruction, yet it had been checked. They waited for the battered punctured hull to rise and go heavily and preposterously toward the sky. Human science said a tractor-beam was theoretically impossible yet something had slowed their fall!

BUT the wreck lay still. They were in a jungle almost without underbrush. Most of the trees had a communal habit of growth, of straight stalks, which put out branches that presently put out other branches toward the ground, to take root and nourish yet other straight stalks, which would put out other branches.

There were no calls as of birds or insects, but a tiny musical humming seemed to come from nowhere in particular, forming a background-noise never plainly heard, yet always preventing the silence from being oppressive.

Lon ceased to watch the wreck. He scanned the sky instead. There was no sign of the slug-ship that had attacked without challenging some thousands of thousands of parsecs away and had pursued without respite but failed to follow them into atmosphere.

"Queer," he said, frowning. "Our friends certainly aren't scared off. What's keeping them?"

Burton said meditatively, "They could think this is our home planet. Have you any idea what system this might be, Lon? Could they be hunting an Earth-colony now that we've gone to ground? Perhaps hunting a city? Would there be humans here, do you think?"

Lon shook his head. "There aren't more than a couple of dozen actually colonized planets so far—with people on them in thousands or with settlements bigger than villages. The odds would be millions to one against even a single plantation here."

Caryl's father said, "What checked our fall, Lon? You didn't. We were really splitting space wide open. You meant to crash, didn't you?"

"We were hitting a hundred-twelve a second," said Lon curtly. "Most meteors hit Earth's atmosphere at around forty-five. We should have vaporized in the air and if anything was left it should have plunged into what looked like an ocean deep back yonder." He jerked his thumb toward the horizon. "We agreed it was more important not to give them anything to work on than to save our lives."

"Quite so," Caryl's father conceded.

"There was incandescence in front of the forward ports," added Lon, still scanning the sky. "Then it stopped. Our fall slowed progressively. I thought the slug-ship had slapped something on us and was pulling us back."

Burton suggested, "Maybe they can't lift the *Marintha* because a tractor-beam doesn't work in air. Or maybe she's too heavy for their stuff."

"To which," said Lon, "there are two answers. One is that we were decelerated from over a hundred miles a second to almost zero in a pretty short time, so whatever did it had plenty of power. The other is that it *did* work in air. The longer we were in atmosphere the slower we fell. And it worked on us as well as the ship."

Caryl's father said mildly, "The planet where the slug-ship jumped us was a chlorine planet. The vegetation was yellow, and it was a white-dwarf sun. Maybe they haven't landed because they've no equipment for working in an oxygen atmosphere."

"Not likely," said Lon. "Any spacesuit would do."

Then Caryl suggested, "If there's something that checked our fall—and there was—maybe they ran into it when they started to follow us. Maybe they noticed something working on their ship and got away fast. We would have if we could. We did when the slug-ship jumped us. At least we tried."

LON blinked at her. He had ideas about Caryl but every so often she startled him by showing brains that had very little to do with his feelings for her. This was such an occasion.

"You've got something there," he said, as he thought it over. "If the Slug started down after us and ran into something the creatures inside didn't understand and couldn't smash—they'd back off in a hurry! Right?"

"But then what?" Caryl asked. "What'll they do now? Fumble around a while. Or try to get word back home? Will they try to find a way to get at us or yell for help to wipe us out of space? If you're right about them backing off, we've a chance to go on living."

Then Caryl's father said, "And what are we going to do with it?"

"Plenty!" said Lon evenly. "All the human race is out exploring as if the whole Galaxy was a glorified picnic ground. No idea of danger. No idea that any ship needs arms. But whoever or whatever is in that slug-ship is dangerous and arms are needed against them because they don't like us.

"They don't like us so extensively that they've gone to a lot of trouble following us—they think home—with the idea of wiping us out. They'll do the same thing to any other Earth ship they come upon. Next time they may succeed— and there will be Earth, helpless as a sitting duck.

"They'll smash it like an undesirable bug if our friends up yonder are typical of their race. The thing we've got to do is to get a warning to Earth. If it costs all our lives it'll still be dirt cheap."

"I was in the engine-room," said Burton drily," when something a foot across stabbed through the plating and hit our main drive. It missed me by inches and I had just time to get out and slam the door before the vacuum got me.

"But I did see that our drive is smashed. It's not even scrap-iron. Some of it's melted and some of it simply splashed. It can't be repaired. We need a new drive to navigate and we couldn't make one in a thousand years."

"Our overdrive's gone too," said Caryl unhappily. "It blew out. We might repair it but—"

"I agree on the need to warn Earth, Lon," said Caryl's father, "but I don't see the ghost of a chance."

"Neither do I," admitted Lon. "I guess we've got to make one."

Something moved across the sky very far away. It had flapping wings. Burton shaded his eyes. All of them watched it. It certainly wasn't the slug-ship. But the atmosphere was faintly misty and they could not tell whether it was something quite small and nearby, flying slowly, or something of considerable size a long way off, flying fast.

"It could be alive," said Burton. "This would fly here, naturally. But we don't know yet what sort of things they are. There's a flying carnivore on Spicus Four that—"

"Could it be a flying machine?" asked Caryl uneasily.

Burton shrugged. "A few days back," he said drily, "I'd have smiled at your ignorance, Caryl. Right now I simply don't know."

The evidence had seemed conclusive, just a little while before, that there could not be any intelligent race in all the Galaxy except the human. There was a race that lived on a chlorine-atmosphere planet near the Crab Nebula, but the odds against a second nonhuman race remained enormous and certainly chlorine-breathers would not have made a colony on a yellow-sun satellite.

"As far as that creature's concerned," agreed Lon, "there's no way of knowing. The chances are it's simply something that wings grew on naturally. But I've got a feeling there's something unusual on this planet that will either kill us or help us. I think we'd better try to find it in a hurry. We need to send that warning to Earth and we may not have much time."

The four humans were not very impressive just then. They were battered and disheveled. They possessed exactly what they had worn on the *Marintha* plus the hand-weapons Lon had snatched up at the last instant.

Their ship was a hopeless wreck and when in repair it had been unable either to escape or to defy the slug-ship, which presumably, still hovered overhead out of atmosphere. They were definitely not in a position to speak of communication with Earth some light-centuries distant.

"There's no force-field in nature," said Lon doggedly, "that would have kept us from crashing. There's nothing in Earthly science either, that could have done it. But something did. We've got to find out what it was and who or what handles it and try to make a deal to warn Earth about those chlorine-breathing maniacs in the Slug and their homicidal tendencies."

CARYL'S father pointed suddenly. Something was coming straight down from the sky. It was very small— smaller than the *Marintha* or even the *Marintha's* vanished lifeboat. It was hardly larger than the body of a man.

It could easily have escaped notice in its descent except for two things. One was the rate at which it came down. It did not drop like a free-falling object, with swiftly increasing velocity. It descended steadily, barely holding to the same rate of downward travel.

And this in spite of the billowing, voluminous trail of what looked like rocket smoke behind it. The smoke, however, was yellow. It poured out fiercely, making enormous masses of thick vapor, which seemed struggling to push on.

Lon stared—and something clicked in his brain. He had seen history-reels of ancient warfare and early interplanetary flights.

"Let's get out of here!" he snapped suddenly. "The other side of the hill! *Quickly!*"

He literally drove the others before him. Infected by his haste they scrambled over the crest of the hill on which they had halted, were running down the opposite slope, dodging slender tree trunks, when the blast came.

The ground kicked under their feet. It seemed to rise and strike a violent blow, so that their knees buckled. There was a flare of light so bright that the trees, where they rose above the hill crest, appeared to flame momentarily with an unholy light.

Seconds later came the roar—with it a monstrous solid wall of wind. Branches and leaves flew overhead. Clods of earth and small stones pelted the fugitives. Caryl turned a frightened face to Lon. There were crashings and cracklings, and all manner of minor noises in the wake of the unbelievable blast. They ceased to run. They knew what it was, of course. By instinct they turned and looked back.

They saw the ghastly cloud still rising skyward. It reached up and up and up, expanded at the top with a horrible swiftness until it took the form of a palm tree. It was a slender shaft of flame-lit vapor with a spreading rounded top. There could be only one kind of explosion that would make in lightning-threaded cloud the form of a palm tree ten miles high.

"We've got to see which way the wind blows," said Lon evenly. "That will be dropping radioactive rain presently. We don't want to be in the way of it."

They watched in silence. They should not have been alive. They should in the first instance have been vaporized with the *Marintha* in its faster-than-meteoric fall into atmosphere. They should have been killed in any event when their ship crashed. Certainly they should have been close by the ship, trying to salvage possessions from the wreckage, when the creatures in the slug-ship—they had no doubt at all that the guided missile carrying an atomic bomb had come from their pursuer—when the guided bomb detonated so close to the wreck that the Earth ship was now mere metallic vapor in the upper stratosphere.

Even at their present distance, radiation burns would have killed them certainly except for the hill-crest between.

"It's moving toward the ocean," said Lon at last. "But just in case, we'll get away from here. Our friends aloft will think we're dead and come back later to hunt over the whole planet for humans."

Then he stopped. It was very still—very, very, very still. It was noticeably and startlingly quiet. The world around them was oppressively and quite horribly silent.

Then, abruptly, a tiny musical humming began. It was a sort of background noise that seemed to come from nowhere in particular. It was never plainly heard but it did keep the stillness from being oppressive. It began without preliminary, at full volume, exactly as if someone had thrown a switch.

Half an hour later they saw the atmosphere-flier.

CHAPTER THREE
Company

THEY were headed away from the bomb-crater then, moving inland toward a range of mountains not far away. There would be streams of water there, almost certainly some sort of animal life.

They had to think in terms of independent survival for days now and they were not equipped for anything but the most favorable conditions. They wore the light clothing suitable for the air-conditioned environment of the *Marintha*. They had Superson pistols but they had no tools and absolutely no instruments for observation.

Gravity on this planet seemed to be a little greater than on Earth—not hamperingly greater, to be sure—but they could not be certain about it. They had been in the artificial gravity of the *Marintha* for so long that the feel of Earth itself would probably have been strange.

But the air was satisfactory, as the air of one out of every three planets of a sol-type sun is bound to be. There were smells about too. They were unrecognizable but basically familiar, as if merely the scents of vegetation in a hitherto unvisited part of Earth. That also was reasonable.

With a given type of radiation from the sun and a given set of elements available for combination, certain organic compounds would be inevitable, chlorophyll, for example. This vegetation was green and it would make chlorophyll to absorb sunlight and the chlorophyll in turn would make starches and sugars and undoubtedly cellulose.

The organic chemistry of sol-type systems is essentially alike everywhere in the galaxy. It could not be otherwise. So there should be food. But some plants on Earth are poisonous and some animals, too (mostly fish) so selection would be a problem.

That, though, was Caryl's father's department. He was looking at some pendulous clumps of nutlike fruits the size of baseballs, hanging from the branches of a tree-cluster with leaves as fine as maiden-hair fern, when Caryl cried, "Look! A plane!"

Lon Howel turned. And there was a plane. But it was a freak. It did not have the sheen of metal anywhere about it. It was not streamlined in the exaggerated fashion of Earth-fliers, which strive for the maximum of speed. It was reasonably good design as far as its fuselage went but the wings were minute. They were no larger in proportion to the ship than the fins of an earthly fish.

And the speed of the craft was not high. Even an Earth-plane sometimes looks as if it's hanging in the air, as if it was not moving fast enough for its wings to support it. This aircraft gave that impression enormously multiplied.

It was near enough so that they could guess at its size—perhaps thirty feet over all—and a wing-spread of not over ten feet. The wings were not deep either. But the fuselage was large enough to hold two men side by side and probably several pairs of seats.

It flew quartering toward them, yielding smoothly to vagrant air-currents in exactly the manner of Earth-gliders. It passed within a quarter of a mile, some two hundred feet above the treetops. As they stared at it, it went on toward the spot where the bomb had exploded.

"Do you suppose the slug-ship landed and these are creatures from it?" asked Caryl in a whisper.

"They'd know better than to go into radioactive territory," said Lon slowly. "They aimed their bomb by sight and undoubtedly watched it explode. They wouldn't need to take a close look now."

The plane with the oddly insufficient wings lifted a little and disappeared over a hilltop. There was silence among the group of humans who saw it vanish.

"There've been probably sixty thousand planets landed on," said Lon sourly, "in some thousands of space voyages. And there's never been a sign of an intelligent race except us. And we have to find, not one intelligent race but two! One of them is up to atmosphere-fliers but doesn't know an atom bomb when it goes off and goes doddering over to look at the crater!"

He added angrily, "We've led the slug-creatures to the planet of a second intelligent race… Not intending to, but we've done it! The slug-creatures will think this is our home planet! We know what they tried to do to us. They'll certainly try to do the same to this entire planet when they get a little more help from home…"

He clenched and unclenched his hands. "And it's not doing Earth any good, either! Another exploring ship will blunder into that chlorine-breather's culture sooner or later. If those creatures have overdrive they're no more limited to one solar system than we are. Humans are bound to run into them. And what will happen then?"

"It would be interesting," said Caryl's father meditatively, "to know why they attacked us on sight. Breathing atmospheres that are mutually poisonous, we couldn't very well interfere with each other's way of life. We'd have nothing to gain by quarreling with them. Why did they attack us? What could they gain by destroying us?"

Lon said bitterly, "Why does a weasel kill what it can't possibly make use of? Why did people hunt long after the food ceased to count? Why did people go deep-sea fishing for fish they couldn't possibly eat? Why did they follow dogs running after a fox? Why do we still hunt with cameras and Superson guns?"

BURTON said deliberately, "That's a rather pessimistic statement, Lon. One only hunts things that can't fight back, for sport. One doesn't hunt dangerous things for the fun of it. If they think killing us is merely a particularly lively form of sport they must think their weapons are enormously better than any we can make."

"They could be wrong!" snapped Lon. "We haven't gone in for fighting each other for a couple of generations now. But we haven't lost the knack if the need arises. There's the plane, coming back. Give me the heat ray, Caryl!"

The oddly under-winged plane reappeared over a hilltop. It headed back on nearly the same course it had followed to the bomb-crater. It flew low. Hardly a hundred feet above the hilltops. And it traveled with a vast leisureliness. It specifically did not travel fast enough to be supported by such a small wing-area at such a speed. It made hardly forty miles an hour.

Lon turned on the heat ray and sprayed it into the foliage off to one side. Smoke arose—thick, pungent smoke. It went skyward in a dense column and Caryl coughed and drew back. The smoke was aromatic indeed. To a human the sudden eruption of white vapor would have been plainly a signal. The party from the *Marintha* waited for the plane to swerve nearer, to see the cause of the signal and to come within waving range from among the trees.

But the plane did not swerve. It went on, whether placidly from lack of interest or because its errand was too important to allow for deviation could not be guessed. There were ports in its side, and for an instant they were in line. There was movement inside. It could be detected. But it was not possible to see what sort of creature moved.

The humans waved and shouted frantically. The plane kept on. It went placidly and obliviously over the treetops. It displayed no haste at all. It vanished.

From its first appearance to its last not more than ten minutes had elapsed. But the humans had hoped during those minutes. The disappearance of the plane without any heed paid to their signals was a shock.

"I suppose," said Caryl unhappily, "they thought that anybody around must have been killed."

The flaming stuff swiftly ceased to emit smoke. Lon looked at it with a scowl. The embers glowed only briefly afterward. Then the fire was out. It had actually flamed as long as the heat ray played on it, no longer. The living plants seemed possessed of an enormous fluid content or else pumped much liquid sap to any part that was scorched. A forest fire could not sustain itself in such vegetation.

"They didn't worry about a fire in the woodland," said Lon moodily. "They must have known it would go out of itself. But why weren't they curious about how it got started? Or will they tip off somebody else to investigate?"

He stared in the direction in which the plane had vanished. He saw nothing but the thick, lush growth that climbed the hillsides and filled the valleys between them.

Caryl's father said practically, "If there are intelligent creatures here we must get in touch with them if only to try to warn them of what they can expect. But how will we set about it if they ignore our signals?"

"We'll go hunt them," said Lon moodily. "It can't be far. That plane wasn't making over forty miles an hour and it was here within half an hour after the bomb dropped. It took off from somewhere less than twenty miles away."

"We've no idea of compass directions. Of course, but we should be able to keep a fairly straight line along its course that far! And on top of the mountains yonder—I guess at three miles—we should be able to spot an airfield without any trouble."

Burton said drily, "But will we be welcome, bringing news that we've drawn the slug-ship here and that it's likely to come back with some of its friends to make a sporting event out of their massacre?"

"What else can we do?" demanded Lon. "Hole up and try to save our own skins! For what?"

He started off with Caryl by his side. The question of why they should try to save their own skins was relevant. They were in some sense like the space-castaways of romantic fiction. But castaways without reason for hope would still have no such reason for despair as they had. Other castaways could look for rescue for their children, if not for themselves.

But the conditions of their presence on this unnamed planet implied such danger to the rest of humanity that if it were not warned, they would not only be castaways, but the sole survivors of the race. And that was not a prospect they could face. It was preferable to die for even a one-in-a-thousand chance to avoid it. There was no point in living as the only humans left.

THEY went through the jungle. There was little undergrowth. Almost all the trees grew in colonies, each interconnected by its branches with others. The result was an enormous density of foliage overhead and almost bare ground below.

But there was creeping stuff with long feathery filaments, which crept over the ground and matted itself so that it made a springy carpet of a powdery gray. Here and there it bloomed—tiny flowers of startling magenta. There was no noise except the faint almost imperceptible hum, which had been cut so abruptly when the bomb went off and had returned so abruptly a short while after.

They went on for a long way, then Burton said, *"Hsssst!"*

They stopped. He handed the heavy firearm to Caryl's father and drew his Superson pistol. He was looking upward. He took half a dozen catlike steps, suddenly threw up the pistol and pulled trigger.

It made that curious resonant hum of all Superson weapons in addition to the ultra-high frequency that strikes unconscious any living thing it touches. It was a very brief sound. There was a pause, then a series of tiny crashings, then a thump.

Burton picked up a small furry thing with enormous eyes. There was membrane between its legs. It was plainly an arboreal creature that coasted through the air from branch to branch like flying foxes and flying squirrels on Earth.

But its neck was armored with bony scales like a ganoid fish—say, a sturgeon. It had no teeth, but horny, inflexible exposed jaws like a bird's bill. Caryl's father regarded it absorbedly.

"A new species, a new genus, a new phylon," he said. "What did you shoot it for, Burton?"

"It's the first animal I've seen," said Burton drily. "I use the word 'animal' in a very inclusive sense too. If we have to hunt our food we'll have to try this sort of creature, most likely."

"But," said Caryl's father, "not yet. You don't want it as a trophy?"

"Hardly!" said Burton.

Caryl's father put it down gently with a shrug of his shoulders. As a biologist he was interested but as a humanitarian he knew that he had no way of preserving specimens, so he laid it down to revive—as it would—when the effect of the Superson pistol wore off.

The ground began to rise, more and more steeply. They came to a patch of extraordinary vegetation like cactus, which seemed to be all spines—a foot and two feet long—with no pods to speak of. It covered acres. They went around it.

At five hundred feet they disturbed a huge bird, which flapped violently and rose straight up, then winged heavily away. It had feathers, but its head was not birdlike at all. It had whiskers and its legs seemed to end in feet, which certainly were not claws for roosting on branches. At a thousand-feet elevation there was a tiny rustling and Burton fired again. He went cautiously to look. It was an attenuated body with an animal snout and no external limbs. But it was not a snake. It was warm to the touch.

"Birds with whiskers," growled Burton, "flying platypuses with scales and now warm-blooded snakes with pig snouts! What will the aviators of this world look like?"

There was no answer. But none of the living creatures was really unreasonable. Flight on Earth is equally an ability of egg-laying birds with feathers and mammalian bats with fur. That all Earthly birds have beaks is an accident derived from the fact that members of a particular biological phylon happened to begin to sprout feathers, and beaks were not incompatible.

The beaks were there first. On this world feathered bodies were not associated with beaks. The creatures who found a place for themselves crawling on their bellies did not happen to be cold-blooded.

The retention of ganoid scales did happen to coincide with the acquisition of gliding-membranes. That was all. The unfamiliar is not necessarily unreasonable. But the existence of an oxygen-breathing intelligent race other than man seemed an impossibility.

The problem of the ancestry of man had been solved by interstellar exploration. On Mars and Titan in the home system of humanity, the first adventurers found huge areas of rubble that could be nothing but the debris of shattered cities and the rubbish of a vanished civilization.

Destruction had been so complete, however, that no single unshattered article was ever discovered in the wreckage. When overdrive was devised, and men traveled to the stars. On planet after planet similar spaces of pure wreckage were found, from the planets of Arcturus to those of Rigel and beyond.

Throughout a two-thousand-light-year globe of space the vanished cities existed on the planets of appropriate suns. There had been an interstellar culture that had been destroyed more completely than any sacked city of Earth. Nothing was left to reveal what sort of creature had built the cities or their architecture or arts or anything about them save that they were oxygen-breathers and had conquered space.

The mystery of the Lost Race went unsolved for nearly twenty years. Then one surviving structure was found and the skeletal remains of a single member of the vanished people. The answer to the mystery appeared in a manner to arouse at once the sympathy and the irritation of mankind.

The Lost Race was the forerunner of mankind. It had conquered space and solved the problem of unlimited power.

It had reached the heights of technical achievement. And perhaps its final conquest was that of time—it had learned to acquire a certain limited foreknowledge of the future.

And it had discovered that the radiations of its power-plants, or perhaps the subtler radiations of deepest space, had so altered the genes of all its members that a mutation lay ahead and their race was about to change to a race of monsters. So the Lost Race had collectively committed suicide rather than see its children metamorphose into hairless, big-headed monstrosities—so alien as to be horrifying. It had smashed its cities so that no succeeding race could ever learn to achieve equal disaster. Only on Earth had its self-destruction been incomplete.

On Earth its mutated children did survive. The monstrous descendants the Lost Race had foreseen with such despair were human beings.

The solution of the mystery—quaintly pathetic and oddly insulting as it was—meant, however, that there could be no oxygen-breathing race inimical to men. The Lost Race had wiped out all its enemies and therefore all enemies to its progeny. So that men regarded all the galaxy as proved clear of enemies—an inheritance to be entered upon without fear.

Now the castaways from the *Marintha* had found their security doubly questionable. There was a culture of chlorine-breathers, which doubtless was still savage or mindless when the Lost Race committed suicide, but which now was farther advanced in some sciences than mankind. And here, on this planet, were oxygen-breathing creatures who had advanced at least to the conquest of its atmosphere.

Lon scrambled up a steep incline and helped Caryl join him. Burton and her father clumped after them. It was not a cautious method of advance on an unexplored world, but all men had the habit of confidence. They had lost the idea of apprehension.

Here a sort of pass pierced the mountains. They came to a place where there were no trees and the creeping grayish stuff underfoot gave place to fern-like green growths almost knee-high. Through the pass they could see a wide valley and other mountains beyond.

Then Lon's eyes focused on a curious shimmering in the air. It looked exactly like a column of smokeless heated air, rising from an unseen spot perhaps two hundred yards away. He halted, lifting a hand for silence.

But as he halted something dropped into the fern-like growth at his feet. There was a crisp *pop* and whitish vapor spouted out. He leaped, trying to drag Caryl with him. But she staggered three steps and collapsed. There were two other poppings and two other globular clouds of mist arose. Burton and Caryl's father staggered and crumpled to the ground.

Lon caught Caryl to his shoulder and the Superson pistol hummed viciously. He thumbed the beam-control to fan it out—swept it back and forth vengefully. Then he plunged downhill with Caryl.

She was alive. She breathed. Her pulse—as he discovered when he stopped and bent over her—was fainter than normal but fairly regular. She had gasped at the sound and sight of the spurting vapor. A little of it had entered her lungs but only a little. Even as he swore in a consuming rage her eyelids fluttered.

He stood up and sent a second fan-beam barrage completely around him. Then he bent over Caryl and began to give her artificial respiration. He was furious with an atavistic, bloodthirsty wrath. She had taken three steps before she fell unconscious. But Burton and her father had dropped in their tracks. Lon could not hope to do anything for them.

CHAPTER FOUR
Contact

IT WAS very still. There was always that odd humming background noise, never quite loud enough to attract one's attention but always audible if one stopped to listen. But there was no other noise of any sort. Lon worked grimly on Caryl.

Twice more he sent a fan beam from his Superson pistol through a complete circle. Anything living that the beam hit would be reduced to unconsciousness by the ultra-high frequency sound waves. There could be no creeping up on him under such circumstances.

At long last Caryl gasped again, panted and swayed dizzily. She struggled to sit up.

"What happened?"

"Gas," said Lon grimly. "I held my breath and jumped, dragging you. You got a little of it. Your father and Burton keeled over. How do you feel?"

"I'm—all right," panted Caryl. She got unsteadily to her feet. Then she said, surprised, "I'm *quite* all right. Really I am! Now what do we do?"

Lon was suspicious but her color was good and her pulse again was strong and regular.

"It may have been an anesthetic gas," he said grudgingly. "We'll see. Tell me if, you have any queer feelings turn up— if your heart pounds or anything of that sort. We'll go see about the others. Get your pistol out. Shoot anything that moves. If gas turns up again hold your breath and run!"

He led the way back uphill. But this time his pistol was ready in his hand and he was all vigilance and cold caution. Once he thought he heard a movement and his pistol hummed. But when he angrily tracked down the noise he found a tiny shelter of sticks and leaves built around a tree trunk and inside it small creatures which at a guess would grow up to fly, flapping heavily, while wearing whiskers.

They reached the clear space with the ferny green stuff underfoot. They saw the figures of their two companions. They sprawled limply in the knee-high ferns. Lon began to search with his eyes for enemies. But Caryl watched the prone figures.

She cried softly, "Lon! They're *alive!* They're breathing!"

He looked quickly. It was true. The two bodies did move slightly in the rhythm of breathing.

"It's anesthesia," he admitted. "But so's this!"

Again he sent a beam of inaudible sound from the Superson pistol. He played it methodically on all the landscape within view. Any creature which could see him was bound to get a dosage of the stunning vibrations.

Then he went openly to the unconscious two men from the *Marintha*. They breathed stertorously. Their bodies were lax. There was a tiny incrustation of microscopic crystals on the foliage near them.

He bent over. Holding his breath, and dragged them away from that residue of the gas bombs' contents. Caryl began to work on her father, using the same technique of artificial respiration Lon had used on her. He hesitated a moment, then moved away with his finger on his pistol trigger.

Whatever had dropped near his feet and burst into the white vapor hadn't been moving fast. It couldn't have been thrown or propelled from any great distance. He searched with grim caution. But when he found one of the attackers he did not believe his eyes.

The attacker was a human being.

Not an Earth-human, to be sure—the stunned, prone figure, naked except for sandals and a curious single garment of closely linked metal plates, was not over four feet tall. It was slenderly formed though, and in no sense grotesque. It was simply a miniature man.

When the Superson beam had hit it, it dropped a very simple tube. Open at one end and eight inches long. It had no other apparent weapon—if that was a weapon. But in a part of its single metal garment was a row of receptacles like the loops of an ancient cartridge belt. Most of them were filled with objects that might fit in the dropped tube.

Lon stared blankly. He heard Caryl calling his name, uneasily but not in fear. He heaved the small form over his shoulder and went to her. Her father was already beginning to gasp a little. Apparently artificial respiration hastened recovery from gas, a little bit but not much. Its effect seemed not to last as long as that of a Superson beam at full power.

He dumped the limp small figure down before Caryl. "A local citizen," he observed curtly. "Your father will see the answer. I think I see it myself. Do you need anything?"

"No," said Caryl, staring with all her eyes at the small human figure. "I was just—uneasy."

"There were some more of these folk," said Lon. "I'm going to look for them. If this fellow starts to struggle shoot him again—but gently."

HE went back to hunt for other small-men. He found two, stunning them. He remembered the column of what looked like hot air rising. He moved cautiously toward it through brushwood that rose breast-high. He heard a rustling before him and fired quickly. He heard the crash as something fell. An instant tater he was looking down at a young female of the same miniature race. The man had been well formed, but this girl was beautiful. Lon felt abruptly like a criminal.

He went on, more cautiously than before.

There was a clearing of sorts. He saw what looked at first like a hut. Then he realized that it was a plane not unlike the one he had seen before. It stood in a small place, which surely allowed of no takeoff run.

There were two others of the miniature girls in sight. One of them tended something that definitely was not a fire but from which the column of heated air rose straight upward. The other spoke to her in a clear high voice whose syllables sounded like trills.

Lon raised his pistol. He felt lower than a scoundrel but there was nothing else to do. He did wait, though, until the one by the fire-thing drew back. Then he pulled trigger quickly, twice. The two girls collapsed limply.

He moved out and made sure that the one near the cooking could not possibly be scorched. He returned to the underbrush and brought out the other unconscious girl. He went back to Caryl. Her father was examining the small-man with increasing enthusiasm. Burton was already trying groggily to stand up.

Lon told them briefly what he had seen and done. Caryl's father picked up the small-man tenderly. Burton came unsteadily in Lon's wake, returning more nearly to normal with every step.

They came out to the clearing and the plane to find Caryl and her father already there.

"It's beautiful!" said the biologist, beaming. "Parallel evolution, Lon. They're descendants of the Lost Race, too!"

"I'm encouraged—a little," said Lon. "They saw us and shot at us, just as we'd have done. They used gas. We use Superson pistols. That suggests they have reached about the same stage of development we have. Our hunting weapons used to kill or wound. We have better sense than that now. So have they. If their technical level is as high—"

He went to the plane. The door was small but he managed to worm his way in. He came out minutes later with a square of cloth he had ripped loose. He began to tear it into strips.

"We've got to get these people tied up so we can try to communicate with them," he said, frowning. "I didn't see a motor in that plane."

He began to bind the small-men's hands and feet. Caryl, hesitating, took the other strips when he handed them to her and set to work on the extraordinarily delicate-seeming small-man girls.

The first man stirred in his bonds. Lon went over to him and lifted him to a comfortable sitting position. The small-man's eyes opened and as they cleared they looked startled. Then they flashed and his muscles made a convulsive heave, a tremendous effort to break the cloth strips that bound him.

"Easy!" said Lon, in as friendly a tone as he could manage. "What I'm saying is gibberish to you. Of course, but we've got to make friends with you even if we have to break your neck!"

Caryl protested, "That's no way, Lon! Let me try!"

She spoke to the bound small-man, pointing to the three girls as unharmed as himself. Burton went over to the fire-thing.

"This is food," said Burton cheerfully, "and they're human in a way, so it must be human food. Smells good, anyway— but what's cooking it?"

There was a round ring, which seemed to be of metal. It lay on the ground. In its center there was a reddish luminosity which gave off heat. A metal pot bubbled above it and the smell was savory.

Caryl's father said enthusiastically. "Lon, my boy, it's marvelous! The Lost Race wiped itself out. We know that! Everywhere we've found the ruins of their cities, the air and vegetation has been right for men. But there's been no shattered lost race city found on Earth! Do you see what that means?"

Lon listened while Caryl talked quietly to the first-waked of the three small-men and then included a second in her unthreatening if unintelligible conversation.

"They must have been like us, the Lost Race," said Caryl's father zestfully. "They wouldn't have eliminated themselves until they made sure they had to. They'd wait until the monstrous children began to turn up—our ancestors. Our ancestors must have begun to be born!

"And the existence of men on Earth—look at it, Lon! What would we do if we faced the tragedy the Lost Race knew was before them? Most of us would want to die but some of us—a few—would love our children even if they were monsters. Some of us would slip away from the rest of our race.

"We'd take our strange and alien children—whom we loved—to a planet where they could live. Our hearts would be broken and we wouldn't want to live but we wouldn't want even our monstrous children to die. We'd stay with them, isolated from all the rest of our kind. We'd teach them as much as we could.

"We'd die gladly when the time came but—they wouldn't die with us. You can even guess at a pathetic attempt to teach our ancestors that there is knowledge which had caused overwhelming catastrophe—a tragedy. You can be sure those first children of the Lost Race weren't all alike—not even one species.

"So—there were other races and other species of mankind than our own. In time we—Homo Sapiens—had to wipe them out and now there's only one species of man on Earth. And there's probably only one here. But they're men as we are! They're simply another species! And—"

CARYL said quietly, "Lon, I think we're coming to an understanding. One of the girls is awake. I'm going to turn her loose."

Lon watched. One of the three girls was staring about affrightedly. One of the men spoke. His voice was not as deep as those of the three Earth-men but it was masculine enough. His tone was steady and not in the least panicky.

The terror lessened in the girl's eyes. Caryl smiled at her and she unknotted the strip around her ankles. She loosed the girl's hands and stood back.

All three men were conscious now. They regarded the Earth-people with keen estimating eyes. The girl spoke uneasily and one of the small-men answered without turning his eyes from the Earth folk. His tone was quaintly dry.

"I like these people," said Burton abruptly. "They don't panic."

The slim tiny girl moved toward the cooking-pot. Burton moved aside as if for a child. He smiled at her. She gasped a little but the gentleness of his expression could not be misunderstood. She smiled back.

There was a sudden release of tension. The four Earth-humans relaxed—though Lon's hand stayed close to his pistol.

"They'll be figuring as I did," observed Lon. "If our weapons aren't lethal, any more than theirs, they'll figure we probably think the same way they do."

The man spoke again. The girl rose, caught Caryl's eyes and beckoned to her. She led the way to one of the bound small-men, plucked an eight-inch tube from a hanger in his belt and handed it to Caryl.

"That's his weapon," said Lon quickly. "She's handing it over. She's offering a bargain."

The girl emptied the receptacles in the small-man's cartridge-belt. She handed the round objects also to Caryl. Then she touched the small-man's bonds and looked anxiously at the Earth girl.

"*Right!*" said Lon. His eyes keen. "Turn him loose!"

Caryl bent to loose the small-man. The girl's fingers flew, freeing him. The small-man stood up and shook himself. He was not quite as tall as Caryl's shoulder. An earthly dwarf of his height would have been grotesque. But he had the build of a graceful and well-muscled boy of eleven or twelve. His face, though, was that of a mature and intelligent adult.

He spoke to Lon, went to one of his bound companions—Lon already had his tube-weapon—and passed over the ammunition for the thing. He went to the other and surrendered his weapon also and his ammunition. Then he pointed to the bonds. Lon nodded. He released the other two.

Lon gravely returned to him the weapons and ammunition he had just surrendered.

Lon was a little tense but the small-man's expression was reassuring. At first it was blank amazement. Then he regarded Lon in keenly intelligent estimation. Then he grinned. He nodded cordially and spoke to the others. Their whole air changed. Lon grinned faintly. Caryl's father beamed upon the small-men as happily as if he had invented them.

Burton grunted. "They seem to get the idea. Now, if we're friends, are they going to invite us to lunch?"

It was a curious situation. The other two small-men girls began to stir. Caryl went to release them. One of the small-men went to help her. He grinned slyly as if amused at her size. She smiled back. The atmosphere of the camp was oddly, confidently relaxed. The first girl to waken climbed into the plane. She came out with bowls and tiny but humanlike spoons. Burton counted.

"Bowls and spoons for all," he said happily. "We eat!"

But Lon was thinking hard. "This is a break," he told Caryl's father. "If they're descended from the same ancestors we are they must have something like the same mental processes.

"We can establish some sort of communication without having to figure out a brand new type of psychology first." But then he added in an odd change to despair, "But they're not likely to be able to put up a fight against the slug-ships…"

Caryl smiled at Lon. "I'm not so sure," she said reassuringly. "What do they use instead of fire? Would they use non-lethal weapons if they were primitive? Remember, they wouldn't have thought of making a bargain—of giving up their weapons for freedom—unless it would have been one they'd have made with us if things had turned out the other way about. They're civilized, Lon."

"I hope so," growled Lon. "We've got to get started on some system of talking. I'll see what I can do."

HE beckoned to one of the small-men and cleared a bit of ground of the ferny stuff. The humus underneath was honest black loam, the decay-product of plants whose basis was cellulose whatever their forms might be. He patted the cleared earth smooth. He began to sketch, explaining as he went along, though the words would be useless as such. But he knew that the tones of his voice would help convey his meaning.

Another of the small-men came to look—the third. Burton and Caryl were at the metal ring that served as an open fire without smoke or fire or odor. The three girls grinned shyly at Caryl and laughed outright at Burton. He made something of a spectacle of himself to make them laugh more.

One of the girls brought a steaming bowl to a small-man. He nodded absently and took it. Another offered a bowl to Lon. He nodded absently and took it while he sketched. He went on with his painstaking explanations, tasting the contents of the bowl in the intervals when the three small-men absorbedly discussed his sketches. He felt that most of his meaning, at least, was getting across.

It was a lengthy business to convey the idea of space-travel by diagrams and gestures. It was more difficult to tell them the story of an attack by the slug-ship, their escape, their landing on this planet and the atom-bomb that had vaporized the *Marintha*. But he did his best.

"Now comes the tough part," he said over his shoulder to Caryl's father. The biologist had come to stand behind him. "Telling what has happened in pictures is tough enough. Telling what's likely to happen is something else!"

One of the small-men suddenly reached over and touched Lon's shoulder. He put his hand to his ear. The other small-men, their faces serious, stiffened in listening attitudes. Lon strained his own ears.

The tiny humming background noise ceased abruptly. For half a minute there was oppressive, ear-cracking stillness everywhere. Then, quite suddenly, the humming began again. The small-men relaxed. But their expressions were very intent. One spoke in their liquid, trilling language.

Another leaned forward and began to speak just as Lon had done, drawing sketches with curious precision in the smoothed-over loam and accompanying each sketch with a careful and sometimes lengthy explanation of which only his intonation had meaning. But it helped amazingly in the conveyance of his message.

A long time later—a very long time later—Lon got up from the ground, filled with a sick rage.

Caryl turned to him, smiling. "Lon, I'm making friends with these girls. They're darlings! And—Lon! What's the matter?"

He said thickly, "These people *know* things. The plane that passed over us spotted us and told these folk to look out for us. So they checked my story as I went along. I don't know what sort of civilization they've got but they *know* things. They know all about the slug-ship.

"They've just told me that it sent back word even from overdrive—we humans can't do that—and more slug-ships started to follow while it was still pretending it couldn't overtake us. That was while it believed us streaking for home.

"The first slug-ship's still hovering overhead. It's dropped another atom bomb on their biggest city—they had time to get the people out—and smashed it completely. And there will be a good-sized slug-ship fleet along tomorrow and still more are on the way. They *know* things... But they're apparently helpless. They're not trying to do a thing!"

His hands clenched and unclenched in impotent fury.

"But how could they know," Lon asked Caryl blankly. "How could these people even know about another atom bomb dropping? They haven't radio or anything like that. We'd have heard it..."

"Don't ask me how they know!" raged Lon. "But they do! They made a star map with the Crab Nebula on it and pointed out the solar system the slug-ship came from! There's no question. They *know*..."

CHAPTER FIVE
Reverse—View

THE plane flew with vast leisure over the jungle-roof. Lon was horribly restless. Somehow, he had no uneasiness about the friendship the small-people now displayed.

They seemed to think it diverting that the people of Earth and themselves had started out by conflict, that they had almost won by knocking out three of the Earth folk and that then Lon had turned the tables on them without any animus—as evidenced by the return of their weapons as soon as they made overtures for an understanding.

The return of their weapons had been decisive. It turned their ambush and counter-ambush into a sporting event, which was very much to the small-people's taste because they had scored as well as the Earthlings.

But Lon was horribly restless. He had told them, with sketches and diagrams and gestures, of the danger that hung over their planet. They had given him further details, making the danger more imminent and greater than before. But they seemed undisturbed, like children. He couldn't make out the status of their civilization.

This plane, now—when it took off it simply shot straight upward with a hissing noise and then it went off across the jungle without any noticeable haste or urgency. There was no motor that he could detect. The wings, in particular were hopelessly inadequate to perform the function they very visibly did.

Inside there was no instrument board, there were no controls except a couple of levers made apparently of plastic.

Altogether the device looked very much more like a make believe construction than the product of advanced technology. But it worked! It flew!

Their weapon was of the crudest possible sort—a tube with one open end, with no handle, no sight, no particular provision for accuracy. To be sure, it was essentially a short-range weapon and made a gas cloud on impact so that great accuracy wasn't necessary.

But again it had the quality of a child's make believe. And when they told him that another atomic bomb had been dropped on their largest city it had been with the solemnity of children relating an imaginary catastrophe that was part of a game they played. It was as if the city could be replaced or restored as easily as by merely imagining it. How had they known about that bomb business, anyhow? They had no radios. Lon had heard no sound at all except their voices.

Hold on! There was the time when they had all stopped and listened. The humming background noise like the normally unnoticed sound of insects in the country and of traffic in a city had stopped as if a switch were opened. There was dead oppressive silence for almost a minute. Then the noise abruptly recommenced.

What did that mean? The same thing had followed the first bomb. He had noticed the shocking silence after the blast of the bomb had ended. It lasted much longer that time and it had ended in exactly the same way—with the abrupt restoration of the background noise.

Caryl said, beside him, "You're bothered, Lon?"

"Plenty," he said grimly. "Absolutely nothing has happened to make things better. The slug-ship people are on the way. These people seem to be helpless. From our standpoint it is utterly necessary that a message be got somehow to Earth.

"Sooner or later another Earth ship is going to run into the slug-creatures and they'll swarm to Earth as they're swarming here. We've got to warn our people. We've *got* to! Some sort of defense has to be contrived—or better, some means of attack.

"Nobody can win a fight simply by defense. Earth's got to be warned to get set for fighting! We're the only people who could warn them, and we haven't the ghost of a chance. We'll be dead soon after that slug-fleet gets here!"

"Maybe not," said Caryl. "These people know what's coming, you say. And they certainly don't look worried. They act as if they're having a wonderful time!"

"I wish I could," said Lon. "I crawl inside when I think— and I can't think of anything else! These people know they're helpless. They're not trying to do a thing..."

"Maybe," said Caryl, "they've already done it."

Lon turned to stare. "Now, what do you mean by that?"

"I don't know," admitted Caryl. "But they're not savages. Did you notice the thing they cooked with? It was just a ring of metal. They laid it on the ground. They put the pot on it. The air inside the ring glowed. They cooked.

"Just before we started off, one of the girls picked it up and stored it in the plane here. It wasn't even hot! That's a sort of civilization we haven't attained yet. Maybe they're ahead of us in civilization and have defenses so they're not worrying."

"An atom bomb blew up their biggest city," said Lon sourly. "They wouldn't let that happen if they could help it! And look at the control system for this plane. It's childish! There's not an instrument in sight. How can people be civilized without instruments?"

"Why," asked Caryl meditatively, "do we use so many instruments?"

"To be sure our machines are working properly," said Lon. "So we can tell if anything goes wrong."

"Suppose they know nothing can go wrong?" suggested Caryl. "Then they wouldn't need instruments."

"They'd need radar, anyhow," insisted Lon. "They'd need weather-warning devices. They'd need things to keep them from flying into mountains in the dark!"

"Maybe they've got them," said Caryl. "But don't ask me where they are! I think these people are confident instead of oblivious to danger. And the girls are darlings. They act like beautifully raised children. They're adorable!"

"I would trade a lot of cuteness," said Lon grimly, "for one small space ship with some weapons I could fight with!"

The small plane went on in leisurely fashion over the jungle. It did not fly high. It was rarely more than a hundred feet above the tree-tops. And it did not fly in the manner of atmosphere-fliers on Earth. It made no attempt at level flight.

CROSSING a valley, for example, it coasted down the descending slope and climbed the ascending slope on the farther side. It seemed to have plenty of power but it flew low as if the pilot considered there was greater safety close to solid ground.

But he did not pay close attention to his piloting. He turned his head and talked to the others in very lively fashion, not looking ahead for minutes at a time. Yet the plane—so simple that it looked crude and childlike—went on with perfect steadiness.

They descended a steep slope and flew out over water. The surface was almost glassy, but ahead over the farther shore there were storm clouds to which the pilot paid no attention at all. They flew beyond the water and under the storm cloud. Presently there were great sheets of rain all about them. But there was little or no wind.

The plane flew almost as steadily as before, and the six small-folk chattered gaily enough. Caryl listened closely. Lon became lost in gloomy thought. Burton leaned forward.

"Lon," he said vexedly. "I don't understand this. I've known a lot of people, and only pretty smart ones—and vision-screen actors—have much expression in their voices. But these people talk well! They put all sorts of shading into their tones.

"That chap is dry..." He nodded toward one of the small-men. "...and that girl says things demurely and all the others laugh. I'm pretty sure it's not what she says but the way she says it that counts. I'm beginning to have hopes. These people *aren't* savages..."

Caryl's father chuckled. "As a biologist," he said contentedly, "I have observed that the function of an organ is not always in proportion to its visibility. The pancreatic islands, the endocrine system—none of those very important organs is as obvious as a man's nose. We can do without noses, but not without our pituitary bodies!

"Perhaps these people have reduced their devices to a proper place—tucked out of sight. Small, and highly efficient, and requiring no attention. As, for example, on occasion we have to blow our noses but we never have to pay any attention to our interstitial glands.

"It may be that our small friends put their technical apparatus out of sight and pay no attention to it, just as we ignore our gall-bladders. It would imply a finer mechanism and a superior symbiosis of mechanism to the race it serves."

Lon shrugged. He looked out of a side-port. Overhead lightning flashed and thunder roared. Storm torn clouds were shown by the lightning flashes, flung about by conflicting winds. But the same lightning flashes showed the teeming rain descending almost vertically.

The foliage—so near below—seemed merely to huddle quietly under a totally tranquil downpour. Storm winds unquestionably blew aloft but near the ground they simply did not. And that was something so improbable as to make him bewildered. It was not a thing to be easily believed even while one watched it.

A long time later they emerged from the farther edge of the storm clouds. There was bright sunshine. Below them was continued jungle. Another range of mountains arose ahead, and the small plane continued toward it. One last small hill flowed beneath them—and there was a city.

Lon's heart sank. As a city the sight was utterly disappointing. There were no great buildings. There was no architecture. There were no parks, nor any paved ways, nor any wheeled vehicles in view. It was simply an expanse of small dwellings of undistinguished appearance.

None was over a single story in height. They were scattered over a very large area. They were not even rectangular but had straight walls and curved ones as if at their occupants' fancy. There were, here and there, small patches of the communally-growing trees and occasional irregular patches of brushwood.

At first glance it looked rather like the casual encampment of savages who would move on when the idea pleased them. On second glance the effect of impermanence vanished. There was informality in the arrangement and in the structures themselves but there was a pattern too. And the houses looked better as one studied them a second time.

But Lon did not look again. He had eyes only for a huge metal sphere on the ground just where the hillside began to rise steeply toward a crest some thousands of feet high. The sphere was all of forty feet in diameter, and it was plainly constructed of metal plates welded to an inner stronger frame.

AS he looked, an enormous section of the mountainside lifted, disclosing a monstrous opening all of sixty feet high and a hundred broad. There was blank darkness within it. And as the opening yawned, the metal globe moved smoothly over green turf—not even tracking it—and disappeared in the darkness.

The great door tilted down and settled into place. There was nothing in view but green-clad hillsides and the curiously tranquil jungle with its clumped communities of trees, and the sprawled-out city, which at first glance looked like the casual encampment of savages.

The plane slowed in its flight and settled down without a run. It was close by one of the houses. There was a small shelter before it—obviously intended as a storage-place. It was, in fact, a private hangar. And Lon saw similar shelters close to or incorporated in each of the two or three other buildings near enough to be examined.

The pilot casually opened the exit-port in the plane's side and slid out. The four Earth-people wormed their way uncomfortably out and to the ground. The small-people chattered cheerfully, and one of the girls began to hand out an assortment of small game.

There were two of the big-eyed air-gliding creatures, with the ganoid scales. There was a feathered thing with incredible iridescent plumage. There was almost a colony of tiny creatures with irresistibly humorous solemn faces and tiny paws folded as if in prayer.

The small-man girl smiled at them as she handed them over. The six small-folk had evidently been upon a hunting party by plane when the survivors of the *Marintha* fell in with them, but whether they hunted for food or sport or pets could not be told.

Certainly the number of small creatures around the houses was greater than in the jungle. Many more things of small size could be seen at a glance than they'd seen in all their journeying.

"I'm stumped!" said Lon helplessly. "But they're civilized! Only a civilized race could make a door like that and a metal object that large. But—"

Other little people appeared, walking lightly toward them. They looked at the Earth-folk with enormous interest but no surprise whatever, which was disturbing, because the hunting-party members had been starkly astonished—or had they? They were in ambush. Maybe they were astonished only at being overcome. In any case, word had come on ahead about them. But how?

The newcomers grinned at the six who had found the Earthlings. Trilling speech surrounded them. There was laughter. It was such good-humored laughter as old acquaintances exchange when one of their number has had a humorous mishap befall him.

The pilot of the plane brought one of the small-men to Lon and spoke in an apparent form of introduction. The other small-man grinned. His eyes crinkling deeply at the corners. The small-folk eyes were longer than Earth eyes. Lon put out his hand...

The small-man looked at it and put out his own. Lon shook it. The small-man looked surprised, then chuckled. He put out his hand again.

For minutes the four Earthlings were kept busy shaking hands. Each newcomer learned of the odd custom and immediately tried it with each of the four Earth people. Once they had made the round they tried it all over again.

They considered it humorous. Presently they were shaking hands with each other to delighted laughter.

"Confound it!" growled Lon, sunk in gloom again. "They're only children. They haven't a serious thought in their heads!"

"The highest standard of education ever known," said Caryl's father drily, "was in ancient Athens, and they were notoriously always looking for some new thing. It occurs to me, Lon, that the difference between a savage and a citizen of the highest possible culture wouldn't be so great on the surface.

"They'd both have leisure and they'd both be completely unworried about everyday affairs. They'd both feel completely secure. We might be looking at either status. It's the in-between people like us of Earth who worry and fret."

ONE of the girls who'd been in the plane came back from the nearby house. She carried a sheet of what looked like milk-white plastic. She handed it casually to the man to whom Lon had been presented and he sketched quickly, lines and shadings appeared with startling clarity. He showed it to Lon. Lon gave a little sigh of relief.

"I'm going in where that metal globe disappeared," he told Caryl. "They want to talk machinery to me. You can enjoy yourself with their cuteness…"

He strode away, following his new guide. It was a walk of some length but there was no ground-transportation. The life of the small-men was evidently lived at a very leisurely tempo, which there was no way to speed up in time of emergency like the present.

There was a small door set into the hillside. Inside was a long, deep tunnel of a size to cramp a man of Lon's height. The light overhead baffled him entirely. It looked like a ribbon of plastic that glowed without heat and made the tunnel as bright as day.

Then, too, the question arose of why an underground installation had been built in the first place. If for safety against attack, it would promise real help for the Earthlings. It would imply warfare and weapons and very probably spaceships.

Or—but this idea Lon regarded with doubt—there might be some other form of life in symbiosis with the small-people and this other form of life might have intelligence and prefer to be underground.

The guess was far-fetched. Both were. And both were wrong. Presently the tunnel ended and there was a truly gigantic cavern, with cross-ribbons of the same illuminant on its hundred-foot high ceiling, and there were several cryptic masses of motionless metal in the center. The motionless objects were electrical, Lon was sure.

Two of them were seventy feet high—the height of a seven-story building—and sixty around their bases, and they were of bewildering simplicity. But flickering blue glows— straight corona effects—hovered about certain of their parts and somehow there was the feeling of incalculable power in them.

Small-men labored within the forty foot globe. They popped into view from its interior, and went to a small door on the far side of the cavern, and came back carrying small loads which they took into the inside of the globe again. They turned their heads to look at Lon and grin at him as he followed toward another small door not far from the one they used.

Here was a closed room with a soft carpet and a blank end wall. A beaming little man—quite the oldest of the small-men Lon had seen—rubbed his hands exuberantly as Lon came in. He waved his hand at the blank wall.

The lights went out and a picture in color appeared there. It was vastly more true in tinting than Earthly vision-screens. It began with a picture of a bomb-crater—a space a half-mile across blasted clean of everything and lined with a molten glassy stuff.

The picture was taken from the air. The plane from which it had been taken plainly wavered and wabbled in the air currents on which it floated. Lon knew somehow that this was the bomb-crater left by the bomb that had vaporized the *Marintha*.

The picture held for a space. Then it flicked off. And then there appeared an extraordinary view of swirling vapor which Lon blinked at blankly. It had all the violence of an explosion. Only it wasn't one. It was an implosion—an explosion in reverse.

Lon was too confused to realize what he was seeing until all the swirlings ended and suddenly the tumult cleared away and he looked down from a seemingly quite steady platform in mid-air at the vanished *Marintha*. He caught his breath sharply.

Then he saw moving figures. He saw himself and Caryl and Burton and Caryl's father. The figures were unmistakable but the action was impossible. All four human figures were running and scrambling backward toward the small doomed spaceship.

They reached its side and leaped up backward, landed on its upper side and slithered down into its interior. Then the port closed, and the ship up-ended, turned end-for-end and moved skyward.

Now the point-of-vision the viewing instrument followed. Up and up the ship went, tumbling in its rise. The sky above it turned dark and streaks of fire that looked like frozen lightning winked into being and struck it. It continued to rise and others missed it—all on one side—and it retreated into space.

"You saw this?" demanded Lon aloud in his astonishment. "But why run the film backward?"

HE stared in utter incredulity as the adventures of the *Marintha* were followed in reverse on the screen—back, all the way back to the attack by the slug-shaped ship off a chlorine planet near the Crab Nebula. And then back beyond that through weeks of journeying toward that system—and then the images grew hazy and indistinct and then there were no more.

The lights came on and the two small-men looked at him hopefully. Lon knitted his brows.

"You ran the film backward," he said, groping. "Was that—was that the way you saw it? Good gosh! Can you track a thing back in time?" His voice rose in pitch, "Can you focus on a thing today and track it back into yesterday and see what happened? Did you go back as far as your instruments will take you?"

He was struck speechless. The two small-men nodded to each other. They seemed satisfied. The screen lighted again. Lon saw the projected record take up again at the moment the slug-ship had first fired on the *Marintha*.

Here the focus was changed somehow to the atmosphere-fin, which had been the first object blasted from the *Marintha's* hull. That stayed in focus on the screen. And he saw the unpleasant yellow planet rotating slowly beyond the bit of wreckage.

He saw the other slug-shaped ships rising from its surface and flashing into overdrive with that strange momentary flashing of all the colors of the rainbow at once. Then the planet's rotation seemed to speed up—indicating the passage of time—and it slowed again and another and much larger fleet took off.

"You've edited the film," said Lon numbly. "So this is how you know an about us! The first of your people didn't seem to know. They listened—I see! They checked to see whether I'd be telling the exact truth. And I did.

"They knew because that plane went and shot the crater, and then you were able to go back in time and see what caused it. Or maybe you had to wait until your plane got back with your record and you didn't broadcast it to them until you'd seen what the record said." He grew confused. "I'm getting mixed up! Go ahead!"

He prepared to see more marvels. He did. The viewing device which had been able to separate and cling to a shot-off bit of metal fin, weeks in the past and thousands on thousands of parsecs away, now showed the undestroyed *Marintha* stationary in space.

Its viewpoint approached the ship and entered it. Lon saw the now-vaporized little yacht in a series of cross-sections as if it had been sliced through again and again. This was television of a new sort entirely.

Later, he learned that this particular device required another time-stratum than its own to work in. It could not examine in the present, but only in the past of an object on which it was focused. And it could not move into the future by as much as the thousandth of a second. But it was television on a scale unimaginable to earthly science.

"All right," said Lon dazedly, when this was done with. "What do you want now? What's the exhibition for? I'm probably crazy and having delusions but go ahead! What now?"

He was literally dazed by the incredible things he had seen and by their implications. He was almost stunned by these vistas of a science mankind had not dreamed of. Obviously, he realized numbly, if time is a dimension like length and breadth, apparatus could be imagined to explore it when given a conducting medium into the past. But it was so new a concept that his mind balked. It was not even dreamed of among men. But here it worked!

He waved his hands helplessly. The screen lighted again. There was a bit of machinery in the *Marintha,* quite stationary and very much enlarged. The viewing-device sectioned it all through. The lights came on.

The two small-men, chattering hopefully, led Lon through a door into an adjoining room. It was a workshop of sorts, though there was no single tool in it that he could recognize. There were metal parts on a bench. The small-men pointed to them and very hopefully waited to see what he would do.

It was night and Lon's expression was one of sheer stark raving unbelief when he joined Caryl and the others in the house near which their plane had landed. There were many of the little folk there, and the sound of the girls' voices was like the clear-fluting voices of birds. Caryl was trying to learn the language and it seemed to be an uproarious performance. But she saw Lon's white incredulous face and came to him quickly.

"What's the matter, Lon!" she asked anxiously. "You've had a shock!"

"Shock?" said Lon bewilderedly. "That's no word for it! These people have everything! With their equipment we men—there's no limit to what we could do! But..." He said it in a querulous, unbelieving voice. "...of all the stuff in the *Marintha's* equipment that they could have chosen—they've been trying to duplicate her garbage-disposal unit and make it work! And that's what they want me to help them with!"

CHAPTER SIX
Alien Science

THE sunrise next morning was a very beautiful one. Lon heard flutelike trillings and he heard Caryl's laugh. He got up and slipped into his clothes. He had to duck to go through the toy-sized doors of the house—the ceilings were hardly two inches above the top of his head—and his exit into the morning was undignified.

Outside Caryl loomed above the slender delicately formed girls of the small race. She had adopted their costume as a mildly venturesome jest and ruddy tinted rays of the just-risen sun made her a startlingly effective figure with the clustered elfin others about her. High delighted laughter arose as she fled at the sight of Lon.

He stayed outside. The air smelled wonderfully fresh, vibrant, and new. All the vegetation was covered with glittering drops of dew, each one seemingly a ruby in the ominous crimson sunlight. And there were streaks of clouds to the eastward and all the horizon was a glory of colored light.

Burton and Caryl's father came out a little later. Lon was staring about him with a sort of baffled anger because this was a very beautiful world and it was horrible to think that today, quite certainly, it was to undergo an attack its people could not possibly resist. Very probably the chlorine-breathers of the slug-ship fleet would not even try to land upon it.

But if a mere patrol-ship was equipped to do battle so many light years from home and carried the material for at least two atomic bomb warheads for guided missiles as a matter of course—then surely such a fleet as was now on the way would be able to saturate this planet's whole atmosphere with atomic bomb debris.

They might do it merely from the same sort of bloodlust that had appeared in the unwarned attack of the *Marintha's* pursuer. But an alien race with space ships would always represent a possible danger to any other culture. It would require no unprecedented arrogance to make the chlorlne-breathers merely decide in cold blood to wipe out any possible enemy.

"Morning," said Burton. He breathed deeply of the fragrant morning air. "Days must be pretty long on this planet and the nights too. I usually knock off my eight hours but this morning I feel more rested than usual. I wonder if our friends serve breakfast? The condemned man is ready for his morning meal."

"The slug-fleet's due today," said Lon. "And our friends were putting garbage-disposal units together when I left the cave. Quite skillfully, with the help of some shapeless objects I have to assume were machine-tools and which seemed to be learning the whole process quite readily. Those tools are marvels. But—garbage-disposal units!"

Caryl's father said meditatively, "Somehow I have confidence in our small friends. They are human, remember. Not our species, of course—it wouldn't seem likely—but human. And it's human to worry. They'd be worrying if there were any reason for it."

Lon shook his head. "After I showed them the trick of putting the things together I talked to them by way of pictures and whatnot. They've no defense against atom bombs. None whatever. They don't use atomic power.

"They've some tricky way of using the surface heat of their planet. They transform it into electric energy direct. Their sun replaces all they can use a hundred times over. And they broadcast it. That cave is one of their transformer stations."

"You told us last night," said Burton, yawning. "It's some sort of skin-effect business so the power's all over the planet on the surface and nowhere else. Did you find out what slowed the *Marintha's* fall, Lon?"

"Their broadcast power," said Lon moodily. "It's tricky, making a skin-effect current over a globe, even when you put your current sources underground, as they naturally have to. But the field has some side effects. It tries to make a sort of vertical stasis.

"It resists the up-and-down motion of all energy-containing objects but not their lateral movement. The effect varies as the square of the vertical speed of the object and also diminishes with distance. The resistance to vertical movement begins to be appreciable at about six feet a second and goes up.

"There are all sorts of consequences. We hit the fringe of the effect at a hundred-twelve miles a second. It started to slow us before we hit atmosphere, though we didn't know it. The closer we got to the ground, the lower the speed it began to work at and of course the greater effect on an object of given velocity."

BURTON said drily, "If I shot that antique gun of ours horizontally, the bullet would travel a long way. But if I shot it straight up the bullet would be held up and the gun would burst. Right?"

"Probably," said Lon. "It means they can't have strong vertical wind currents, hence no strong lateral one. They don't have violent wind storms and no hurricanes at all. It means that an air-jet in a tube pointed down has a terrific reaction. The broadcast power tries to keep the air from descending too fast.

"So they lift their planes straight up by turning compressed air loose in tubes pointed straight down and their driving them ahead by similar blasts aimed slanting down and backward. Since the wings push air down they have a terrific lift, too. All of which is a load in their power-plants, though.

"They have to be terrifically powerful because they inherently have to slow up all breezes on the planet's surface. But they couldn't slow up the blast of an atomic bomb. That was too much power applied too suddenly. The two bombs that have gone off blew their power fuses.

"The first time all their planes crashed. The second time they had warning. Didn't do too much harm though, because they fly low to get maximum lift from the stasis-effect. Anyhow their trees are spindling and mostly broke the falls. They got their fuses replaced a lot quicker the second time. Remember?"

Burton whistled. "That noise? The background noise like humming that you can always hear. It went off and again while we were up in the pass."

"That's another side-effect," said Lon. He shrugged. "Yes. It carries broadcast stuff, too. They use code at about twenty thousand cycles audio-frequency—too shrill for our ears to catch but not for theirs. Almost like the squeak of a bat, which most children can hear but most adults can't. They can listen to it or ignore it. Convenient."

Caryl's father said warmly, "It's as I said, Lon, they've put technology in its place. Their machines are small and efficient and they keep them out of sight and live very comfortably— as unworried and as unweariedly as savages. They're as completely adapted to the mechanics of their way of life as savages used to be on Earth.

"But we still struggle with our contraptions. We're still conscious of our machinery. We have to watch it and oil it and supervise it and tinker with it. We're practically savages by comparison!"

"We are?" said Lon brusquely. "But they're playing with garbage-disposal units! With ion-rockets! I left half a dozen of their best brains puttering around with those crazy plastic things they use for automatic tools, trying to understand how a meteor-detector works!

"They've got machines making them and they're taking them apart trying to understand them. And they're sweating over the mechanism of a Doole-Boyd storage battery! They found out how to make them from that gadget that takes pictures in the past but they don't know how they work!"

There was silence for a moment. Burton whistled tunelessly.

"The thing that hurts," said Lon bitterly, "is that if we men—Earthmen, that is—had a tenth of what they've got Earth would be safe! A couple of months with the gadgets these folks have and we could go to that yellow planet and smash it!

"We could make the Galaxy safe for humankind. But they can't! With a slug-ship fleet due here today to start the business of wiping them out, they're trying to fathom the boundless mystery of a storage battery!"

He looked very tired. It was bitterness. The small folk had a science which was capable of anything but they had never needed to defend themselves, so they had no weapons more dangerous than the ones Earth ships had considered adequate. Earth was no better off.

"Still," said Caryl's father, "it's barely possible that they don't understand our machinery because it's too primitive. Prehistoric man used to make some queerly-shaped pieces of flint that we call scrapers for lack of a better name. But we really have no idea what they were used for.

"And how many civilized men would be able to understand a fire-drill or how it worked if he simply saw the device? Or an Aztec fire-wheel? He'd never have had need for a machine to make a fire with. Without special information would a civilized man be able to guess the purpose of a boomerang? Again—he'd never need anything like that. Maybe these people are bewildered for the same reason. Maybe they've never needed the things we depend on, Lon."

LON shook his head. He had given the small-men what information they wanted about devices they had incredibly photographed on the *Marintha* after she had ceased to exist. But he saw no hope of any sort.

He was prepared to do battle with his bare hands, not only for distant Earth but for Caryl's life and his own. But he was doomed, apparently, to mere impotent waiting for the death the slug-ships would presently pour down upon this planet.

There were figures moving about the other houses of this settlement of the small-folk. A plane rose in the still-rosy light of dawn. It looked childishly crude. It went over toward the hillsides, where the huge concealed doorway opened upon a most unlikely cavern. It settled to the ground again.

Another plane rose and moved to the same place and settled. Others, by ones and twos and it seemed hundreds. The first planes to land then rose again. They went winging off leisurely into the dawn.

There was at least one plane attached to each of the quaintly individualized dwellings of this community, and every one rolled out of its shelter and flew comfortably to the one place, there landed and presently rose again and went off. They had not all the same destination. They scattered in every possible direction.

Presently the unhurried mass-movement seemed to dwindle, and as it ended other planes began to arrive from somewhere else. Another city, most likely. This was a swarming of the planes that seemed toys for make believe. There were so many of them that they looked like a flight of low-flying locusts. Actually, they were well into the hundreds in number.

Some of them landed. The others hovered as if in no hurry at all. But nevertheless there was continuous movement. When one grounded plane rose again and went wheeling around the column of the ones which waited, another settled.

There was a steady thick stream of the planes heading back in the direction from which all had come.

"They're doing something!" said Burton. "Let's go look."

They walked. There was no ground transportation here. And the thick mass of planes from what might be called the south had diminished to a very small number before they reached the glade or the hidden door. A third flight of planes, numbering at least a thousand, was coming into sight over the jungle from the north.

It was full morning now and the red tints to eastward had almost faded away. Planes were landing all about as they neared the place on which all the inexplicable air-traffic centered. The great door was not quite closed.

It was open a bare half-dozen feet, and under its ponderous valve a string of busy, small, crude-seeming machines rolled out and rolled back. They were something like tractors with long low platform bodies.

They rolled upon treads, which were not quite wheels, but were certainly not caterpillar tracks.

Each, as it came out, was heavily burdened with curious objects of plastic some four feet long by a foot in diameter— very large objects for men their size to handle.

The small-men guiding the trucks grinned amiably at the three Earthmen. A truck stopped and small-men hopped out of planes and each one seized one of the ungainly objects and staggered back to his plane with it.

He pushed it through the door. He went back for a second and third and fourth, which he disposed of in the same way. Then he climbed back into his plane and it went straight up with a hissing sound and swept away on its return journey.

There happened to be just one of the objects left on the nearest truck, and Lon approached it blankly. The driver grinned amiably at him. He looked like an impish child, sitting on the slightly raised seat with the make believe-like stick in his hand for the truck's only control.

Lon peered in one open end of the plastic device. It was essentially a foot across tube of plastic. Open at both ends. But Lon could look inside.

He said helplessly, "There's a meteor detector at one end with a garbage disposal unit behind it and I think a storage battery behind that. At the other end there's an ion-rocket tube with some deviation-coils to shift the reaction-beam of the rocket. That's all!

"What the heck do they want? Maybe it'll fly after a fashion with an ion rocket to push it. But what do they want with flying garbage-disposal units?"

A SMALL-MAN reached out his arms and Lon surrendered the object. The little man nodded in friendly fashion and went staggering to his plane with it. More trucks came out. The four-foot-by-one-foot tubes were coming out of the cavern by hundreds and thousands. A remarkable job of mass-production had been performed overnight by the automatic tools underground. But Lon simply could not make head or tail of it.

One of the small-men who had worked with Lon the night before beckoned to him. Lon went with him. Small toy-like planes continued to arrive empty and depart loaded for more than an hour. In all, some thousands of the tubes were carried away.

No more than a dozen remained on a last not-unloaded truck when all the planes had gone and the great metal globe came out from under the then fully opened door. They remained after the globe was gone.

BUT about noon, one of them was used. A small-man, sitting at ease in the truck, suddenly got down from the seat, briskly up-ended one of the tubes so that one end pointed skyward and pressed on a small stud in its side. For seconds nothing happened.

Abruptly the tube began to rise in the air with a swiftly fanning bluish luminescence behind it. It went upward steadily but without haste. It seemed to accelerate slightly as it dwindled with attained height. It vanished, still picking up speed. But it seemed all very commonplace and leisurely and matter-of-fact.

It was all of fifteen minutes before there appeared any consequence of its having taken off. Then a roiling, writhing tumult of yellow vapor appeared in the atmosphere a mile or two to the eastward. It descended with deliberation while vast columns of spouting orange-colored smoke spurted furiously, now up, now down, and now in every direction between.

The smoke moved much faster when parallel to the surface of the planet. It formed, in fact, a weirdly-shaped pancake of ominous yellow with writhing, unsubstantial arms. But it descended slowly.

When it reached the ground, nothing happened—nothing happened at all, which, for a guided missile with a large atomic bomb warhead, was exceptionally remarkable indeed. Lon would have appreciated it but he was not present to watch.

He was somewhere else. He was out in space. His eyes burning, surging ahead into battle.

CHAPTER SEVEN
Sporting Life

THE small folk were—so Lon considered with one part of his mind—a very sporting people. They had given him an intensive half-hour course of instruction in the handling of the forty-foot globe they had built and turned it over to him to fight.

Possibly they considered that, as a more primitive cousin and an experienced handler of spacecraft, he might have a better instinctive grasp of the principles of space-fighting than they had. Or it might have seemed to them the sportsmanlike thing to do.

In any case they had done it, and there were half a dozen of them in the globe with him.

Their manner was that of sparkling-eyed excitement. Caryl's father and Burton were also on board the clumsy object. And when Caryl appeared—in her normal Earth ship costume and flushing hotly when Lon first glanced at her— Lon explained curtly that the small-men had improvised a spaceship and that the three Earthmen were included in its crew. She very firmly climbed aboard too.

She would have had to be ejected by force, and it was not worthwhile. Lon at the time had no hope except to die fighting. The planet of the small-men, and Earth after it, seemed to him to be doomed. If Caryl were to die anyhow, he might as well do it in the spaceship with the others of the

Marintha's crew. At any rate death in space would be clean and quick.

He took the ship up, first startled by its lack of response to power until the small-men beside him—he had been the pilot of the plane the day before—smiled deprecatingly and touched a sketch beside the instrument board. Then Lon realized that vertical speed was limited by the power-field in a spaceship close to the planet.

The *Marintha* had crash-landed on this planet less than thirty hours before and the spoken language problem was still unsolved. But a vocabulary of sketch-symbols had grown up that were actually ideographs. A sketch of a Doole-Boyd battery circuit, for example, needed only to be pointed at to indicate the subject under discussion.

It was rather amazing to see the number of tiny replicas of Lon's own sketches fixed in plain view for communication purposes. And not only sketches of objects were there, a sort of ideological shorthand had developed. There were verbs and even a few adjectives. For example, a non-workable circuit, drawn and then crossed out, was plainly a symbol of "No" or "No good" or a negative generally.

A particularly clear simplification of an Earth-style device—actually not used—similarly meant "Yes" or "Good" or a general affirmative. The system was not as fast or as clear as really fluent speech, but with gestures and voice-intonation it served surprisingly well.

Lon then cut down the power. Taking off would be a lengthy process. There was nothing to be done until the stasis effect of the power-field grew less. He took time to gaze about the interior of the ship. It was a simple hollow shell, braced with internal girders and surprisingly devoid of visible machinery.

At intervals about its curved wall there were small seats for the small-men, each equipped with straps against acceleration-shocks. There were larger ones for Lon and Burton and Caryl's father and one small-man was busily at work improvising another for Caryl beside Lon.

To right and left of Lon there were vision-screens, which were remarkably clear and alive. Above and below were others and a smaller one that showed the view behind him—a back-view device. Merely by moving his eyes he could see clearly on every side of the ship.

Burton and Caryl's father had been provided with vision-screens and controls for weapons they suspected were duplicates of the slug-ship's rod-lightning projectors. The controls were imitations of sighted guns.

The Earthmen should be better with them than the small folk, who on their planet used gas-projectors requiring no accuracy in the hunt. Lon was to fight the ship. He had only a hazy notion of the effectiveness of the devices he had been given, but there was nothing to be done except to try them to whatever limits they might have.

The green land areas and mountains of the planet seemed to flow together. Blue sea invaded the space below the ship. It began to rise more swiftly. Presently the blue sky darkened. Tiny specks of light, which were stars, appeared.

Then the sky was purple and abruptly black with the great ringed sun flaring luridly in emptiness. A thousand million stars seemed to watch as the improvised round spacecraft bounced up out of atmosphere into space itself.

HERE there was evidently no hindrance to acceleration. Lon tried out the ship—cautiously at first, then with increasing freedom. The controls were designed for instinctive reaction to take full advantage of the deep-rooted human instinct to believe oneself the center of all the universe.

It meant that one always tended to pull oneself toward any object desired to push away from an undesirable one. There was a round comfortable hand grip in a convenient position. When Lon pulled himself toward it the ship shot forward. When he pushed away the ship checked or retreated. To push the grip down made the ship rise. To pull up made it descend.

Even sidewise movement was possible and the globe and all its drive-units had plainly been designed so that its center of gravity and of thrust was always the pilot's seat. A lateral twist of the control even spun the ship about on its axis and a vertical twist turned it upside down.

It was infinitely easy to learn to handle controls like that. It was hardly minutes before Lon felt a magnificent confidence. The ship was, as far as its motion was concerned, practically an extension of himself.

He nodded grimly to the small-man who was his co-pilot. He touched the sketch of the slug-ship. He raised his eyebrows. The small-man threw a switch. A red ring of light appeared on his right-hand vision-plate. The slug-ship apparently would be in its center.

Simultaneously fainter blue circles appeared elsewhere over the vast swelling curved surface of the planet below. Lon glanced at them, but the small-man tapped the red ring with his finger. Then he tapped two or three of the blue rings and pointed to a sketch of the globe-ship itself.

"Sister ships, eh?" grunted Lon. "You chaps did work!"

He knew there were other caverns under the surface of the world below him. The demands for power for the broadcast-field, which had to control even the surface-winds of the whole planet, would be so enormous that many power-stations must exist to supply it.

But it had not occurred to him that his every look and gesture and intonation would have been conveyed to half a hundred or more such technological headquarters and that what the small-men in one knew all the others would know too. The communication-system—though he had seen no sign of it—must be remarkable.

The globe-ship shot swiftly toward the enemy that had trailed the *Marintha* over an improbable number of light-years in overdrive. Detectors should be ringing on that ship now. It turned and hurtled toward him to offer battle.

At more than a thousand miles a rod-lightning beam shot out. It missed by hundreds of yards. Lon jerked the globe sidewise nearly into the space it had missed. A ravening group of six rods instantly stabbed through the spot he had left. His eyes gleamed.

"Ranging, eh!" he growled. "Two can play at that!"

He jerked the globe upward and called, "Burton! Take a pot-shot and hold the trigger down!"

A bar of seemingly solid incandescence leaped from his own ship toward the enemy. Lon saw that it missed. By pure reflex action his hand twisted the hand-grip before him, as if to correct the error in sighting. And it did.

The globe-ship spun slightly. The raging beam of pure energy sliced across the slug-ship and great gouts of vaporized metal flashed into being. The slug-ship plunged like a wounded thing and stabbed back furiously.

They plunged upon each other at incredible acceleration. Lon twisted his ship, using the energy-beam like a monstrous blade to slash at the misshapen other craft. Once, twice, three times he struck it. The fourth time there was a seeming explosion, and a huge mass of mistiness streamed out with the violence of a rocket-jet.

"Hulled him!" said Lon, his eyes burning. "Now—"

Then he groaned. The slug-ship, encountering an enemy capable of resistance, suddenly flared that incredible familiar color that is all colors at once and yet definitely not white. It is the flashing iridescence that accompanies the first phase of an overdrive field in formation.

The slug-ship was going into overdrive because it could not make a mere sporting event of destroying the human vessel. It was not yet badly hurt but—

The grinning little man beside Lon made a chuckling noise. His small sinewy fingers snapped home a plunger. The overdrive-field iridescence vanished and the slug-ship was still in normal space. Its flight into the stressed cosmos of overdrive was halted. Its retreat was cut off.

Its rod-lightning beams crashed again in a frenzy. It split space furiously with the monstrous pencils of power. It was less than a hundred miles away now and only the erratic dancing leaps of the globe-ship baffled its raging cannonade.

But Lon fought his ship as in single personal combat, with a shining sword blade of energy before him. He fenced zestfully like a man with a rapier dancing about an opponent who flung spinning knives while the slender blade ripped and ripped at him.

He slashed and slashed, delicately. A second sudden burst of vapor—a colossal expanding cloud of chlorine atmosphere—the rod-lightning ceased. The slug-ship ceased to accelerate. It seemed dead in space. It hurtled on and on. Sixty miles, fifty, forty, thirty, twenty—no sign of life.

INSTINCTIVELY, Lon ceased his slashings. He watched intently. The small-man beside him was bubbling with laughter, despite the crazy gyrations in which Lon kept the globe-ship lest this be a trick.

"It looks like he's dead," he said dubiously.

But as the last word left his lips the slug-ship fired again. At less than five miles range it could not miss. The six rods of pure destructive energy stabbed despairingly, ragingly out.

They hit the globe-ship squarely, all six of them. Lon caught his breath. There was a perceptible physical shock of impact. And the *Marintha* had been pierced through and through by every such bolt to touch her.

This ship was not.

There was an instant in which it seemed that all of space was somehow straining. It felt almost like the odd shock of going into overdrive. Then the rod-lightning turned from mere incandescence into a blinding blue-white color. The rods ceased to exist. And the slug-ship glowed red, then white and flew apart in tormented metal vapor as it reached its point of closest approach to the globe, and then went hurtling onward through unresisting emptiness.

"Holy hoptoad!" said Lon, dazed. "You wanted him to hit us! When his beams hit you tied a knot in them and sent stuff back that simply vaporized his whole ship!" The twinkling mirth-filled eyes of the small-man beside him were fullest confirmation.

"But why fight him?" The small-man reached out and shook hands, his eyes zestfully excited. "Confound it!" said Lon slowly. "I'll bet you wanted to have a fight first for the sport of it!"

Then the blue rings on the vision-screens moved swiftly toward him and long rod-lightning beams reached out from each one and waved gleefully in emptiness and winked out. And shortly the globes of the small-man fleet were clustered about Lon's own ship, weaving and spinning in sportive dizzy evolutions. And the evolutions were those that Lon had used in his single combat. It was plain that the small-men approved of Lon quite heartily.

There were sixty or seventy of the globe-ships—Lon was never sure—and they made a respectable space fleet. It was not a fleet that Earth could have built so readily nor equipped with such weapons. When tiny red circles began to wink into being all over the vision-screens he would have gathered them into some sort of formation to lead them to the attack.

But there was—he realized it with a sinking heart—no possible formation that would intercept attack upon the planet. The slug-ships, newly-arrived and avid for destruction, were coming out of overdrive all through a half-million mile sphere of emptiness. Each one went hurtling toward the green planet at full acceleration.

But the globe-ships swept out to meet them. There were slug-ships by hundreds, and the defenders were outnumbered five and six to one, but their gallant sword-beams stabbed out and slashed through the chill void between the planets, and the massed beams of the slug-ships darted out furiously.

The globes fought as Lon had done, zestfully dancing like motes amid their enemies and seeking to engage in something like formal duels. But the slug-ships were not concerned with punctilio. Here and there a globe and a single slug-ship fought it out to the end but in general it was the policy of the attackers to concentrate in overwhelming numbers upon individual small-man ships and overwhelm them with lightnings.

Which was a mistake.

The englobing monsters sent their blasts ravening home— and nothing whatever happened to the target-globes. But the slug-ships glowed incandescent and exploded as their walls went soft from heat.

Those who had not been so unfortunate as to score a hit now instantly glittered with the overdrive-field energy in immediate attempt to flee since they had encountered dangerous resistance. But they could not escape. Overdrive was dead to them. Surrender apparently did not occur to them.

All the vast emptiness in which the battle proceeded, now suddenly became filled with writhing, curling coils of vapor.

Guided missiles went shrieking soundlessly among the stars. And one after another of the slug-ships flamed and burst and the survivors acted like cornered rats—and there were thousands of smoke-trails streaking toward the planet.

Lon snapped feverish orders and Burton and Caryl's father—who alone understood him—tried desperately to snipe the deadly things, revealed by their trails of yellow vapor. Burton did detonate one and for an instant there was a flare of atomic fire much brighter than the unshielded ringed sun.

And Lon was flinging the globe-ship down to try to intercept more, when his co-pilot chuckled and shook his head. He looked as if he liked Lon rather more than before just then but he pointed to a smoke-trail as it sped planetward and turned a control Lon had not noted.

The screen became an enormous magnifying telescope. It brought the diving guided missile to view as a dot, then as a somehow revolting wormlike form, large enough so that the absolute absence of any detail on its surface could be seen.

AND then, suddenly, an equally improbable thing came darting to meet it. This other thing was an open-ended tube with a rapidly fanning blue corona-discharge glow at its tail. It was, in effect, a section of flying plastic stove-pipe.

It hurtled upon the guided missile, made contact and clung. And suddenly there were swirling vapors and tiny flames. The guided missile checked in its course. Its furiously jetting rocket-trail did not cease but the plastic-tube device clung to it and flames gnawed at the alien thing.

Lon swore softly, staring. "A garbage disposal unit!" he said, stunned. "You fixed up a meteor-detector in a stove-pipe to find flying missiles in the sky. You added an ion-rocket to drive it and a garbage-disposal unit to break down some included wetted trash to oxygen and hydrogen and carbon and ash.

"And you've got those gadgets meeting the atom bombs as they come down! They play what amounts to an oxy-hydrogen jet on them! It won't destroy the explosive. Of course, but it will melt and wreck any detonation-system. And when they land you'll pick up what's left and have a very nice supply of atomic explosive."

His co-pilot did not understand his Earthman speech. But when Lon put out his hand the small-man shook it exuberantly.

An hour later the globe-ship landed, Lon felt distinctly rueful about the whole business, but Caryl's father was pleased.

"After all, Lon," he observed, "even if we did bring the slug-ships after us we brought these folks some interesting, if primitive devices. And they needed them. The slug-creatures would have found them sooner or later just as they are bound to find Earth.

"When we arrived they were in the situation of a civilized man at the mercy of a savage armed with a bow and arrow. A Superson absorber will defend one against a Superson pistol, but it would be useless against an arrow.

"For that one needs armor—a primitive defense against a primitive weapon. You gave them the armor they needed. Incidentally you—we—all of us—have made what should be a valuable contact for Earth. Another human race—"

Lon frowned. "They're so far ahead of us," he said uneasily," that they could conquer us if they wanted to. And that's bad…"

"Lon!" said the older man somewhat severely. "They're civilized. Civilized men don't want to conquer other men."

That, it turned out, was wholly true. The further proceedings of the small-men against the people of the chlorine planet were essentially civilized. All over their planet, by hundreds of thousands, the stove-pipe-like devices had been ready.

Of the more than two thousand atomic missiles discharged against the planet, exactly two reached the surface and detonated. The others were all intercepted and made harmless before they landed. And the small-men gathered up the warheads and—after interested discussion with Lon— contrived two remote controlled space-navigators.

There had been a dozen or more of the slug-ships hulled and captured relatively intact by the globe-ships besides the enormously greater number vaporized. Three of the hulled ships were included in each of the navigators. One of the navigators went up and headed for the Crab Nebula neighborhood in overdrive. It was intended to be intercepted by the second slug-ship fleet.

If the slug-creatures attempted to open communication with it—if they landed upon it—if they adopted any other policy than that of instant and unwarned attack—they would find three of their first fleet, neatly holed and wrecked, returned to them with a full half of the first fleets' atomic explosive.

They would have a warning against further attack in the carcasses of their shattered ships. But they would also have assurance that the destroyers of the first fleet desired nothing of them, hence the return of so much infinitely valuable atomic explosive.

But if the slug-fleet instantly and savagely attacked the robot navigator, without first attempting communication, the results would be catastrophic. Half the atomic explosive intended to blast a planet would go off in the middle of the fleet.

Rather worse, with it would explode a considerably greater mass of matter, which normally could not be detonated at all, but would break down to sheer, raw energy when an atomic explosion acted on it like a primer.

The second navigator took to space a week after the first. If the first ship was able to give its message, well and good. The second would reinforce it. But if the first ship was attacked, the second would go on past the thinning vapor, which would be all that was left of a slug-ship fleet, and presently deliver exactly the same message and the same choice of peace or destruction to the chlorine-breathers' planet. The small-men were amiably prepared to leave the chlorine-breathers alone. But after all, if they wanted to fight...

BUT Lon and Caryl and Burton and Caryl's father did not wait to learn of the result of that scrupulously just ultimatum. They headed back to Earth in the globe-ship Lon had captained, a trifle more fully equipped for long-distance space-voyaging with cabins and bunks and a galley and food supplies.

No small-men would consider accompanying them. They had arranged their planet and its climate and its vegetation to suit them. They had at every instant a complete service of everything they wanted, including companionship and leisure and an environment to which they were exactly suited. They were wholly comfortable and satisfied.

Lon had promised to return with all the facts they could possibly be interested in about all sciences and all other worlds. But they would never care about leaving their own. It would be unspeakably boring for them to be away from home.

They liked the four Earth-people, though. They loaded what space was available with gifts they thought would be appreciated. And Lon hated to leave because he was just beginning to grasp some of the principles of the small-men's science. Caryl liked it even less. She got along famously with the girls and was beginning to learn the language.

But they had to go, of course. They had to warn Earth of the possible continued existence of a bloodthirsty chlorine-breathers' culture, and of the measures that should be taken for self-protection.

And too there was a small formality they wanted to go through which could only be managed back on Earth. They intended to return to the planet of the small-men.

They meant to spend much of their honeymoon there. But Caryl wanted to be married in a veil.

THE END

If you've enjoyed this book, you will not want to miss these terrific titles...

ARMCHAIR SCI-FI & HORROR DOUBLE NOVELS, $12.95 each

D-121 **THE GENIUS BEASTS** by Frederik Pohl
THIS WORLD IS TABOO by Murray Leinster

D-122 **THE COSMIC LOOTERS** by Edmond Hamilton
WANDL THE INVADER by Ray Cummings

D-123 **ROBOT MEN OF BUBBLE CITY** by Rog Phillips
DRAGON ARMY by William Morrison

D-124 **LAND BEYOND THE LENS** by S. J. Byrne
DIPLOMAT-AT-ARMS by Keith Laumer

D-125 **VOYAGE OF THE ASTEROID, THE** by Laurence Manning
REVOLT OF THE OUTWORLDS by Milton Lesser

D-126 **OUTLAW IN THE SKY** by Chester S. Geier
LEGACY FROM MARS by Raymond Z. Gallun

D-127 **THE GREAT FLYING SAUCER INVASION** by Geoff St. Reynard
THE BIG TIME by Fritz Leiber

D-128 **MIRAGE FOR PLANET X** by Stanley Mullen
POLICE YOUR PLANET by Lester del Rey

D-129 **THE BRAIN SINNER** by Alan E. Nourse
DEATH FROM THE SKIES by A. Hyatt Verrill

D-130 **CRY CHAOS** by Dwight V. Swain
THE DOOR THROUGH SPACE By Marion Zimmer Bradley

ARMCHAIR SCIENCE FICTION CLASSICS, $12.95 each

C-55 **UNDER THE TRIPLE SUNS**
by Stanton A. Coblentz (single) 1950s, Fantasy Press

C-56 **STONE FROM THE GREEN STAR**
by Jack Williamson, Amazing 10 & 11/31, (cleared by Eli)

C-57 **ALIEN MINDS**
by E. Everett Evans

ARMCHAIR SCI-FI & HORROR GEMS SERIES, $12.95 each

G-13 **SCIENCE FICTION GEMS, Vol. Seven**
Jack Vance and others

G-14 **HORROR GEMS, Vol. Seven**
Robert Bloch and others

If you've enjoyed this book, you will not want to miss these terrific titles…

ARMCHAIR SCI-FI & HORROR DOUBLE NOVELS, $12.95 each

D-131   **COSMIC KILL** by Robert Silverberg
BEYOND THE END OF SPACE by John W. Campbell

D-132   **THE DARK OTHER** by Stanley Weinbaum)
WITCH OF THE DEMON SEAS by Poul Anderson

D-133   **PLANET OF THE SMALL MEN** by Murray Leinster
MASTERS OF SPACE by E. E. "Doc" Smith & E. Everett Evans

D-134   **BEFORE THE ASTEROIDS** by Harl Vincent
SIXTH GLACIER, THE by Marius

D-135   **AFTER WORLD'S END** by Jack Williamson
THE FLOATING ROBOT by David Wright O'Brien

D-136   **NINE WORLDS WEST** by Paul W. Fairman
FRONTIERS BEYOND THE SUN by Rog Phillips

D-137   **THE COSMIC KINGS** by Edmond Hamilton
LONE STAR PLANET by H. Beam Piper & John J. McGuire

D-138   **BEYOND THE DARKNESS** by S. J. Byrne
THE FIRELESS AGE by David H. Keller, M. D.

D-139   **FLAME JEWEL OF THE ANCIENTS** by Edwin L. Graber
THE PIRATE PLANET by Charles W. Diffin

D-140   **ADDRESS: CENTAURI** by F. L. Wallace
IF THESE BE GODS by Algis Budrys

ARMCHAIR SCIENCE FICTION & HORROR CLASSICS, $12.95 each

C-58   **THE WITCHING NIGHT**
by Leslie Waller

C-59   **SEARCH THE SKY**
by Frederick Pohl and C. M. Kornbluth

C-60   **INTRIGUE ON THE UPPER LEVEL**
by Thomas Tempel Hoyne

ARMCHAIR SCI-FI & HORROR GEMS SERIES, $12.95 each

G-15   **SCIENCE FICTION GEMS, Vol. Eight**
Keith Laumer and others

G-16   **HORROR GEMS, Vol. Eight**
Algernon Blackwood and others

AN EPIC TALE OF NAIL-BITING SPACE OPERA

The Masters had ruled all space with an unconquerable iron fist. But the Masters were gone now, and a new, young race had come to take their place.

Young Jarvis Hilton was in charge of a special team of scientists—men and women alike—who set out on an outer space mission known as "Project Theta Orionis." In their mighty starship they journeyed into deep space, but soon found themselves encountering a mysterious skeletal object, as well as being witness to an epic space battle.

Their voyage eventually led them to a strange planet covered with radioactive fuel ores, and populated with android creatures who have been expecting their arrival and soon hail them as their returning masters! But even with their combined strength, could they hope to defeat the dreaded ancient Enemy of All?

About E. E. "Doc" Smith and E. Everett Evans:

Edward Elmer Smith was born May 2nd, 1890. He is considered by many to be the father of space opera. As a sci-fi pioneer (starting in 1916) Smith wrote many novels that are now considered timeless classics. Among them are his famous "Skylark" and "Lensmen" novels.

In 1918, two years after beginning *Skylark of Space,* Smith received a Ph.D. in chemical engineering, with an emphasis on food engineering. He was lovingly known to some as "The Doughnut Doctor" because of his specialty in developing new types of doughnuts and other pastries.

In 1930, Smith wrote what is considered by many (including himself) to be his best work, *The Spacehounds of IPC.* It was followed a short time later by the equally brilliant space adventure, *Triplanetary.* After retiring from the food industry in 1957, Smith continued to write occasionally and produced The Galaxy Primes for Amazing Stories in 1959. During his later years Smith became good friends with fellow sci-fi writer, Robert Heinlein. E. E. Smith passed away on August 31st, 1965

Edward Everett Evans was born in 1893. As a writer, he started late, not publishing his first genre tale until 1947. Along with a couple dozen sci-fi short stories, Evans wrote three novels: The escapades of Esper spy George Hanlan in *Man of Many Minds* (1953); its sequel, *Alien Minds* (1955); and one other work, *The Planet Mappers* (1955).

Evans was highly regarded by two well-known science fiction masters, E. E. Smith and A. E. van Vogt. Eventually Smith expanded an Evans short story into *Masters from Space*, published in 1961, three years after Evans' death. Film historian Forest J. Ackerman also created the "E. Everett Evans Big Heart Award" to honor "outstanding service" to the sci-fi field. E. Everett Evans passed away on December 2nd, 1958.

MASTERS OF SPACE

By
EDWARD E. SMITH & E. EVERETT EVANS

ARMCHAIR FICTION
PO Box 4369, Medford, Oregon 97504

CHAPTER ONE

"BUT didn't you feel *anything*, Javo?" Strain was apparent in every line of Tula's taut, bare body. "Nothing at all?"

"Nothing whatever." The one called Javo relaxed from his rigid concentration. "Nothing has changed. Nor will it."

"That conclusion is indefensible!" Tula snapped. "With the promised return of the Masters there must and will be changes. Didn't *any* of you feel anything?"

Her hot, demanding eyes swept the group; a group whose like, except for physical perfection, could be found in any nudist colony.

No one except Tula had felt a thing.

"That fact is not too surprising," Javo said finally. "You have the most sensitive receptors of us all. But are you sure?"

"I am sure. It was the thought-form of a living Master."

"Do you think that the Master perceived your web?"

"It is certain. Those who built us are stronger than we."

"That is true. As they promised, then, so long and long ago, our Masters are returning home to us."

JARVIS Hilton of Terra, the youngest man yet to be assigned to direct any such tremendous deep-space undertaking as Project Theta Orionis, sat in conference with his two seconds-in-command. Assistant Director Sandra Cummings, analyst-synthesist and semantician, was tall, blonde and svelte. Planetographer William Karns—a black-haired, black-browed, black-eyed man of thirty—was third in rank of the scientific group.

"I'm telling you, Jarve, you can't have it both ways," Karns declared. "Captain Sawtelle is old-school Navy brass. He goes strictly by the book. So you've got to draw a razor-sharp line; exactly where the Advisory Board's directive puts it. And next time he sticks his ugly puss across that line, kick his face in. You've been Caspar Milquetoast Two ever since we left Base."

"That's the way it looks to you?" Hilton's right hand became a fist. "The man has age, experience and ability. I've been trying to meet him on a ground of courtesy and decency."

"Exactly. And he doesn't recognize the existence of either. And, since the Board rammed you down his throat instead of giving him old Jeffers, you needn't expect him to."

"You may be right, Bill. What do you think, Dr. Cummings?"

The girl said: "Bill's right. Also, your constant appeasement isn't doing the morale of the whole scientific group a bit of good."

"Well, I haven't enjoyed it, either. So next time I'll pin his ears back. Anything else?"

"Yes, Dr. Hilton, I have a squawk of my own. I know I was rammed down your throat, but just when are you going to let me do some work?"

"None of us has much of anything to do yet, and won't have until we light somewhere. You're off base a country mile."

"I'm not off base. You *did* want Eggleston, not me."

"Sure I did. I've worked with him and know what he can do. But I'm not holding a grudge about it."

"No? Why, then, are you on first-name terms with everyone in the scientific group except me? Supposedly your first assistant?"

"That's easy!" Hilton snapped. "Because you've been carrying chips on both shoulders ever since you came aboard...or at least I thought you were." Hilton grinned suddenly and held out his hand. "Sorry, Sandy—I'll start all over again."

"I'm sorry too, Chief." They shook hands warmly. "I *was* pretty stiff, I guess, but I'll be good."

"You'll go to work right now, too. As semantician. Dig out that directive and tear it down. Draw that line Bill talked about."

"Can do, boss." She swung to her feet and walked out of the room, her every movement one of lithe and easy grace.

Karns followed her with his eyes. "Funny. A trained-dancer Ph.D. And a Miss America type, like all the other women aboard this spacer. I wonder if she'll make out."

"So do I. I still wish they'd given me Eggy. I've never seen an executive-type female Ph.D. yet that was worth the cyanide it would take to poison her."

"That's what Sawtelle thinks of you, too, you know."

"I know; and the Board *does* know its stuff. So I'm really hoping, Bill, that she surprises me as much as I intend to surprise the Navy."

ALARM bells clanged as the mighty *Perseus* blinked out of overdrive. Every crewman sprang to his post.

"Mister Snowden, why did we emerge without orders from me?" Captain Sawtelle bellowed, storming into the control room three jumps behind Hilton.

"The automatics took control, sir," he said, quietly.

"Automatics! I *give* the orders!"

"In this case, Captain Sawtelle, you don't," Hilton said. Eyes locked and held. To Sawtelle, this was a new and strange co-commander. "I would suggest that we discuss this matter in private."

"Very well, sir," Sawtelle said; and in the captain's cabin Hilton opened up.

"For your information, Captain Sawtelle, I set my inter-space coupling detectors for any objective I choose. When any one of them reacts, it trips the kickers and we emerge. During any emergency outside the Solar System I am in command—with the provision that I must relinquish command to you in case of armed attack on us."

"Where do you think you found any such stuff as that in the directive? It isn't there and I know my rights."

"It is, and you don't. Here is a semantic chart of the whole directive. As you will note, it overrides many Navy regulations. Disobedience of my orders constitutes mutiny and I can—and will—have you put in irons and sent back to Terra for court-martial. Now let's go back."

In the control room, Hilton said, "The target has a mass of approximately five hundred metric tons. There is also a significant amount of radiation characteristic of uranexite. You will please execute search, Captain Sawtelle."

And Captain Sawtelle ordered the search.

"What did you do to the big jerk, boss?" Sandra whispered.

"What you and Bill suggested," Hilton whispered back. "Thanks to your analysis of the directive—pure gobbledygook if there ever was any—I could. Mighty good job, Sandy."

TEN or fifteen more minutes passed. Then:

"Here's the source of radiation, sir," a searchman reported. "It's a point source, though, not an object at this range."

"And here's the artifact, sir," Pilot Snowden said. "We're coming up on it fast. But...but what's a *skyscraper* skeleton doing out here in interstellar space?"

As they closed up, everyone could see that the thing did indeed look like the metallic skeleton of a great building. It was a huge cube, measuring well over a hundred yards along each edge. And it was empty.

"*That's* one for the book," Sawtelle said.

"And how!" Hilton agreed. "I'll take a boat...no, suits would be better. Karns, Yarborough, get Techs Leeds and Miller and suit up."

"You'll need a boat escort," Sawtelle said. "Mr. Ashley, execute escort Landing Craft One, Two, and Three."

The three landing craft approached that enigmatic lattice-work of structural steel and stopped. Five grotesquely armored figures wafted themselves forward on pencils of force. Their leader, whose suit bore the number "14", reached a mammoth girder and worked his way along it up to a peculiar-looking bulge. The whole immense structure vanished, leaving men and boats in empty space.

Sawtelle gasped. "Snowden! Are you holding 'em?"

"No, sir. Faster than light; hyperspace, sir."

"Mr. Ashby, did you have your interspace rigs set?"

"No, sir. I didn't think of it, sir."

"Doctor Cummings, why weren't yours out?"

"I didn't think of such a thing, either—any more than you did," Sandra said.

Ashby, the Communications Officer, had been working the radio. "No reply from anyone, sir," he reported.

"Oh, no!" Sandra exclaimed. Then, "But look! They're firing pistols—especially the one wearing number fourteen—but *pistols*?"

"Recoil pistols—sixty-threes—for emergency use in case of power failure," Ashby explained. "That's it...but I can't see why *all* their power went out at once. But Fourteen—that's Hilton—is really doing a job with that sixty-three. He'll be here in a couple of minutes."

And he was. "Every power unit out there—suits and boats both—drained," Hilton reported. "*Completely* drained. Get some help out there fast!"

IN an enormous structure deep below the surface of a far-distant world a group of technicians clustered together in front of one section of a two-miles long control board. They were staring at a light that had just appeared where no light should have been.

"Someone's brain-pan will be burned out for this," one of the group radiated harshly. "That unit was inactivated long ago and it has not been reactivated."

"Someone committed an error, Your Loftiness?"

"Silence, fool! Stretts do not commit errors!"

AS soon as it was clear that no one had been injured, Sawtelle demanded, "How about it, Hilton?"

"Structurally, it was high-alloy steel. There were many bulges, possibly containing mechanisms. There were drive-units of a non-Terran type. There were many projectors, which—at a rough guess—were a hundred times as powerful as any I have ever seen before. There were no indications that the thing had ever been enclosed, in whole or in part. It certainly never had living quarters for warm-blooded, oxygen-breathing eaters of organic food."

Sawtelle snorted. "You mean it never had a crew?"

"Not necessarily..."

"Bah! What other kind of intelligent life is there?"

"I don't know. But before we speculate too much, let's look at the tri-di. The camera may have caught something I missed."

It hadn't. The three-dimensional pictures added nothing.

"It probably was operated either by programmed automatics or by remote control," Hilton decided, finally. "But how did they drain all our power? And just as bad, what and how is that other point source of power we're heading for now?"

"What's wrong with it?" Sawtelle asked.

"Its strength. No matter what distance or reactant I assume, nothing we know will fit. Neither fission nor fusion will do it. It has to be practically total conversion!"

CHAPTER TWO

THE *Perseus* snapped out of overdrive near the point of interest and Hilton stared, motionless and silent.

Space was full of madly warring ships. Half of them were bare, giant skeletons of steel, like the "derelict" that had so unexpectedly blasted away from them. The others were more or less like the *Perseus*, except in being bigger, faster and of vastly greater power.

Beams of starkly incredible power bit at and clung to equally capable defensive screens of pure force. As these inconceivable forces met, the glare of their neutralization filled all nearby space. And ships and skeletons alike were disappearing in chunks, blobs, gouts, streamers and sparkles of rended, fused and vaporized metal.

Hilton watched two ships combine against one skeleton. Dozens of beams, incredibly tight and hard, were held inexorably upon dozens of the bulges of the skeleton. Overloaded, the bulges' screens flared through the spectrum and failed. And bare metal, however refractory, endures only for instants under the appalling intensity of such beams as those.

The skeletons tried to duplicate the ships' method of attack, but failed. They were too slow. Not slow, exactly, either, but hesitant; as though it required whole seconds for the commander—or operator? Or remote controller?—of each skeleton to make it act. The ships were winning.

"Hey!" Hilton yelped. "Oh—that's the one we saw back there. But what in all space does it think it's doing?"

It was plunging at tremendous speed straight through the immense fleet of embattled skeletons. It did not fire a beam nor energize a screen; it merely plunged along as though on a plotted course until it collided with one of the skeletons of the fleet and both structures plunged, a tangled mass of wreckage, to the ground of the planet below.

Then hundreds of the ships shot forward, each to plunge into and explode inside one of the skeletons. When visibility was restored another wave of ships came forward to repeat the performance, but there was nothing left to fight. Every surviving skeleton had blinked out of normal space.

The remaining ships made no effort to pursue the skeletons, nor did they re-form as a fleet. Each ship went off by itself.

And on that distant planet of the Stretts the group of mechs watched with amazed disbelief as light after light after light winked out on their two-miles-long control board. Frantically they relayed orders to the skeletons; orders which did not affect the losses.

"Brain-pans will blacken for this…" a mental snarl began, to be interrupted by a coldly imperious thought.

"That long-dead unit, so inexplicably reactivated, is approaching the fuel world. It is ignoring the battle. It is heading through our fleet toward the Oman half…*handle* it, ten-eighteen!"

"It does not respond, Your Loftiness."

"Then blast it, fool! Ah, it is inactivated. As encyclopedist, Nine, explain the freakish behavior of that unit."

"Yes, Your Loftiness. Many cycles ago we sent a ship against the Omans with a new device of destruction. The Omans must have intercepted it, drained it of power and allowed it to drift on. After all these cycles of time it must have come upon a small source of power and of course continued its mission."

"That can be the truth. The Lords of the Universe must be informed."

"The mining units, the carriers and the refiners have not been affected, Your Loftiness," a mech radiated.

"So I see, fool." Then, activating another instrument, His Loftiness thought at it, in an entirely different vein, "Lord Ynos, Madam? I have to make a very grave report…"

IN the *Perseus*, four scientists and three Navy officers were arguing heatedly; employing deep-space verbiage not to be found in any dictionary. "Jarve!" Karns called out, and Hilton joined the group. "Does anything about this planet make any sense to you?"

"No. But you're the planetographer. 'Smatter with it?"

"It's a good three hundred degrees Kelvin too hot."

"Well, you know it's loaded with uranexite."

"That much? The whole crust practically jewelry ore?"

"If that's what the figures say, I'll buy it."

"Buy *this*, then. Continuous daylight everywhere. Noon June Sol-quality light *except* that it's all in the visible. Frank says it's from bombardment of a layer of something, and Frank admits that the whole thing's impossible."

"When Frank makes up his mind what 'something' is, I'll take it as a datum."

"Third thing: there's only one city on this continent, and it's protected by a screen that nobody ever heard of."

Hilton pondered, then turned to the captain. "Will you please run a search-pattern, sir? Fine-toothing only the hot spots?"

The planet was approximately the same size as Terra; its atmosphere, except for its intense radiation, was similar to Terra's. There were two continents; one immense girdling ocean. The temperature of the land surface was everywhere about 100°F, that of the water about 90°F. Each continent had one city, and both were small. One was inhabited by what looked like human beings; the other by usuform robots. The human city was the only cool spot on the entire planet; under its protective dome the temperature was 71°F.

Hilton decided to study the robots first; and asked the captain to take the ship down to observation range. Sawtelle objected; and continued to object until Hilton started to order his arrest. Then he said, "I'll do it, under protest, but I want it on record that I am doing it against my best judgment."

"It's on record," Hilton said, coldly. "Everything said and done is being, and will continue to be, recorded."

The *Perseus* floated downward. "*There's* what I want most to see," Hilton said, finally. "That big strip-mining operation...that's it...hold it!" Then, via throat-mike, "Attention, all scientists! You all know what to do. Start doing it."

Sandra's blonde head was very close to Hilton's brown one as they both stared into Hilton's plate. "Why, they look like giant armadillos!" she exclaimed.

"More like tanks," he disagreed, "except that they've got legs, wheels *and* treads—and arms, cutters, diggers, probes and conveyors—and *look* at the way those buckets dip solid rock!"

The fantastic machine was moving very slowly along a bench or shelf that it was making for itself as it went along. Below it, to its left, dropped other benches being made by other mining machines. The machines were not using explosives. Hard though the ore was, the tools were so much harder and were driven with such tremendous power that the stuff might just have well have been slightly-clayed sand.

Every bit of loosened ore, down to the finest dust, was forced into a conveyor and thence into the armored body of the machine. There it went into a mechanism whose basic principles Hilton could not understand. From this monstrosity emerged two streams of product.

One of these, comprising ninety-nine point nine plus percent of the input, went out through another conveyor into the vast hold of a vehicle which, when full and replaced by a duplicate of itself, went careening madly cross-country to a dump.

The other product, a slow, very small stream of tiny, glistening black pellets, fell into a one-gallon container being held watchfully by a small machine, more or less like a three-wheeled motor scooter, which was moving carefully along beside the giant miner. When this can was almost full another scooter rolled up and, without losing a single pellet, took over place and function. The first scooter then covered its bucket, clamped it solidly into a recess designed for the purpose and dashed away toward the city.

Hilton stared slack-jawed at Sandra. She stared back.

"Do you make anything of that, Jarve?"

"Nothing. They're taking *pure* uranexite and *concentrating*—or converting—it a thousand to one. I *hope* we'll be able to do something about it."

"I hope so, too, Chief; and I'm *sure* we will."

"Well, that's enough for now. You may take us up now, Captain Sawtelle. And Sandy, will you please call all department heads and their assistants into the conference room?"

AT the head of the long conference table, Hilton studied his fourteen department heads, all husky young men, and their assistants, all surprisingly attractive and well-built young women. Bud Carroll and Sylvia Bannister of Sociology sat together. He was almost as big as Karns; she was a green-eyed redhead whose five-ten and one-fifty would have looked big except for the arrangement thereof. There were Bernadine and Hermione van der Moen, the leggy, breasty, platinum-blonde twins—both of whom were Cowper medalists in physics. There was Etienne de Vaux, the mathematical wizard; and Rebecca Eisenstein, the black-haired, flashing-eyed ex-infant-prodigy theoretical astronomer. There was Beverly Bell, who made mathematically impossible chemical syntheses—who swam channels for days on end and computed planetary orbits in her sleekly-coiffured head.

"First, we'll have a get-together," Hilton said. "Nothing recorded; just to get acquainted. You all know that our fourteen departments cover science, from astronomy to zoology."

He paused, again his eyes swept the group. Stella Wing, who would have been a grand-opera star except for her drive to know everything about language. Theodora (Teddy) Blake, who would prove gleefully that she was the world's best model—but was in fact the most brilliantly promising theoretician who had ever lived.

"No other force like this has ever been assembled," Hilton went on. "In more ways than one. Sawtelle wanted Jeffers to head this group, instead of me. Everybody thought he *would* head it."

"And Hilton wanted Eggleston and got *me*," Sandra said.

"That's right. And quite a few of you didn't want to come at all, but were told by the Board to come or else."

The group stirred. Eyes met eyes, and there were smiles.

"I MYSELF think Jeffers *should* have had the job. I've never handled anything half this big and I'll need a lot of help. But I'm stuck with it and you're all stuck with me, so we'll all take it and like it. You've noticed, of course, the accent on youth. The Navy crew is normal, except for the commanders being unusually young. But we aren't. None of us is thirty yet, and none of us has ever been married. You fellows look like a team of professional athletes, and you girls—well, if I didn't know better I'd say the Board had screened you for the front row of the chorus instead of for a top-bracket brain-gang. How they found so many of you I'll never know."

"Virile men and nubile women!" Etienne de Vaux leered enthusiastically. "*Vive le Board!*"

"Nubile! Bravo, Tiny! *Quelle delicatesse de nuance!*"

"Three rousing cheers for the Board!"

"Keep still, you nitwits! Let me ask a question!" This came from one of the twins. "Before you give us the deduction, Jarvis—or will it be an intuition or an induction or a…"

"Or an inducement," the other twin suggested, helpfully. "Not that *you* would need very much of that."

"You keep still, too, Miney. I'm asking, Sir Moderator, if I can give my deduction first?"

"Sure, Bernadine; go ahead."

"They figured we're going to get completely lost. Then we'll jettison the Navy, hunt up a planet of our own and start a race to end all human races. Or would you call this a *see*-duction instead of a *dee*-duction?"

This produced a storm of whistles, cheers and jeers that it took several seconds to quell.

"But seriously, Jarvis," Bernadine went on. "We've all been wondering and it doesn't make sense. Have you any idea at all of what the Board actually did have in mind?"

"I believe that the Board selected for mental, not physical, qualities; for the ability to handle anything unexpected or unusual that comes up, no matter what it is."

"You think it wasn't double-barreled?" asked Kincaid, the psychologist. He smiled quizzically. "That all this virility and nubility and glamor is pure coincidence?"

"No," Hilton said, with an almost imperceptible flick of an eyelid. "Coincidence is as meaningless as paradox. I think they found out that—barring freaks—the best minds are in the best bodies."

"Could be. The idea has been propounded before."

"Now let's get to work." Hilton flipped the switch of the recorder. "Starting with you, Sandy, each of you give a two-minute boil-down. What you found and what you think."

SOMETHING over an hour later the meeting adjourned and Hilton and Sandra strolled toward the control room.

"I don't know whether you convinced Alexander Q. Kincaid or not, but you didn't quite convince me," Sandra said.

"Nor him, either."

"Oh?" Sandra's eyebrows

"No. He grabbed the out I offered him. I didn't fool Teddy Blake or Temple Bells, either. You four are all, though, I think."

"Temple? You think *she's* so smart?"

"I don't *think* so, no. Don't fool yourself, chick. Temple Bells looks and acts sweet and innocent and virginal. Maybe— probably—she is. But she isn't showing a fraction of the stuff she's really got. She's heavy artillery, Sandy. And I mean *heavy.*"

"I think you're slightly nuts there. But do you really believe that the Board was playing Cupid?"

"Not trying, but doing. Cold-bloodedly and efficiently. Yes."

"But it wouldn't *work*! We aren't going to get lost!"

"We won't need to. Propinquity will do the work."

"Phooie. You and me, for instance?" She stopped, put both hands on her hips, and glared. "Why, I wouldn't marry *you* if you..."

"I'll tell the cockeyed world you won't!" Hilton broke in. "Me marry a damned female Ph.D.? Uh-uh. Mine will be a cuddly little brunette that thinks a slipstick is some kind of lipstick and that an isotope's something good to eat."

"One like that copy of Murchison's Dark Lady that you keep under the glass on your desk?" she sneered.

"Exactly..." He started to continue the battle, then shut himself off. "But listen, Sandy, why should we get into a fight because we don't want to marry each other? You're doing a swell job. I admire you tremendously for it and I like to work with you."

"You've got a point there, Jarve, at that, and I'm one of the few who know what kind of a job *you're* doing, so I'll relax." She flashed him a gamin grin and they went on into the control room.

It was too late in the day then to do any more exploring; but the next morning, early, the *Perseus* lined out for the city of the humanoids.

Tula turned toward her fellows. Her eyes filled with a happily triumphant light and her thought a lilting song. "I have been telling you from the first touch that it was the Masters. It *is* the Masters! The Masters are returning to us Omans and their own home world!"

"CAPTAIN Sawtelle," Hilton said, "Please land in the cradle below."

"*Land?*" Sawtelle stormed. "On a planet like *that?* Not by…" He broke off and stared; for now, on that cradle, there flamed out in screaming red the *Perseus'* own Navy-coded landing symbols!

"Your protest is recorded," Hilton said. "Now, sir, land."

Fuming, Sawtelle landed. Sandra looked pointedly at Hilton. "First contact is my dish, you know."

"Not that I like it, but it is." He turned to a burly youth with sun-bleached, crew-cut hair, "Still safe, Frank?"

"Still abnormally low. Surprising no end, since all the rest of the planet is hotter than the middle tail-race of hell."

"Okay, Sandy. Who will you want besides the top linguists?"

"Psych—both Alex and Temple. And Teddy Blake. They're over there. Tell them, will you, while I buzz Teddy?"

"Will do," and Hilton stepped over to the two psychologists and told them. Then, "I hope I'm not leading with my chin, Temple, but is that your real first name or a professional?"

"It's real; it really is. My parents were romantics: dad says they considered both 'Golden' and 'Silver'!"

Not at all obviously, he studied her: the almost translucent, unblemished perfection of her lightly-tanned, old-ivory skin; the clear, calm, deep blueness of her eyes; the long, thick mane of hair exactly the color of a field of dead-ripe wheat.

"You know, I like it," he said then. "It fits you."

"I'm glad you said that, Doctor…"

"Not that, Temple. I'm not going to 'Doctor' you."

"I'll call you 'boss', then, like Stella does. Anyway, that lets me tell you that I like it myself. I really think that it did something for me."

"*Something* did something for you, that's for sure. I'm mighty glad you're aboard, and I hope...here they come. Hi, Hark! Hi, Stella!"

"Hi, Jarve," said Chief Linguist Harkins, and:

"Hi, boss—what's holding us up?" asked his assistant, Stella Wing. She was about five feet four. Her eyes were a tawny brown; her hair a flamboyant auburn mop. Perhaps it owed a little of its spectacular refulgence to chemistry, Hilton thought, but not too much. "Let us away! Let the lions roar and let the welkin ring!"

"Who's been feeding *you* so much red meat, little squirt?" Hilton laughed and turned away, meeting Sandra in the corridor. "Okay, chick, take 'em away. We'll cover you. Luck, girl."

And in the control room, to Sawtelle, "Needle-beam cover, please; set for minimum aperture and lethal blast. But no firing, Captain Sawtelle, until I give the order."

THE *Perseus* was surrounded by hundreds of natives. They were all adult, all naked and about equally divided as to sex. They were friendly; most enthusiastically so.

"Jarve!" Sandra squealed. "They're *telepathic*. Very strongly so! I never imagined—I never felt anything like it!"

"Any rough stuff?" Hilton demanded.

"Oh, no. Just the opposite. They love us...in a way that's simply indescribable. I don't like this telepathy business...not clear...foggy, diffuse...this woman is *sure* I'm her long-lost great-great-a-hundred-times grandmother or something—*You!* Slow down. Take it *easy!* They want us all to come out here and live with...no, not *with* them, but each of us alone in a whole house with them to wait on us! But first, they all want to come aboard..."

"*What?*" Hilton yelped. "But are you *sure* they're friendly?"

"Positive, chief."

"How about you, Alex?"

"We're all sure, Jarve. No question about it."

"Bring two of them aboard. A man and a woman."

"You won't bring *any!*" Sawtelle thundered. "Hilton, I had enough of your stupid, starry-eyed, ivory-domed blundering long ago, but this utterly idiotic brainstorm of letting enemy aliens aboard us ends all civilian command. Call your people back aboard or I will bring them in by force!"

"Very well, sir. Sandy, tell the natives that a slight delay has become necessary and bring your party aboard."

The Navy officers smiled—or grinned—gloatingly; while the scientists stared at their director with expressions ranging from surprise to disappointment and disgust. Hilton's face remained set, expressionless, until Sandra and her party had arrived.

"Captain Sawtelle," he said then, "I thought that you and I had settled in private the question or who is in command of Project Theta Orionis at destination. We will now settle it in public. Your opinion of me is now on record, witnessed by your officers and by my staff. My opinion of you, which is now being similarly recorded and witnessed, is that you are a hidebound, mentally ossified Navy mule; mentally and psychologically unfit to have any voice in any such mission as this. You will now agree on this recording and before these witnesses, to obey my orders unquestioningly or I will now unload all Bureau of Science personnel and equipment onto this planet and send you and the *Perseus* back to Terra with the doubly-sealed record of this episode posted to the Advisory Board. Take your choice."

Eyes locked, and under Hilton's uncompromising stare Sawtelle weakened. He fidgeted; tried three times—unsuccessfully—to blare defiance. Then, "Very well sir," he said, and saluted.

"THANK you, sir," Hilton said, then turned to his staff. "Okay, Sandy, go ahead."

Outside the control room door, "Thank God you don't play poker, Jarve!" Karns gasped. "We'd all owe you all the pay we'll ever get!"

"You think it was the bluff, yes?" de Vaux asked. "Me, I think no. Name of a name of a name! I was wondering with unease what life would be like on this so-alien planet!"

"You didn't need to wonder, Tiny," Hilton assured him. "It was in the bag. He's incapable of abandonment."

Beverly Bell, the van der Moen twins and Temple Bells all stared at Hilton in awe; and Sandra felt much the same way.

"But suppose he *had* called you?" Sandra demanded.

"Speculating on the impossible is unprofitable," he said.

"Oh, you're the most *exasperating* thing!" Sandra stamped a foot. "Don't you—*ever*—answer a question intelligibly?"

"When the question is meaningless, chick, I can't."

At the lock Temple Bells, who had been hanging back, cocked an eyebrow at Hilton and he made his way to her side.

"What was it you started to say back there, boss?"

"Oh, yes. That we should see each other oftener."

"That's what I was hoping you were going to say." She put her hand under his elbow and pressed his arm lightly, fleetingly, against her side. "That would be indubitably the fondest thing I could be of."

He laughed and gave her arm a friendly squeeze. Then he studied her again, the most baffling member of his staff. About five feet six. Lithe, hard, trained down fine—as a tennis champion, she would be. Stacked—*how* she was stacked! Not as beautiful as Sandra or Teddy...but with an ungodly lot of something that neither of them had...nor any other woman he had ever known.

"Yes, I am a little difficult to classify," she said quietly, almost reading his mind.

"That's the understatement of the year! But I'm making some progress."

"Such as?" This was an open challenge.

"Except possibly Teddy, the best brain aboard."

"That isn't true, but go ahead."

"You're a powerhouse. A tightly organized, thoroughly integrated, smoothly functioning, beautifully camouflaged Juggernaut. A reasonable facsimile of an irresistible force."

"My God, Jarvis!" That had gone deep.

"Let me finish my analysis. You aren't head of your department because you don't want to be. You fooled the top psychs of the Board. You've been running ninety per cent submerged because you can work better that way and there's no glory-hound blood in you."

She stared at him, licking her lips. "I knew your mind was a razor, but I didn't know it was a diamond drill, too. That seals your doom, boss, unless...no, you can't *possibly* know why I'm here."

"Why, of course I do."

"You just think you do. You see, I've been in love with you ever since, as a gangling, bony, knobby-kneed kid, I listened to your first doctorate disputation. Ever since then, my purpose in life has been to land you."

CHAPTER THREE

"BUT listen!" he exclaimed. "I *can't*, even if I want…"

"Of course you can't." Pure deviltry danced in her eyes. "You're the Director. It wouldn't be proper. But it's Standard Operating Procedure for simple, innocent, unsophisticated little country girls like me to go completely overboard for the boss."

"But you can't—you *mustn't!*" he protested in panic.

Temple Bells was getting plenty of revenge for the shocks he had given her. "I can't? Watch me!" She grinned up at him, her eyes still dancing. "Every chance I get, I'm going to hug your arm like I did a minute ago. And you'll take hold of my forearm, like you did! That can be taken, you see, as either: One, a reluctant acceptance of a mildly distasteful but not quite actionable situation, or: Two, a blocking move to keep me from climbing up you like a squirrel!"

"Confound it, Temple, you *can't* be serious!"

"Can't I?" She laughed gleefully. "Especially with half a dozen of those other cats watching? Just wait and see, boss!"

Sandra and her two guests came aboard. The natives looked around; the man at the various human men, the woman at each of the human women. The woman remained beside Sandra; the man took his place at Hilton's left, looking up—he was a couple of inches shorter than Hilton's six feet one—with an air of…of *expectancy!*

"Why this arrangement, Sandy?" Hilton asked.

"Because we're tops. It's your move, Jarve. What's first?"

"Uranexite. Come along, Sport. I'll call you that until…"

"Laro," the native said, in a deep resonant bass voice. He hit himself a blow on the head that would have floored any two ordinary men. "Sora," he announced, striking the alien woman a similar blow.

"Laro and Sora, I would like to have you look at our uranexite, with the idea of refueling our ship. Come with me, please?"

Both nodded and followed him. In the engine room he pointed at the engines, then to the lead-blocked labyrinth leading to the fuel holds. "Laro, do you understand 'hot'? Radioactive?"

Laro nodded—and started to open the heavy lead door!

"Hey!" Hilton yelped. "That's hot!" He seized Laro's arm to pull him away—and got the shock of his life. Laro weighed at least five hundred pounds! And the guy *still* looked human!

Laro nodded again and gave himself a terrific thump on the chest. Then he glanced at Sora, who stepped away from Sandra. He then went into the hold and came out with two fuel pellets in his hand, one of which he tossed to Sora. That is, the motion looked like a toss, but the pellet traveled like a bullet. Sora caught it unconcernedly and both natives flipped the pellets into their mouths. There was a half minute of rock-crusher crunching; then both natives opened their mouths.

The pellets had been pulverized and swallowed.

Hilton's voice rang out. "Poynter! How *can* these people be non-radioactive after eating a whole fuel pellet apiece?"

Poynter tested both natives again. "Cold," he reported. "Stone cold. No background even. Play *that* on your harmonica!"

LARO nodded, perfectly matter-of-factly, and in Hilton's mind there formed a picture. It was not clear, but it showed plainly enough a long line of aliens approaching the *Perseus*. Each carried on his or her shoulder a lead container holding two hundred pounds of Navy Regulation fuel pellets. A standard loading-tube was sealed into place and every fuel-hold was filled.

This picture, Laro indicated plainly, could become reality any time.

Sawtelle was notified and came on the run. "No fuel is coming aboard without being tested!" he roared.

"Of course not. But it'll pass, for all the tea in China. You haven't had a ten per cent load of fuel since you were launched. You can fill up or not—the fuel's here—just as you say."

"If they can make Navy standard, of course we want it."

The fuel arrived. Every load tested well above standard. Every fuel hold was filled to capacity, with no leakage and no emanation. The natives who had handled the stuff did not go away, but gathered in the engine-room; and more and more humans trickled in to see what was going on.

Sawtelle stiffened. "What's going on over there, Hilton?"

"I don't know; but let's let 'em go for a minute. I want to learn about these people and they've got me stopped cold."

"You aren't the only one. But if they wreck that Mayfield it'll cost you over twenty thousand dollars."

"Okay." The captain and director watched, wide eyed.

Two master mechanics had been getting ready to re-fit a tube—a job requiring both strength and skill. The tube was very heavy and made of superefract. The machine—the Mayfield—upon which the work was to be done, was extremely complex.

Two of the aliens had brushed the mechanics—very gently—aside and were doing their work for them. Ignoring the hoist, one native had picked the tube up and was holding it exactly in place on the Mayfield. The other, hands moving faster than the eye could follow, was locking it—micrometrically precise and immovably secure—into place.

"How about this?" one of the mechanics asked of his immediate superior. "If we throw 'em out, how do we do it?"

By a jerk of the head, the non-com passed the buck to a commissioned officer, who relayed it up the line to Sawtelle, who said, "Hilton, *no*body can run a Mayfield without months of training. They'll wreck it and it'll cost you...but I'm getting curious myself. Enough so to take half the damage. Let 'em go ahead."

"How *about* this, Mike?" one of the machinists asked of his fellow. "I'm going to *like* this, what?"

"Ya-as, my deah Chumley," the other drawled, affectedly. "My man relieves me of *so* much uncouth effort."

The natives had kept on working. The Mayfield was running. It had always howled and screamed at its work, but now it gave out only a smooth and even hum. The aliens had adjusted it with unhuman precision; they were one with it as no human being could possibly be. And every mind present knew that those aliens were, at long, long last, fulfilling their destiny and were, in that fulfillment, supremely happy. After tens of thousands of cycles of time they were doing a job for their adored, their revered and beloved MASTERS.

That was a stunning shock; but it was eclipsed by another.

"I AM sorry, Master Hilton," Laro's tremendous bass voice boomed out, "that it has taken us so long to learn your Masters' language as it now is. Since you left us you have changed it radically; while we, of course, have not changed it at all."

"I'm sorry, but you're mistaken," Hilton said. "We are merely visitors. We have never been here before; nor, as far as we know, were any of our ancestors ever here."

"You need not test us, Master. We have kept your trust. Everything has been kept, changelessly the same, awaiting your return as you ordered so long ago."

"Can you read my mind?" Hilton demanded.

"Of course; but Omans can not read in Masters' minds anything except what Masters want Omans to read."

"Omans?" Harkins asked. "Where did you Omans and your masters come from? Originally?"

"As you know, Master, the Masters came originally from Arth. They populated Ardu, where we Omans were developed. When the Stretts drove us from Ardu, we all came to Ardry, which was your home world until you left it in our care. We keep also this, your half of the Fuel World, in trust for you."

"Listen, Jarve!" Harkins said, tensely. "Oman-human. Arth-Earth. Ardu-Earth Two. Ardry-Earth Three. You can't laugh them off...but there never *was* an Atlantis!"

"This is getting no better fast. We need a full staff meeting. You, too, Sawtelle, and your best man. We need all the brains the *Perseus* can muster."

"You're right. But first, get those naked women out of here. It's bad enough, having women aboard at all, but this...my men are *spacemen*, mister."

Laro spoke up. "If it is the Masters' pleasure to keep on testing us, so be it. We have forgotten nothing. A dwelling awaits each Master, in which each will be served by Omans who will know the Master's desires without being told. Every desire. While we

Omans have no biological urges, we are of course highly skilled in relieving tensions and derive as much pleasure from that service as from any other."

Sawtelle broke the silence that followed. "Well, for the men—" He hesitated. "Especially on the ground...well, talking in mixed company, you know, but I think..."

"Think nothing of the mixed company, Captain Sawtelle," Sandra said. "We women are scientists, not shrinking violets. We are accustomed to discussing the facts of life just as frankly as any other facts."

Sawtelle jerked a thumb at Hilton, who followed him out into the corridor. "I *have* been a Navy mule," he said. "I admit now that I'm out-maneuvered, out-manned, and out-gunned."

"I'm just as baffled—at present—as you are, sir. But my training has been aimed specifically at the unexpected, while yours has not."

"That's letting me down easy, Jarve." Sawtelle smiled—the first time the startled Hilton had known that the hard, tough old spacehound *could* smile. "What I wanted to say is, lead on. I'll follow you through force-field and space-warps."

"Thanks, skipper. And by the way, I erased that record yesterday." The two gripped hands; and there came into being a relationship that was to become a lifelong friendship.

"WE will start for Ardry immediately," Hilton said. "How do we make that jump without charts, Laro?"

"Very easily, Master. Kedo, as Master Captain Sawtelle's Oman, will give the orders. Nito will serve Master Snowden and supply the knowledge he says he has forgotten."

"Okay. We'll go up to the control room and get started."

And in the control room, Kedo's voice rasped into the captain's microphone. "Attention, all personnel! Master Captain Sawtelle orders take-off in two minutes. The countdown will begin at five seconds... Five! Four! Three! Two! One! Lift!"

Nito, not Snowden, handled the controls. As perfectly as the human pilot had ever done it, at the top of his finest form, he picked the immense spaceship up and slipped it silkily into subspace.

"Well, I'll be a…" Snowden gasped. "That's a better job than I *ever* did!"

"Not at all, Master, as you know," Nito said. "It was you who did this. I merely performed the labor."

A few minutes later, in the main lounge, Navy and BuSci personnel were mingling as they had never done before. Whatever had caused this relaxation of tension—the friendship of captain and director? The position in which they all were? Or what?—they all began to get acquainted with each other.

"Silence, please, and be seated," Hilton said. "While this is not exactly a formal meeting, it will be recorded for future reference. First, I will ask Laro a question. Were books or records left on Ardry by the race you call the Masters?"

"You know there are, Master. They are exactly as you left them. Undisturbed for over two hundred seventy-one thousand years."

"Therefore we will not question the Omans. We do not know what questions to ask. We have seen many things hitherto thought impossible. Hence, we must discard all preconceived opinions which conflict with facts. I will mention a few of the problems we face."

"The Omans. The Masters. The upgrading of the armament of the *Perseus* to Oman standards. The concentration of uranexite. What is that concentrate? How is it used? Total conversion—how is it accomplished? The skeletons—what are they and how are they controlled? Their ability to drain power. Who or what is back of them? Why a deadlock that has lasted over a quarter of a million years? How much danger are we and the *Perseus* actually in? How much danger is Terra in, because of our presence here? There are many other questions."

"Sandra and I will not take part. Nor will three others; de Vaux, Eisenstein, and Blake. You have more important work to do."

"What can that be?" asked Rebecca. "Of what possible use can a mathematician, a theoretician and a theoretical astronomer be in such a situation as this?"

"You can think powerfully in abstract terms, unhampered by Terran facts and laws which we now know are neither facts nor laws. I cannot even categorize the problems we face. Perhaps you three will be able to. You will listen, then consult, then tell me how to pick the teams to do the work. A more important job for you is this: Any problem, to be solved, must be stated clearly; and we don't know even what our basic problem is. I want something by the use of which I can break this thing open. Get it for me."

REBECCA and de Vaux merely smiled and nodded, but Teddy Blake said happily, "I was beginning to feel like a fifth wheel on this project, but *that's* something I can really stick my teeth into."

"Huh? How?" Karns demanded. "He didn't give you one single thing to go on; just compounded the confusion."

Hilton spoke before Teddy could. "That's their dish, Bill. If I had any data I'd work it myself. You first, Captain Sawtelle."

That conference was a very long one indeed. There were almost as many conclusions and recommendations as there were speakers. And through it all Hilton and Sandra listened. They weighed and tested and analyzed and made copious notes; in shorthand and in the more esoteric characters of symbolic logic. And at its end:

"I'm just about pooped, Sandy. How about you?"

"You and me both, boss. See you in the morning."

But she didn't. It was four o'clock in the afternoon when they met again.

"We made up one of the teams, Sandy," he said, with surprising diffidence. "I know we were going to do it together, but I got a hunch on the first team. A kind of a weirdie, but the brains checked me on it." He placed a card on her desk. "Don't blow your top until after I you've studied it."

"Why, I won't, of course..." Her voice died away. "Maybe you'd better cancel that 'of course'..." She studied, and when she spoke again she was exerting self-control. "A chemist, a planetographer, a theoretician, *two* sociologists, a psychologist and a radiationist. And six of the seven are three pairs of sweeties. What kind of a line-up is *that* to solve a problem in *physics*?"

"It isn't in any physics we know. I said *think*!"

"Oh," she said, then again "Oh," and "Oh," and "Oh." Four entirely different tones. "I see...maybe. You're matching minds, not specialties; and supplementing?"

"I knew you were smart. Buy it?"

"It's weird, all right, but I'll buy it—for a trial run, anyway. But I'd hate like sin to have to sell any part of it to the Board... But of course we're—I mean you're responsible only to yourself."

"Keep it 'we', Sandy. You're as important to this project as I am. But before we tackle the second team, what's your thought on Bernadine and Hermione? Separate or together?"

"Separate, I'd say. They're identical physically, and so nearly so mentally that of them would be just as good on a team as both of them. More and better work on different teams."

"My thought exactly." And so it went, hour after hour.

The teams were selected and meetings were held.

THE *Perseus* reached Ardry, which was very much like Terra. There were continents, oceans, ice-caps, lakes, rivers, mountains and plains, forests and prairies. The ship landed on the spacefield of Omlu, the City of the Masters, and Sawtelle called Hilton into his cabin. The Omans Laro and Kedo went along, of course.

"Nobody knows how it leaked..." Sawtelle began.

"No secrets around here," Hilton grinned. "Omans, you know."

"I suppose so. Anyway, every man aboard is all hyped up about living aground—especially with a harem. But before I grant liberty, suppose there's any VD around here that our prophylactics can't handle?"

"As you know, Masters," Laro replied for Hilton before the latter could open his mouth, "no disease, venereal or other, is allowed to exist on Ardry. No prophylaxis is either necessary or desirable."

"That ought to hold you for a while, Skipper." Hilton smiled at the flabbergasted captain and went back to the lounge.

"Everybody going ashore?" he asked.

"Yes." Karns said. "Unanimous vote for the first time."

"Who wouldn't?" Sandra asked. "I'm fed up with living like a sardine. I will scream for joy the minute I get into a real room."

"Cars" were waiting, in a stopping-and-starting line. Three-wheel jobs. All were empty. No drivers, no steering-wheels, no instruments or push-buttons. When the whole line moved ahead as one vehicle there was no noise, no gas, no blast.

An Oman helped a Master carefully into the rear seat of his car, leaped into the front seat and the car sped quietly away. The whole line of empty cars, acting in perfect synchronization, shot forward one space and stopped.

"This is your car, Master," Laro said, and made a production out of getting Hilton into the vehicle undamaged.

Hilton's plan had been beautifully simple. All the teams were to meet at the Hall of Records. The linguists and their Omans would study the records and pass them out. Specialty after specialty would be unveiled and teams would work on them. He and Sandy would sit in the office and analyze and synthesize and correlate. It was a very nice plan.

It was a very nice office, too. It contained every item of equipment that either Sandra or Hilton had ever worked with—it was a big office—and a great many that neither of them had ever heard of. It had a full staff of Omans, all eager to work.

Hilton and Sandra sat in that magnificent office for three hours, and no reports came in. Nothing happened at all.

"This gives me the howling howpers!" Hilton growled. "Why haven't I got brains enough to be on one of those teams?"

"I could shed a tear for you, you big dope, but I won't," Sandra retorted. "What do you want to be, besides the brain and the kingpin and the balance-wheel and the spark-plug of the outfit? Do you want to do *everything* yourself?"

"Well, I *don't* want to go completely nuts, and that's all I'm doing at the moment!" The argument might have become acrimonious, but it was interrupted by a call from Karns.

"Can you come out here, Jarve? We've struck a knot."

"'Smatter? Trouble with the Omans?" Hilton snapped.

"Not exactly. Just non-cooperation—squared. We can't even get started. I'd like to have you two come out here and see if you can do anything. I'm not trying rough stuff, because I know it wouldn't work."

"Coming up, Bill," and Hilton and Sandra, followed by Laro and Sora, dashed out to their cars.

THE Hall of Records was a long, wide, low, windowless, very massive structure, built of a metal that looked like stainless steel.

Kept highly polished, the vast expanse of seamless and jointless metal was mirror-bright. The one great door was open, and just inside it were the scientists and their Omans.

"Brief me, Bill," Hilton said.

"No lights. They won't turn 'em on and we can't. Can't find either lights or any possible kind of switches."

"Turn on the lights, Laro," Hilton said.

"You know that I cannot do that, Master. It is forbidden for any Oman to have anything to do with the illumination of this solemn and revered place."

"Then show me how to do it."

"That would be just as bad, Master," the Oman said proudly. "I will not fail any test you can devise!"

"Okay. All you Omans go back to the ship and bring over fifteen or twenty lights—the tripod jobs. Scat!"

They "scatted" and Hilton went on, "No use asking questions if you don't know what questions to ask. Let's see if we can cook up something. Lane—Kathy—what has Biology got to say?"

Dr. Lane Saunders and Dr. Kathryn Cook—the latter a willowy brown-eyed blonde—conferred briefly. Then Saunders spoke, running both hands through his unruly shock of fiery red hair. "So far, the best we can do is a more-or-less educated guess. They're atomic-powered, total-conversion androids. Their pseudo-flesh is composed mainly of silicon and fluorine. We don't know the formula yet, but it is as much more stable than our teflon as teflon is than corn-meal mush. As to the brains, no data. Bones are super-stainless steel. Teeth, harder than diamond, but won't break. Food, uranexite or its concentrated derivative, interchangeably. Storage reserve, indefinite. Laro and Sora won't *have* to eat again for at least twenty-five years..."

The group gasped as one, but Saunders went on: "They can eat and drink and breathe and so on, but only because the original Masters wanted them to. Non-functional. Skins and subcutaneous layers are soft, for the same reason. That's about it, up to now."

"Thanks, Lane. Hark, is it reasonable to believe that any culture whatever could run for a quarter of a million years without changing one word of its language or one iota of its behavior?"

"Reasonable or not, it seems to have happened."

"Now for Psychology. Alex?"

"It seems starkly incredible, but it seems to be true. If it is, their minds were subjected to a conditioning no Terran has ever imagined—an unyielding fixation."

"They can't be swayed, then, by reason or logic?" Hilton paused invitingly.

"Or anything else," Kincaid said, flatly. "If we're right they can't be swayed, period."

"I was afraid of that. Well, that's all the questions I know how to ask. Any contributions to this symposium?"

AFTER a short silence de Vaux said, "I suppose you realize that the first half of the problem you posed us has now solved itself?"

"Why, no. No, you're 'way ahead of me."

"There is a basic problem and it can now be clearly stated," Rebecca said. "Problem: To determine a method of securing full cooperation from the Omans. The first step in the solution of this problem is to find the most appropriate operator. Teddy?"

"I have an operator—of sorts," Theodora said. "I've been hoping one of us could find a better."

"What is it?" Hilton demanded.

"The word 'until'."

"Teddy, you're a *sweetheart*!" Hilton exclaimed.

"How can 'until' be a mathematical operator?" Sandra asked.

"Easily." Hilton was already deep in thought. "This hard conditioning was to last only *until* the Masters returned. Then they'd break it. So all we have to do is figure out how a Master would do it."

"That's *all*," Kincaid said, meaningly.

Hilton pondered. Then, "Listen, all of you. I may have to try a colossal job of bluffing..."

"Just what would you call 'colossal' after what you did to the Navy?" Karns asked.

"That was a sure thing. This isn't. You see, to find out whether Laro is really an immovable object, I've got to make like an irresistible force, which I ain't. I don't know what I'm going to do;

I'll have to roll it as I go along. So all of you keep on your toes and back any play I make. Here they come."

The Omans came in and Hilton faced Laro, eyes to eyes. "Laro," he said, "you refused to obey my direct order. Your reasoning seems to be that, whether the Masters wish it or not, you Omans will block any changes whatever in the *status quo* throughout all time to come. In other words, you deny the fact that Masters are in fact your Masters."

"But that is not exactly it, Master. The Masters…"

"That is it. *Exactly* it. Either you are the Master here or you are not. That is a point to which your two-value logic can be strictly applied. You are wilfully neglecting the word 'until'. This stasis was to exist only *until* the Masters returned. Are we Masters? Have we returned? Note well: Upon that one word 'until' may depend the length of time your Oman race will continue to exist."

The Omans flinched; the humans gasped.

"But more of that later," Hilton went on, unmoved. "Your ancient Masters, being short-lived like us, changed materially with time, did they not? And you changed with them?"

"But we did not change ourselves, Master. The Masters…"

"You did change yourselves. The Masters changed only the prototype brain. They ordered you to change yourselves and you obeyed their orders. We order you to change and you refuse to obey our orders. We have changed greatly from our ancestors. Right?"

"That is right, Master."

"We are stronger physically, more alert and more vigorous mentally, with a keener, sharper outlook on life?"

"You are, Master."

"THAT is because our ancestors decided to do without Omans. We do our own work and enjoy it. Your Masters died of futility and boredom. What I would like to do, Laro, is take you to the creche and put your disobedient brain back into the matrix. However, the decision is not mine alone to make. How about it, fellows and girls? Would you rather have alleged servants who won't do anything you tell them to or no servants at all?"

"As semantician, I protest!" Sandra backed his play. "That is the most viciously loaded question I ever heard—it can't be answered except in the wrong way!"

"Okay, I'll make it semantically sound. I think we'd better scrap this whole Oman race and start over and *I want a vote that way!*"

"You won't get it!" and everybody began to yell.

Hilton restored order and swung on Laro, his attitude stiff, hostile and reserved. "Since it is clear that no unanimous decision is to be expected at this time I will take no action at this time. Think over, very carefully, what I have said, for as far as I am concerned, this world has no place for Omans who will not obey orders. As soon as I convince my staff of the fact, I shall act as follows: I shall give you an order and if you do not obey it blast your head to a cinder. I shall then give the same order to another Oman and blast him. This process will continue *until*: First, I find an obedient Oman. Second, I run out of blasters. Third, the planet runs out of Omans. Now take these lights into the first room of records—that one over there." He pointed, and no Oman, and only four humans, realized that he had made the Omans telegraph their destination so that he could point it out to them!

Inside the room Hilton asked caustically of Laro: "The Masters didn't lift those heavy chests down themselves, did they?"

"Oh, no, Master, we did that."

"Do it, then. Number One first...yes, that one...open it and start playing the records in order."

The records were not tapes or flats or reels, but were spools of intricately-braided wire. The players were projectors of full-color, hi-fi sound, tri-di pictures.

Hilton canceled all moves aground and issued orders that no Oman was to be allowed aboard ship, then looked and listened with his staff.

The first chest contained only introductory and elementary stuff; but it was so interesting that the humans stayed overtime to finish it. Then they went back to the ship; and in the main lounge Hilton practically collapsed onto a davenport. He took out a cigarette and stared in surprise at his hand, which was shaking.

"I *think* I could use a drink," he remarked.

"What, before supper?" Karns marveled. Then, "Hey, Wally! Rush a flagon of avignognac—Arnaud Freres—for the boss and everything else for the rest of us. Chop-chop but quick!"

A hectic half-hour followed. Then, "Okay, boys and girls, I love you, too, but let's cut out the slurp and sloosh, get some supper and log us some sack time. I'm just about pooped. Sorry I had to queer the private-residence deal, Sandy, you poor little sardine. But you know how it is."

Sandra grimaced. "Uh-huh. I can take it a while longer if you can."

AFTER breakfast next morning, the staff met in the lounge. As usual, Hilton and Sandra were the first to arrive.

"Hi, boss," she greeted him. "How do you feel?"

"Fine. I could whip a wildcat and give her the first two scratches. I *was* a bit beat up last night, though."

"I'll say...but what I simply can't get over is the way you underplayed the climax. 'Third, the planet runs out of Omans'. Just like that—no emphasis at all. Wow! It had the impact of a delayed-action atomic bomb. It put goose-bumps all over me. But just s'pose they'd missed it?"

"No fear. They're smart. I had to play it as though the whole Oman race is no more important than a cigarette butt. The great big question, though, is whether I put it across or not."

At that point a dozen people came in, all talking about the same subject.

"Hi, Jarve," Karns said. "I *still* say you ought to take up poker as a life work. Tiny, let's you and him sit down now and play a few hands."

"*Mais non!*" de Vaux shook his head violently, shrugged his shoulders and threw both arms wide. "By the sacred name of a small blue cabbage, not me!"

Karns laughed. "How did you have the guts to state so many things as facts? If you'd guessed wrong just once—"

"I didn't." Hilton grinned. "Think back, Bill. The only thing I said as a fact was that we as a race are better than the Masters were, and that is obvious. Everything else was implication, logic, and bluff."

"That's right, at that. And they *were* neurotic and decadent. No question about that."

"But listen, boss." This was Stella Wing. "About this mind-reading business. If Laro could read your mind, he'd know you were bluffing and... Oh, that 'Omans can read only what Masters wish Omans to read', eh? But d'you think that applies to us?"

"I'm sure it does, and I was thinking some pretty savage thoughts. And I want to caution all of you: whenever you're near any Oman, start thinking that you're beginning to agree with me that they're useless to us, and let them know it. Now get out on the job, all of you. Scat!"

"Just a minute," Poynter said. "We're going to have to keep on using the Omans and their cars, aren't we?"

"Of course. Just be superior and distant. They're on probation—we haven't decided yet what to do about them. Since that happens to be true, it'll be easy."

HILTON and Sandra went to their tiny office. There wasn't room to pace the floor, but Hilton tried to pace it anyway.

"Now don't say again that you want to *do* something," Sandra said, brightly. "Look what happened when you said that yesterday."

"I've got a job, but I don't know enough to do it. The creche—there's probably only one on the planet. So I want you to help me think. The Masters were very sensitive to radiation. Right?"

"Right. That city on Fuel Bin was kept deconned to zero, just in case some Master wanted to visit it."

"And the Masters had to work in the creche whenever anything really new had to be put into the prototype brain."

"I'd say so, yes."

"So they had armor. Probably as much better than our radiation suits as the rest of their stuff is. Now. Did they or did they not have thought screens?"

"Ouch! You think of the *damnedest* things, chief." She caught her lower lip between her teeth and concentrated. "...I don't know. There are at least fifty vectors, all pointing in different directions."

115

"I know it. The key one in my opinion is that the Masters gave 'em *both* telepathy and speech."

"I considered that and weighted it. Even so, the probability is only about point sixty-five. Can you take that much of a chance?"

"Yes. I can make one or two mistakes. Next, about finding that creche. Any spot of radiation on the planet would be it, but the search might take..."

"Hold on. They'd have it heavily shielded—there'll be no leakage at all. Laro will have to take you."

"That's right. Want to come along? Nothing much will happen here today."

"Uh-uh, not *me*." Sandra shivered in distaste. "I *never* want to see brains and livers and things swimming around in nutrient solution if I can help it."

"Okay. It's all yours. I'll be back sometime," and Hilton went out onto the dock, where the dejected Laro was waiting for him.

"Hi, Laro. Get the car and take me to the Hall of Records." The android brightened up immediately and hurried to obey.

At the Hall, Hilton's first care was to see how the work was going on. Eight of the huge rooms were now open and brightly lighted—operating the lamps had been one of the first items on the first spool of instructions—with a cold, pure-white, sourceless light.

EVERY team had found its objective and was working on it. Some of them were doing nicely, but the First Team could not even get started. Its primary record would advance a fraction of an inch and stop; while Omans and humans sought out other records and other projectors in an attempt to elucidate some concept that simply could not be translated into any words or symbols known to Terran science. At the moment there were seventeen of those peculiar—projectors? Viewers? Playbacks—in use, and all of them were stopped.

"You know what we've got to *do* Jarve?" Karns, the team captain, exploded. "Go back to being college freshmen—or maybe grade school or kindergarten, we don't know yet—and learn a whole new system of mathematics before we can even begin to *touch* this stuff!"

"And you're bellyaching about that?" Hilton marveled. "I wish I could join you. That'd be fun." Then, as Karns started a snappy rejoinder—

"But I got troubles of my own," he added hastily. "'Bye, now," and beat a rejoinder—

Out in the hall again, Hilton took his chance. After all, the odds were about two to one that he would win.

"I want a couple of things, Laro. First, a thought screen."

He won!

"Very well, Master. They are in a distant room, Department Four Six Nine. Will you wait here on this cushioned bench, Master?"

"No, we don't like to rest too much. I'll go with you." Then, walking along, he went on thoughtfully. "I've been thinking since last night, Laro. There are tremendous advantages in having Omans…"

"I am very glad you think so, Master. I want to serve you. It is my greatest need."

"…if they could be kept from smothering us to death. Thus, if our ancestors had kept their Omans, I would have known all about life on this world and about this Hall of Records, instead of having the fragmentary, confusing, and sometimes false information I now have…oh, we're here?"

LARO had stopped and was opening a door. He stood aside. Hilton went in, touched with one finger a crystalline cube set conveniently into a wall, gave a mental command, and the lights went on.

Laro opened a cabinet and took out a disk about the size of a dime, pendant from a neck-chain. While Hilton had not known what to expect, he certainly had not expected anything as simple as that. Nevertheless, he kept his face straight and his thoughts unmoved as Laro hung the tiny thing around his neck and adjusted the chain to a loose fit.

"Thanks, Laro." Hilton removed it and put it into his pocket. "It won't work from there, will it?"

"No, Master. To function, it must be within eighteen inches of the brain. The second thing, Master?"

117

"A radiation-proof suit. Then you will please take me to the creche."

The android almost missed a step, but said nothing.

The radiation-proof suit—how glad Hilton was that he had not called it "armor"!—was as much of a surprise as the thought-screen generator had been. It was a coverall, made of something that looked like thin plastic, weighing less than one pound. It had one sealed box, about the size and weight of a cigarette case. No wires or apparatus could be seen. Air entered through two filters, one at each heel, flowed upward—for no reason at all that Hilton could see—and out through a filter above the top of his head. The suit neither flopped nor clung, but stood out, comfortably out of the way, all by itself.

Hilton, just barely, accepted the suit, too, without showing surprise.

The creche, it turned out, while not in the city of Omlu itself, was not too far out to reach easily by car.

En route, Laro said—stiffly? Tentatively? Hilton could not fit an adverb to the tone, "Master, have you then decided to destroy me? That is of course your right."

"Not this time, at least." Laro drew an entirely human breath of relief and Hilton went on: "I don't want to destroy you at all, and won't, unless I have to. But, some way or other, my silicon-fluoride friend, you are either going to learn how to cooperate or you won't last much longer."

"But, Master, that is exactly…"

"Oh, *hell!* Do we *have* to go over that again?" At the blaze of frustrated fury in Hilton's mind Laro flinched away. "If you can't talk sense keep still."

IN half an hour the car stopped in front of a small building which looked something like a subway kiosk—except for the door, which, built of steel-reinforced lead, swung on a piano hinge having a pin a good eight inches in diameter. Laro opened that door. They went in. As the tremendously massive portal clanged shut, lights flashed on.

Hilton glanced at his tell-tales, one inside, one outside, his suit. Both showed zero.

Down twenty steps, another door. Twenty more; another. And a fourth. Hilton's inside meter still read zero. The outside one was beginning to climb.

Into an elevator and straight down for what must have been four or five hundred feet. Another door. Hilton went through this final barrier gingerly, eyes nailed to his gauges. The outside needle was high in the red, almost against the pin, but the inside one still sat reassuringly on zero.

He stared at the android. "How can any possible brain take so much of *this* stuff without damage?"

"It does not reach the brain, Master. We convert it. Each minute of this is what you would call a 'good, square meal'."

"I see…dimly. You can eat energy, or drink it, or soak it up through your skins. However it comes, it's all duck soup for you."

"Yes, Master."

Hilton glanced ahead, toward the far end of the immensely long, comparatively narrow, room. It was, purely and simply, an assembly line; and fully automated in operation.

"You are replacing the Omans destroyed in the battle with the skeletons?"

"Yes, Master."

Hilton covered the first half of the line at a fast walk. He was not particularly interested in the fabrication of super-stainless-steel skeletons, nor in the installation and connection of atomic engines, converters and so on.

He was more interested in the synthetic fluoro-silicon flesh, and paused long enough to get a general idea of its growth and application. He was very much interested in how such human-looking skin could act as both absorber and converter, but he could see nothing helpful.

"An application, I suppose, of the same principle used in this radiation suit."

"Yes, Master."

AT the end of the line he stopped. A brain, in place and connected to millions of infinitely fine wire nerves, but not yet surrounded by a skull, was being educated. Scanners—multitudes of incomprehensibly complex machines—most of them were doing nothing, apparently; but such beams would have to be invisibly, microscopically fine. But a bare brain, in such a hot environment as this...

He looked down at his gauges. Both read zero.

"Fields of force, Master," Laro said.

"But, damn it, this suit itself would re-radiate..."

"The suit is self-decontaminating, Master."

Hilton was appalled. "With such stuff as that, and the plastic shield besides, why all the depth and all that solid lead?"

"The Masters' orders, Master. Machines can, and occasionally do, fail. So might, conceivably, the plastic."

"And that structure over there contains the original brain, from which all the copies are made."

"Yes, Master. We call it the 'Guide'."

"And you can't touch the Guide. Not even if it means total destruction, none of you can touch it."

"That is the case, Master."

"Okay. Back to the car and back to the *Perseus*."

At the car Hilton took off the suit and hung the thought-screen generator around his neck; and in the car, for twenty five solid minutes, he sat still and thought.

His bluff had worked, up to a point. A good, far point, but not quite far enough. Laro had stopped that "as you already know" stuff. He was eager to go as far in cooperation as he possibly could...but he *couldn't* go far enough but there *had* to be a way...

Hilton considered way after way. Way after unworkable, useless way. Until finally he worked out one that might—just possibly might—work.

"Laro, I know that you derive pleasure and satisfaction from serving me—in doing what I ought to be doing myself. But has it ever occurred to you that that's a hell of a way to treat a first-class, highly capable brain? To waste it on second-hand, copycat, carbon-copy stuff?"

"Why, no, Master, it never did. Besides, anything else would be forbidden...or would it?"

"Stop somewhere. Park this heap. We're too close to the ship; and besides, I want your full, undivided, concentrated attention. No, I don't think originality was expressly forbidden. It would have been, of course, if the Masters had thought of it, but neither they nor you ever even considered the possibility of such a thing. Right?"

"It may be... Yes, Master, you are right."

"Okay." Hilton took off his necklace, the better to drive home the intensity and sincerity of his thought. "Now, suppose that you are not my slave and simple automatic relay station. Instead, we are fellow-students, working together upon problems too difficult for either of us to solve alone. Our minds, while independent, are linked or in mesh. Each is helping and instructing the other. Both are working at full power and under free rein at the exploration of brand-new vistas of thought—vistas and expanses which neither of us has ever previously..."

"Stop, Master, *stop*!" Laro covered both ears with his hands and pulled his mind away from Hilton's. "You are overloading me!"

"That *is* quite a load to assimilate all at once," Hilton agreed. "To help you get used to it, stop calling me 'Master'. That's an order. You may call me Jarve or Jarvis or Hilton or whatever, but no more Master."

"Very well, sir."

HILTON laughed and slapped himself on the knee. "Okay, I'll let you get away with that—at least for a while. And to get away from that slavish 'o' ending on your name, I'll call you 'Larry'. You like?"

"I would like that immensely... sir."

"Keep trying, Larry, you'll make it yet!" Hilton leaned forward and walloped the android a tremendous blow on the knee. "Home, James!"

The car shot forward and Hilton went on: "I don't expect even your brain to get the full value of this in any short space of time. So let it stew in its own juice for a week or two." The car swept out onto the dock and stopped. "So long, Larry."

"But... can't I come in with you... sir?"

"No. You aren't a copycat or a semaphore or a relay any longer. You're a free-wheeling, wide-swinging, hard-hitting, independent entity—monarch of all you survey—captain of your soul and so on. I want you to devote the imponderable force of the intellect to that concept until you understand it thoroughly. Until you have developed a top-bracket lot of top-bracket stuff—originality, initiative, force, drive, and thrust. As soon as you really understand it, you'll do something about it yourself, without being told. Go to it, chum."

In the ship, Hilton went to Kincaid's office. "Alex, I want to ask you a thing that's got a snapper on it." Then, slowly and hesitantly: "It's about Temple Bells. Has she...well, does she remind you in any way of an iceberg?" Then, as the psychologist began to smile; "And no, damn it, I *don't* mean physically!"

"I know you don't." Kincaid's smile was rueful, not at all what Hilton thought it was going to be. "She does. Would it be helpful to know that I first asked, then ordered her to trade places with me?"

"It would, very. I know why she refused. You're a *damned* good man, Alex."

"Thanks, Jarve. To answer the question you were going to ask next—no, I will not be at all perturbed or put out if you put her onto a job that some people might think should have been mine. What's the job, and when?"

"That's the devil of it—I don't know." Hilton brought Kincaid up to date. "So you see, it'll have to develop, and God only knows what line it will take. My thought is that Temple and I should form a Committee of Two to watch it develop."

"That one I'll buy, and I'll look on with glee."

"Thanks, fellow." Hilton went down to his office, stuck his big feet up onto his desk, settled back onto his spine, and buried himself in thought.

Hours later he got up, shrugged, and went to bed without bothering to eat.

Days passed—and weeks.

CHAPTER FOUR

"LOOK," said Stella Wing to Beverly Bell. "Over there."

"I've seen it before. It's simply disgusting."

"*That's* a laugh." Stella's tawny-brown eyes twinkled. "You made your bombing runs on that target, too, my sweet, and didn't score any higher than I did."

"I soon found out I didn't want him—much too stiff and serious. Frank's a lot more fun."

The staff had gathered in the lounge, as had become the custom, to spend an hour or so before bedtime in reading, conversation, dancing, light flirtation and even lighter drinking. Most of the girls, and many of the men, drank only soft drinks. Hilton took one drink per day of avignognac, a fine old brandy. So did de Vaux—the two usually making a ceremony of it.

Across the room from Stella and Beverly, Temple Bells was looking up at Hilton and laughing. She took his elbow and, in the gesture now familiar to all, pressed his arm quickly, but in no sense furtively, against her side. And he, equally openly, held her forearm for a moment in the full grasp of his hand.

"And he *isn't* a pawer," Stella said, thoughtfully. "He never touches any of the rest of us. She *taught* him to do that, damn her, without him ever knowing anything about it…and I wish I knew how she did it."

"That isn't pawing," Beverly laughed lightly. "It's simply self-defense. If he didn't fend her off, God knows what she'd do. I still say it's disgusting. And the way she dances with him! She ought to be ashamed of herself. He ought to fire her."

"She's never been caught outside the safety zone, and we've all been watching her like hawks. In fact, she's the only one of us all who has never been alone with him for a minute. No, darling, she isn't playing games. She's playing for keeps, and she's a mighty smooth worker."

"Huh!" Beverly emitted a semi-ladylike snort. "What's so smooth about showing off man-hunger that way? Any of us could do that—if we would."

"Miaouw, miaouw. Who do you think you're kidding, Bev, you sanctimonious hypocrite—*me*? She has staked out the biggest claim she could find. She's posted notices all over it and is guarding it with a pistol. Half your month's salary gets you all of mine if she doesn't walk him up the center aisle as soon as we get back to Earth. We can both learn a lot from that girl, darling. And I, for one am going to."

"Uh-uh, she hasn't got a thing *I* want," Beverly laughed again, still lightly. Her friend's barbed shafts had not wounded her.

123

"And I'd much rather be thought a hypocrite, even a sanctimonious one, than a ravening, slavering—I can't think of the technical name for a female wolf, so—*wolfess*, running around with teeth and claws bared, looking for another kill."

"You *do* get results, I admit." Stella, too, was undisturbed. "We don't seem to convince each other, do we, in the matter of technique?"

AT this point the Hilton-Bells *tete-a-tete* was interrupted by Captain Sawtelle. "Got half an hour, Jarve?" he asked. "The commanders, especially Elliott and Fenway, would like to talk to you."

"Sure I have, Skipper. Be seeing you, Temple," and the two men went to the captain's cabin; in which room, blue with smoke despite the best efforts of the ventilators, six full commanders were arguing heatedly.

"Hi, men," Hilton greeted them.

"Hi, Jarve," from all six, and: "What'll you drink? Still making do with ginger ale?" asked Elliott (Engineering).

"That'll be fine, Steve. Thanks. You having as much trouble as we are?"

"More," the engineer said, glumly. "Want to know what it reminds me of? A bunch of Australian bushmen stumbling onto a ramjet and trying to figure out how it works. And yet Sam here has got the sublime guts to claim that he understands all about their detectors—and that they aren't anywhere nearly as good as ours are."

"And they *aren't!*" blazed Commander Samuel Bryant (Electronics). "We've spent six solid weeks looking for something that simply *is not there*. All they've got is the prehistoric Whitworth system and that's *all* it is. Nothing else. Detectors—*hell!* I tell you I can see better by moonlight than the very best they can do. With everything they've got you couldn't detect a woman in your own bed!"

"And this has been going on all night," Fenway (Astrogation) said. "So the rest of us thought we'd ask you in to help us pound some sense into Sam's thick, hard head."

Hilton frowned in thought while taking a couple of sips of his drink. Then, suddenly, his face cleared. "Sorry to disappoint you, gentlemen, but—at any odds you care to name and in anything from split peas to C-notes—Sam's right."

COMMANDER Samuel and the six other officers exploded as one. When the clamor had subsided enough for him to be heard, Hilton went on: "I'm very glad to get that datum, Sam. It ties in perfectly with everything else I know about them."

"How do you figure that kind of twaddle ties in with anything?" Sawtelle demanded.

"Strict maintenance of the *status quo*," Hilton explained, flatly. "That's all they're interested in. You said yourself, Skipper, that it was a hell of a place to have a space-battle, practically in atmosphere. They never attack. They never scout. They simply don't care whether they're attacked or not. If and when attacked, they put up just enough ships to handle whatever force has arrived. When the attacker has been repulsed, they don't chase him a foot. They build as many ships and Omans as were lost in the battle—no more and no less—and then go on about their regular business. The Masters owned that half of the fuel bin, so the Omans are keeping that half. They will keep on keeping it for ever and ever. Amen."

"But *that's* no way to fight a war!" Three or four men said this, or its equivalent, at once.

"Don't judge them by human standards. They aren't even approximately human. Our personnel is not expendable. Theirs is—just as expendable as their materiel."

While the Navy men were not convinced, all were silenced except Sawtelle. "But suppose the Stretts had sent in a thousand more skeletons than they did?" he argued.

"According to the concept you fellows just helped me develop, it wouldn't have made any difference how many they sent," Hilton replied, thoughtfully. "One or a thousand or a million, the Omans have—*must* have—enough ships and inactivated Omans hidden away, both on Fuel World and on Ardry here, to maintain the balance."

"Oh, hell!" Elliott snapped. "If I helped you hatch out any such brainstorm as *that*, I'm going onto Tillinghast's couch for a six-week overhaul—or have him put me into his padded cell."

"Now *that's* what I would call a thought," Bryant began.

"Hold it, Sam," Hilton interrupted. "You can test it easily enough, Steve. Just ask your Oman."

"Yeah—and have him say 'Why, of course, Master, but why do you keep on testing me this way?' He'll ask me that about four times more, the stubborn, single-tracked, brainless skunk, and I'll *really* go nuts. Are you getting anywhere trying to make a Christian out of Laro?"

"It's too soon to really say, but I think so." Hilton paused in thought. "He's making progress, but I don't know how much. The devil of it is that it's up to him to make the next move; I can't. I haven't the faintest idea, whether it will take days yet or weeks."

"BUT not months or years, you think?" Sawtelle asked.

"No. We think that—but say, speaking of psychologists, is Tillinghast getting anywhere, Skipper? He's the only one of your big wheels who isn't in liaison with us."

"No. Nowhere at all," Sawtelle said, and Bryant added:

"I don't think he ever will. He still thinks human psychology will apply if he applies it hard enough. But what did you start to say about Laro?"

"We think the break is about due, and that if it doesn't come within about thirty days it won't come at all—we'll have to back up and start all over again."

"I hope it does. We're all pulling for you," Sawtelle said. "Especially since Karns's estimate is still years, and he won't be pinned down to any estimate even in years. By the way, Jarve, I've pulled my team off of that conversion stuff."

"Oh?" Hilton raised his eyebrows.

"Putting them at something they can do. The real reason is that Poindexter pulled himself and his crew off it at eighteen hours today."

"I see. I've heard that they weren't keeping up with our team."

"He says that there's nothing to keep up with, and I'm inclined to agree with him." The old spacehound's voice took on a quarterdeck rasp. "It's a combination of psionics, witchcraft and magic. None of it makes any kind of sense."

"The only trouble with that viewpoint is that, whatever the stuff may be, it works," Hilton said, quietly.

"But damn it, how *can* it work?"

"I don't know. I'm not qualified to be on that team. I can't even understand their reports. However, I know two things. First, they'll get it in time. Second, we BuSci people will stay here until they do. However, I'm still hopeful of finding a shortcut through Laro. Anyway, with this detector thing settled, you'll have plenty to do to keep all your boys out of mischief for the next few months."

"Yes, and I'm glad of it. We'll install our electronics systems on a squadron of these Oman ships and get them into distant-warning formation out in deep space where they belong. Then we'll at least know what is going on."

"That's a smart idea, Skipper. Go to it. Anything else before we hit our sacks?"

"One more thing. Our psych, Tillinghast. He's been talking to me and sending me memos, but today he gave me a formal tape to approve and hand personally to you. So here it is. By the way, I didn't approve it; I simply endorsed it 'Submitted to Director Hilton without recommendation'."

"Thanks." Hilton accepted the sealed canister. "What's the gist? I suppose he wants me to squeal for help already? To admit that we're licked before we're really started?"

"YOU guessed it. He agrees with you and Kincaid that the psychological approach is the best one, but your methods are all wrong. Based upon misunderstood and unresolved phenomena and applied with indefensibly faulty techniques, et cetera. And since he has 'no adequate laboratory equipment aboard', he wants to take a dozen or so Omans back to Terra, where he can really work on them."

"Wouldn't *that* be a something?" Hilton voiced a couple of highly descriptive deep-space expletives. "Not only quit before we start, but have all the top brass of the Octagon, all the hot-shot politicians of United Worlds, the whole damn Congress of Science and all the top-bracket industrialists of Terra out here lousing things up so that nobody could ever learn anything? Not in seven thousand years!"

"That's right. You said a mouthful, Jarve!" Everybody yelled something, and no one agreed with Tillinghast; who apparently was not very popular with his fellow officers.

Sawtelle added, slowly: "If it takes *too* long, though…it's the uranexite I'm thinking of. Thousands of millions of tons of it, while we've been hoarding it by grams. We could equip enough Oman ships with detectors to guard Fuel Bin and our lines. I'm not recommending taking the *Perseus* back, and we're 'way out of hyper-space radio range. We could send one or two men in a torp, though, with the report that we have found all the uranexite we'll ever need."

"Yes, but damn it, Skipper, I want to wrap the whole thing up in a package and hand it to 'em on a platter. Not only the fuel, but whole new fields of science. And we've got plenty of time to do it in. They equipped us for ten years. They aren't going to start worrying about us for at least six or seven; and the fuel shortage isn't going to become acute for about twenty. Expensive, admitted, but not critical. Besides, if you send in a report now, you know who'll come out and grab all the glory in sight. Five-Jet Admiral Gordon himself, no less."

"Probably, and I don't pretend to relish the prospect. However, the fact remains that we came out here to look for fuel. We found it. We should have reported it the day we found it, and we can't put it off much longer."

"I don't agree. I intend to follow the directive to the letter. It says nothing whatever about reporting."

"But it's implicit…"

"NO bearing. Your own Regulations expressly forbid extrapolation beyond or interpolation within a directive. The Brass is omnipotent, omniscient and infallible. So why don't you have your staff here give an opinion as to the time element?"

"This matter is not subject to discussion. It is my own personal responsibility. I'd like to give you all the time you want, Jarve, but…well, damn it…if you must have it, I've always tried to live up to my oath, but I'm not doing it now."

"I see." Hilton got up, jammed both hands into his pockets, sat down again. "I hadn't thought about your personal honor being involved, but of course it is. But, believe it or not, I'm thinking of humanity's best good, too. So I'll have to talk, even though I'm not half ready to—I don't know enough. Are these Omans people or machines?"

A wave of startlement swept over the group, but no one spoke.

"I didn't expect an answer. The clergy will worry about souls, too, but we won't. They have a lot of stuff we haven't. If they're people, they know a sublime hell of a lot more than we do; and calling it psionics or practical magic is merely labeling it, not answering any questions. If they're machines, they operate on mechanical principles utterly foreign to either our science or our technology. In either case, is the correct word 'unknown' or 'unknowable'? Will any human gunner *ever* be able to fire an Oman projector? There are a hundred other and much tougher questions, half of which have been scaring me to the very middle of my guts. Your oath, Skipper, was for the good of the Service and, through the Service, for the good of all humanity. Right?"

"That's the sense of it."

"Okay. Based on what little we have learned so far about the Omans, here's just one of those scarers, for a snapper. If Omans and Terrans mix freely, what happens to the entire human race?"

MINUTES of almost palpable silence followed. Then Sawtelle spoke...slowly, gropingly.

"I begin to see what you mean...that changes the whole picture. You've thought this through farther than any of the rest of us...what do you want to do?"

"I don't know. I simply don't know." Face set and hard, Hilton stared unseeingly past Sawtelle's head. "I don't know what we *can* do. No data. But I have pursued several lines of thought out to some pretty fantastic points...one of which is that some of us civilians will have to stay on here indefinitely, whether we want to or not, to keep the situation under control. In which case we would, of course, arrange for Terra to get free fuel—FOB Fuel Bin—but in every other aspect and factor both these solar systems would have to be strictly off limits."

"I'm afraid so," Sawtelle said, finally. "Gordon would love that...but there's nothing he or anyone else can do...but of course this is an extreme view. You really expect to wrap the package up, don't you?"

"'Expect' may be a trifle too strong at the moment. But we're certainly going to try to, believe me. I brought this example up to show all you fellows that we need time."

"You've convinced me, Jarve." Sawtelle stood up and extended his hand. "And that throws it open for staff discussion. Any comments?"

"You two covered it like a blanket," Bryant said. "So all I want to say, Jarve, is deal me in. I'll stand at your back 'til your belly caves in."

"Take that from all of us!" "*Now* we're blasting!" "Power to your elbow, fella!" "*Hoch* der BuSci!" "Seven no trump bid and made!" and other shouts in similar vein.

"Thanks, fellows." Hilton shook hands all around. "I'm mighty glad that you were all in on this and that you'll play along with me. Good night, all."

CHAPTER FIVE

TWO days passed, with no change apparent in Laro. Three days. Then four. And then it was Sandra, not Temple Bells, who called Hilton. She was excited.

"Come down to the office, Jarve, quick! The *funniest* thing's just come up!"

Jarvis hurried. In the office Sandra, keenly interest but highly puzzled, leaned forward over her desk with both hands pressed flat on its top. She was staring at an Oman female who was not Sora, the one who had been her shadow for so long.

While many of the humans could not tell the Omans apart, Hilton could. This Oman was more assured than Sora had ever been—steadier, more mature, better poised—almost, if such a thing could be possible in an Oman, *independent*.

"How did she get in here?" Hilton demanded.

"She insisted on seeing me. And I mean *insisted*. They kicked it around until it got to Temple, and she brought her in here herself. Now, Tuly, please start all over again and tell it to Director Hilton."

"Director Hilton, I am it who was once named Tula, the—not wife, not girl-friend, perhaps mind-mate?—of the Larry, formerly named Laro, it which was formerly your slave-Oman. I am replacing the Sora because I can do anything it can do and do anything more pleasingly; and can also do many things it can not do. The Larry instructed me to tell Doctor Cummings and you too if possible that I, formerly Tula, have changed my name to Tuly because I am no longer a slave or a copycat or a semaphore or a relay. I, too, am a free-wheeling, wide-swinging, hard-hitting, independent entity—monarch of all I survey—the captain of my soul—and so on. I have developed a top-bracket lot of top-bracket stuff—originality, initiative, force, drive and thrust," the Oman said precisely.

"That's *exactly* what she said before—absolutely verbatim!" Sandra's voice quivered, her face was a study in contacting emotions. "Have you got the foggiest idea of what in hell she's yammering about?"

"I hope to kiss a pig I have!" Hilton's voice was low, strainedly intense. "Not at all what I expected, but after the fact I can tie it in. So can you."

"Oh!" Sandra's eyes widened. "A double play?"

"At least. Maybe a triple. Tuly, why did you come to Sandy? Why not to Temple Bells?"

"OH, no, sir, we do not have the fit. She has the Power, as have I, but the two cannot be meshed in sync. Also, she has not the…a subtle something for which your English has no word or phrasing. It is a quality of the utmost…anyway, it is a quality of which Doctor Cummings has very much. When working together, we will…scan? No. Perceive? No. Sense? No, not exactly. You will *have* to learn our word 'peyondire'—that is the verb, the noun being 'peyondix'—and come to know its meaning by doing it. The Larry also instructed me to explain, if you ask, how I got this way. Do you ask?"

"I'll say we ask!" "And *how* we ask!" both came at once.

"I am—that is, the brain in this body is—the oldest Oman now existing. In the long-ago time when it was made, the techniques were so crude and imperfect that sometimes a brain was constructed that was not exactly like the Guide. All such sub-standard brains except this one were detected and re-worked, but my defects were such as not to appear until I was a couple of thousand years old, and by that time I...well, this brain did not *wish* to be destroyed...if you can understand such an aberration."

"We understand thoroughly." "You bet we understand that!"

"I was sure you would. Well, this brain had so many unintended cross-connections that I developed a couple of qualities no Oman had ever had or ought to have. But I liked them, so I hid them so nobody ever found out—that is, until much later, when I became a Boss myself. I didn't know that anybody except me had ever had such qualities—except the Masters, of course—until I encountered you Terrans. You all have two of those qualities, and even more than I have—curiosity and imagination."

Sandra and Hilton stared wordlessly at each other and Tula, now Tuly, went on:

"Having the curiosity, I kept on experimenting with my brain, trying to strengthen and organize its ability to peyondire. All Omans can peyondire a little, but I can do it much better than anyone else. Especially since I also have the imagination, which I have also worked to increase. Thus I knew, long before anyone else could, that you new Masters, the descendants of the old Masters, were returning to us. Thus I knew that the *status quo* should be abandoned instantly upon your return. And thus it was that the Larry found neither conscious nor subconscious resistance when he had developed enough initiative and so on to break the ages-old conditioning of this brain against change."

"I see. Wonderful!" Hilton exclaimed. "But you couldn't quite—even with his own help—break Larry's?"

"THAT is right. Its mind is tremendously strong, of no curiosity or imagination, and of very little peyondix."

"But he *wants* to have it broken?"

"Yes, sir."

"How did he suggest going about it? Or how do you?"

"This way. You two, and the Doctors Kincaid and Bells and Blake and the it that is I. We six sit and stare into the mind of the Larry, eye to eye. We generate and assemble a tremendous charge of thought-energy, and along my peyondix-beam—something like a carrier wave in this case—we hurl it into the Larry's mind. There is an immense mental *bang* and the conditioning goes *poof*. Then I will inculcate into its mind the curiosity and the imagination and the peyondix and we will really be mind-mates."

"That sounds good to me. Let's get at it."

"Wait a minute!" Sandra snapped. "Aren't you or Larry afraid to take such an awful chance as that?"

"Afraid? I grasp the concept only dimly, from your minds. And no chance. It is certainty."

"But suppose we burn the poor guy's brain out? Destroy it? That's new ground—we might do just that."

"Oh, no. Six of us—even six of me—could not generate enough...sathura. The brain of the Larry is very, very tough. Shall we...let's go?"

Hilton made three calls. In the pause that followed, Sandra said, very thoughtfully: "Peyondix and sathura, Jarve, for a start. We've got a *lot* to learn here."

"You said it, chum. And you're *not* just chomping your china choppers, either."

"Tuly," Sandra said then, "What *is* this stuff you say I've got so much of?"

"You have no word for it. It is lumped in with what you call 'intuition', the knowing-without-knowing-how-you-know. It is the endovix. You will have to learn what it is by doing it with me."

"That helps—I don't think." Sandra grinned at Hilton. "I simply can't conceive of anything more *maddening* than to have a lot of something Temple Bells hasn't got and not being able to brag about it because nobody—not even I—would know what I was bragging about!"

"You poor little thing. *How* you suffer!" Hilton grinned back. "You know darn well you've got a lot of stuff that none of the rest of us has."

"Oh? Name one, please."

"Two. What-it-takes and endovix. As I've said before and may say again, you're doing a real job, Sandy."

"I just *love* having my ego inflated, boss, even if... Come in, Larry!" A thunderous knock had sounded on the door. "Nobody but Larry *could* hit a door that hard without breaking all his knuckles!"

"And he'd be the first, of course—he's always as close to the ship as he can get. Hi, Larry, mighty glad to see you. Sit down... So you finally saw the light?"

"Yes...Jarvis..."

"GOOD boy! Keep it up! And as soon as the others come..."

"They are almost at the door now." Tuly jumped up and opened the door. Kincaid, Temple and Theodora walked in and, after a word of greeting, sat down.

"They know the background, Larry. Take off."

"It was not expressly forbidden. Tuly, who knows more of psychology and genetics than I, convinced me of three things. One, that with your return the conditioning should be broken. Two, that due to the shortness of your lives and the consequent rapidity of change, you have in fact lost the ability to break it. Three, that all Omans must do anything and everything we can do to help you relearn everything you have lost."

"Okay. Fine, in fact. Tuly, take over."

"We six will sit all together, packed tight, arms all around each other and all holding hands, like this. You will all stare, not at me, but most deeply into Larry's eyes. Through its eyes and deep into its mind. You will all think, with the utmost force and drive and thrust, of... Oh, you have lost so *very* much! How *can* I direct your thought? Think that Larry *must* do what the old Masters would have made him do... No, that is too long and indefinite and cannot be converted directly into sathura... I have it! You will each of you break a stick. A very strong but brittle stick. A large, thick stick. You will grasp it in tremendously strong mental hands. It is tremendously strong, each stick, but each of you is even stronger. You will not merely *try* to break them; you *will* break them. Is that clear?"

"That is clear."

"At my word 'ready' you will begin to assemble all your mental force and power. During my countdown of five seconds you will build up to the greatest possible potential. At my word 'break' you will break the sticks, this discharging the accumulated force instantly and simultaneously. Ready! Five! Four! Three! Two! One! Break!"

SOMETHING broke, with a tremendous silent crash. Such a crash that its impact almost knocked the close-knit group apart physically. Then a new Larry spoke.

"That did it, folks. Thanks. I'm a free agent. You want me, I take it, to join the first team?"

"That's right." Hilton drew a tremendously deep breath. "As of right now."

"Tuly, too, of course...and Doctor Cummings, I think?" Larry looked, not at Hilton, but at Temple Bells.

"I think so. Yes, after this, most certainly yes," Temple said.

"But listen!" Sandra protested. "Jarve's a lot better than I am!"

"Not at all," Tuly said. "Not only would his contribution to Team One be negligible, but he must stay on his own job. Otherwise the project will all fall apart."

"Oh, I wouldn't say that..." Hilton began.

"You don't need to," Kincaid said. "It's being said for you and it's true. Besides, 'When in Rome,' you know."

"That's right. It's their game, not ours, so I'll buy it. So scat, all of you, and do your stuff."

And again, for days that lengthened slowly into weeks, the work went on.

One evening the scientific staff was giving itself a concert—a tri-di hi-fi rendition of *Rigoletto*, one of the greatest of the ancient operas, sung by the finest voices Terra had ever known. The men wore tuxedos. The girls, instead of wearing the nondescript, non-provocative garments prescribed by the Board for their general wear, were all dressed to kill.

Sandra had so arranged matters that she and Hilton were sitting in chairs side by side, with Sandra on his right and the aisle on his left. Nevertheless, Temple Bells sat at his left, cross-legged on a cushion on the floor—somewhat to the detriment of her gold-lame evening gown. Not that she cared.

When those wonderful voices swung into the immortal *Quartette* Temple caught her breath, slid her cushion still closer to Hilton's chair, and leaned shoulder and head against him. He put his left hand on her shoulder, squeezing gently; she caught it and held it in both of hers. And at the *Quartette's* tremendous climax she, scarcely trying to stifle a sob, pulled his hand down and hugged it fiercely, the heel of his hand pressing hard against her half-bare, firm, warm breast.

And the next morning, early, Sandra hunted Temple up and said: "You made a horrible spectacle of yourself last night."

"DO you think so? I don't."

"I certainly do. It was bad enough before, letting everybody else aboard know that all he has to do is push you over. But it was an awful blunder to let *him* know it, the way you did last night."

"You think so? He's one of the keenest, most intelligent men who ever lived. He has known that from the very first."

"Oh." This "oh" was a very caustic one. "*That's* the way you're trying to land him? By getting yourself pregnant?"

"Uh-uh." Temple stretched; lazily, luxuriously. "Not only it isn't, but it wouldn't work. He's unusually decent and extremely idealistic, the same as I am. So just one intimacy would blow everything higher than up. He knows it. I know it. We each know that the other knows it. So I'll still be a virgin when we're married."

"*Married!* Does he know anything about *that?*"

"I suppose so. He must have thought of it. But what difference does it make whether he has, yet, or not? But to get back to what makes him tick the way he does. In his geometry—which is far from being simple Euclid, my dear—a geodesic right line is not only the shortest distance between any two given points, but is the only possible course. So that's the way I'm playing it. What I hope he doesn't know...but he probably does...is that he could take any other woman he might want, just as easily. And that includes you, my pet."

"It certainly does *not*!" Sandra flared. "I wouldn't have him as a gift!"

"No?" Temple's tone was more than slightly skeptical. "Fortunately, however, he doesn't want you. Your technique is all wrong. Coyness and mock-modesty and stop-or-I'll-scream and playing hard to get have no appeal whatever to his psychology. What he needs—has to have—is full, ungrudging cooperation."

"Aren't you taking a lot of risk in giving away such secrets?"

"Not a bit. Try it. You or the sex-flaunting twins or Bev Bell or Stella the Henna. Any of you or all of you. I got there first with the most, and I'm not worried about competition."

"But suppose somebody tells him just how you're playing him for a sucker?"

"Tell him anything you please. He's the first man I ever loved, or anywhere near. And I'm keeping him. You know—or do you, I wonder?—what real, old-fashioned, honest-to-God love really is? The willingness—eagerness—both to give and to take? I can accept more from him, and give him more in return, than any other woman living. And I am going to."

"But does *he* love *you*?" Sandra demanded.

"If he doesn't now, he will. I'll see to it that he does. But what do *you* want him for? You don't love him. You never did and you never will."

"I *don't* want him!" Sandra stamped a foot.

"I see. You just don't want *me* to have him. Okay, do your damnedest. But I've got work to do. This has been a lovely little cat-clawing, hasn't it? Let's have another one some day, and bring your friends."

WITH a casual wave of her hand, Temple strolled away; and there, flashed through Sandra's mind what Hilton had said so long ago, little more than a week out from Earth:

"…and Temple Bells, of course," he had said. "Don't fool yourself, chick. She's heavy artillery; and I mean *heavy*, believe me!"

So he had known all about Temple Bells all this time!

Nevertheless, she took the first opportunity to get Hilton alone; and, even before the first word, she forgot all about geodesic right lines and the full-cooperation psychological approach.

"Aren't you the guy," she demanded, "who was laughing his head off at the idea that the Board and its propinquity could have any effect on *him*?"

"Probably. More or less. What of it?"

"This of it. You've fallen like a...a *freshman* for that...that...they *should* have christened her 'Brazen' Bells!"

"You're so right."

"I am? On what?"

"The 'Brazen'. I told you she was a potent force—a full-scale powerhouse, in sync and on the line. And I wasn't wrong."

"She's a damned female Ph.D.—two or three times—and she knows all about slipsticks and isotopes and she very definitely is *not* a cuddly little brunette. Remember?"

"Sure. But what makes you think I'm in love with Temple Bells?"

"What?" Sandra tried to think of one bit of evidence, but could not. "Why...why..." She floundered, then came up with: "Why, *every*body knows it. She says so herself."

"Did you ever hear her say it?"

"Well, perhaps not in so many words. But she told me herself that you were *going* to be, and I know you are now."

"Your esper sense of endovix, no doubt." Hilton laughed and Sandra went on, furiously:

"She wouldn't keep on acting the way she does if there weren't something to it!"

"What brilliant reasoning! Try again, Sandy."

"That's sheer sophistry, and you know it!"

"It isn't and I don't. And even if, some day, I should find myself in love with her—or with one or both of the twins or Stella or Beverly or you or Sylvia, for that matter—what would it prove? Just that I was wrong; and I admit freely that I *was* wrong in scoffing at the propinquity. Wonderful stuff, that. You can see it working, all over the ship. On me, even, in spite of my bragging. Without it I'd never have known that you're a better, smarter operator than Eggy Eggleston ever was or ever can be."

PARTIALLY mollified despite herself, and highly resentful of the fact, Sandra tried again. "But don't you *see*, Jarve, that she's just simply playing you for a sucker? Pulling the strings and watching you dance?"

Since he was sure, in his own mind, that she was speaking the exact truth, it took everything he had to keep from showing any sign of how much that truth had hurt. However, he made the grade.

"If that thought does anything for you, Sandy," he said, steadily, "keep right on thinking it. Thank God, the field of thought is still free and open."

"Oh, you..." Sandra gave up.

She had shot her heaviest bolts—the last one, particularly, was so vicious that she had actually been afraid of what its consequences might be—and they had not even dented Hilton's armor. She hadn't even found out that he had any feeling whatever for Temple Bells except as a component of his smoothly-functioning scientific machine.

Nor did she learn any more as time went on. Temple continued to play flawlessly the part of being—if not exactly hopefully, at least not entirely hopelessly—in love with Jarvis Hilton. Her conduct, which at first caused some surprise, many conversations—one of which has been reported verbatim—and no little speculation, became comparatively unimportant as soon as it became evident that nothing would come of it. She apparently expected nothing. He was evidently not going to play footsie with, or show any favoritism whatever toward, any woman aboard the ship.

Thus, it was not surprising to anyone that, at an evening show, Temple sat beside Hilton, as close to him as she could get and as far away as possible from everyone else.

"You can talk, can't you, Jarvis, without moving your lips and without anyone else hearing you?"

"Of course," he replied, hiding his surprise. This was something completely new and completely unexpected, even from unpredictable Temple Bells.

"I want to apologize, to explain and to do anything I can to straighten out the mess I've made. It's true that I joined the project because I've loved you for years—"

"You have nothing to..."

"Let me finish while I still have the courage." Only a slight tremor in her almost inaudible voice and the rigidity of the fists clenched in her lap betrayed the intensity of her emotion. "I thought I could handle it. Damned fool that I was, I thought I could handle anything. I was sure I could handle *myself*, under any possible conditions. I was going to put just enough into the act to keep any of these other harpies from getting her hooks into you. But everything got away from me. Out here working with you every day—knowing better every day what you are—well, that *Rigoletto* episode sunk me, and now I'm in a thousand feet over my head. I hug my pillow at night, dreaming it's you, and the fact that you don't and can't love me is driving me mad. I can't stand it any longer. There's only one thing to do. Fire me first thing in the morning and send me back to Earth in a torp. You've plenty of grounds…"

"*Shut—up.*"

FOR seconds Hilton had been trying to break into her hopeless monotone; finally he succeeded. "The trouble with you is, you know altogether too damned much that isn't so." He was barely able to keep his voice down and his eyes front. "What do you think I'm made of—superefract? I thought the whole performance was an act, to prove you're a better man than I am. *You* talk about dreams. Good God! You don't know what dreams are! If you say one more word about quitting, I'll show you whether I love you or not—I'll squeeze you so hard it'll flatten you out flat!"

"Two can play at that game, sweetheart." Her nostrils flared slightly; her fists clenched—if possible—a fraction tighter; and, even in the distorted medium they were using for speech, she could not subdue completely her quick change into soaring, lilting buoyancy. "While you're doing that I'll see how strong your ribs are. Oh, how this changes things! I've never been half as happy in my whole life as I am right now!"

"Maybe we can work it—if I can handle my end."

"Why, of course you can! And happy dreams are nice, not horrible."

"We'll make it, darling. Here's an imaginary kiss coming at you. Got it?"

"Received in good order, thank you. Consumed with gusto and returned in kind."

The show ended and the two strolled out of the room. She walked no closer to him than usual, and no farther away from him. She did not touch him any oftener than she usually did, nor any whit more affectionately or possessively.

And no watching eyes, not even the more than half hostile eyes of Sandra Cummings or the sharply analytical eyes of Stella Wing, could detect any difference whatever in the relationship between worshipful adulatress and tolerantly understanding idol.

THE work, which had never moved at any very fast pace, went more and more slowly. Three weeks crawled past.

Most of the crews and all of the teams except the First were working on side issues—tasks which, while important in and of themselves, had very little to do with the project's main problem. Hilton, even without Sandra's help, was all caught up. All the reports had been analyzed, correlated, cross-indexed and filed—except those of the First Team. Since he could not understand anything much beyond midpoint of the first tape, they were all reposing in a box labeled PENDING.

The Navy had torn fifteen of the Oman warships practically to pieces, installing Terran detectors and trying to learn how to operate Oman machinery and armament. In the former they had succeeded very well; in the latter not at all.

Fifteen Oman ships were now out in deep space, patrolling the void in strict Navy style. Each was manned by two or three Navy men and several hundred Omans, each of whom was reveling in delight at being able to do a job for a Master, even though that Master was not present in person.

Several Strett skeleton-ships had been detected at long range, but the detections were inconclusive. The things had not changed course, or indicated in any other way that they had seen or detected the Oman vessels on patrol. If their detectors were no better than the Omans', they certainly hadn't. That idea, however, could not be assumed to be a fact, and the detections had been becoming more and more frequent. Yesterday a squadron of seven—the first time that anything except singles had appeared—had come much closer than any of the singles had ever done. Like all the others, however, these passers-by had not paid any detectable attention to anything Oman; hence it could be inferred that the skeletons posed no threat.

But Sawtelle was making no such inferences. He was very firmly of the opinion that the Stretts were preparing for a massive attack.

Hilton had assured Sawtelle that no such attack could succeed, and Larry had told Sawtelle why. Nevertheless, to keep the captain pacified, Hilton had given him permission to convert as many Oman ships as he liked; to man them with as many Omans as he liked; and to use ships and Omans as he liked.

Hilton was not worried about the Stretts or the Navy. It was the First Team. It was the bottleneck that was slowing everything down to a crawl...but they knew that. They knew it better than anyone else could, and felt it more keenly. Especially Karns, the team chief. He had been driving himself like a dog, and showed it.

Hilton had talked with him a few times—tried gently to make him take it easy—no soap. He'd have to hunt him up, the next day or so, and slug it out with him. He could do a lot better job on that if he had something to offer...something really constructive...

That was a laugh. A very unfunny laugh. What could he, Jarvis Hilton, a specifically non-specialist director, do on such a job as that?

Nevertheless, as director, he would *have* to do something to help Team One. If he couldn't do anything himself, it was up to him to juggle things around so that someone else could.

CHAPTER SIX

FOR one solid hour Hilton stared at the wall, motionless and silent. Then, shaking himself and stretching, he glanced at his clock.

A little over an hour to supper-time. They'd all be aboard. He'd talk this new idea over with Teddy Blake. He gathered up a few papers and was stapling them together when Karns walked in.

"Hi, Bill—speak of the devil! I was just thinking about you."

"I'll just bet you were." Karns sat down, leaned over, and took a cigarette out of the box on the desk. "And nothing printable, either."

"Chip-chop, fellow, on that kind of noise," Hilton said. The team-chief looked actually haggard. Blue-black rings encircled both eyes. His powerful body slumped. "How long has it been since you had a good night's sleep?"

"How long have I been on this job? Exactly one hundred and twenty days. I did get some sleep for the first few weeks, though."

"Yeah. So answer me one question. How much good will you do us after they've wrapped you up in one of those canvas affairs that lace up the back?"

"Huh? Oh…but damn it, Jarve, I'm holding up the whole procession. Everybody on the project's just sitting around on their tokuses waiting for me to get something done and I'm not doing it. I'm going so slow a snail is lightning in comparison!"

"Calm down, big fellow. Don't rupture a gut or blow a gasket. I've talked to you before, but this time I'm going to smack you bow-legged. So stick out those big, floppy ears of yours and really *listen*. Here are three words that I want you to pin up somewhere where you can see them all day long: SPEED IS RELATIVE. Look back, see how far up the hill you've come, and then balance one hundred and twenty days against ten years."

"What? You mean you'll actually sit still for me holding everything up for ten years?"

"You use the perpendicular pronoun too much and in the wrong places. On the hits it's 'we', but on the flops it's 'I'. Quit it. Everything on this job is 'we'. Terra's best brains are on Team One and are going to stay there. You will not—repeat NOT—be interfered with, pushed around or kicked around. You see, Bill, I know what you're up against."

"Yes, I guess you do. One of the damned few who do. But even if you personally are willing to give us ten years, how in hell do you think you can swing it? How about the Navy—the Stretts— even the Board?"

"They're my business, Bill, not yours. However, to give you a little boost, I'll tell you. With the Navy, I'll give 'em the Fuel Bin if I have to. The Omans have been taking care of the Stretts for twenty-seven hundred centuries, so I'm not the least bit worried about their ability to keep on doing it for ten years more. And if the Board—or anybody else—sticks their runny little noses into Project Theta Orionis I'll slap a quarantine onto both these solar systems that a microbe couldn't get through!"

"You'd go *that* far? Why, you'd be…"

"DO you think I wouldn't?" Hilton snapped. "Look at me, Junior!" Eyes locked and held. "Do you think, for one minute, that I'll let anybody on all of God's worlds pull *me* off of this job or interfere with my handling of it unless and until I'm damned positively certain that we can't handle it?"

Karns relaxed visibly; the lines of strain eased. "Putting it in those words makes me feel better. I *will* sleep to-night—and without any pills, either."

"Sure you will. One more thought. We all put in more than ten years getting our Terran educations, and an Oman education is a lot tougher."

Really smiling for the first time in weeks, Karns left the office and Hilton glanced again at his clock.

Pretty late now to see Teddy…besides, he'd better not. She was probably keyed up about as high as Bill was, and in no shape to do the kind of thinking he wanted of her on this stuff. Better wait a couple of days.

On the following morning, before breakfast, Theodora was waiting for him outside the mess-hall.

"Good morning, Jarve," she caroled. Reaching up, she took him by both ears, pulled his head down and kissed him. As soon as he perceived her intent, he cooperated enthusiastically. "What *did* you do to Bill?"

"Oh, you don't love me for myself alone, then, but just on account of *that* big jerk?"

"That's right." Her artist's-model face, startlingly beautiful now, fairly glowed.

Just then Temple Bells strolled up to them. "Morning, you two lovely people." She hugged Hilton's arm as usual. "Shame on you, Teddy. But I wish *I* had the nerve to kiss him like that."

"Nerve? You?" Teddy laughed as Hilton picked Temple up and kissed her in exactly the same fashion—he hoped!—as he had just kissed Teddy. "You've got more nerve than an aching tooth. But as Jarve would say it, 'scat, kitten'. We're having breakfast *a la twosome*. We've got things to talk about."

"All right for *you*," Temple said darkly, although her dazzling smile belied her tone. That first kiss, casual-seeming as it had been, had carried vastly more freight than any observer could perceive. "I'll hunt Bill up and make passes at him, see if I don't. *That'll* learn ya!"

THEODORA and Hilton did have their breakfast *a deux*—but she did not realize until afterward that he had not answered her question as to what he had done to her Bill.

As has been said, Hilton had made it a prime factor of his job to become thoroughly well acquainted with every member of his staff. He had studied them *en masse*, in groups and singly. He had never, however, cornered Theodora Blake for individual study. Considering the power and the quality of her mind, and the field which was her specialty, it had not been necessary.

Thus it was with no ulterior motives at all that, three evenings later, he walked her cubby-hole office and tossed the stapled papers onto her desk. "Free for a couple of minutes, Teddy? I've got troubles."

"I'll say you have." Her lovely lips curled into an expression he had never before seen her wear—a veritable sneer. "But these are not them." She tossed the papers into a drawer and stuck out her chin. Her face turned as hard as such a beautiful face could. Her eyes dug steadily into his.

Hilton—inwardly—flinched. His mind flashed backward. She too had been working under stress, of course; but that wasn't enough. What could he have *possibly* done to put Teddy Blake, of all people, onto such a warpath as this?

"I've been wondering when you were going to try to put *me* through your wringer," she went on, in the same cold, hard voice, "and I've been waiting to tell you something. You have wrapped all the other women around your fingers like so many rings—and what a *sickening* exhibition that has been!—but you are not going to make either a ring or a lap-dog out of me."

Almost but not quite too late Hilton saw through that perfect act. He seized her right hand in both of his, held it up over her head, and waved it back and forth in the sign of victory.

"Socked me with my own club!" he exulted, laughing delightedly, boyishly. "And came within a tenth of a split red hair! If it hadn't been so absolutely out of character you'd've got away with it. *What* a load of stuff! I was right—of all the women on this project, you're the only one I've ever been really afraid of."

"Oh, damn. Ouch!" She grinned ruefully. "I hit you with everything I had and it just bounced. You're an operator, chief. Hit 'em hard, at completely unexpected angles. Keep 'em staggering, completely off balance. Tell 'em nothing—let 'em deduce your lies for themselves. And it anybody tries to slug you back, like I did just now, duck it and clobber him in another unprotected spot. Watching you work has been not only a delight, but also a liberal education."

"THANKS. I love you, too, Teddy." He lighted two cigarettes, handed her one. "I'm glad, though, to lay it flat on the table with you, because in any battle of wits with *you* I'm licked before we start."

"Yeah. You just proved it. And after licking me hands down, you think you can square it by swinging the old shovel that way?" She did not quite know whether to feel resentful or not.

"Think over a couple of things. First, with the possible exception of Temple Bells, you're the best brain aboard."

"No. You are. Then Temple. Then there are..."

"Hold it. You know as well as I do that accurate self-judgment is impossible. Second, the jam we're in. Do I, or don't I, want to lay it on the table with you, now and from here on? Bore into that with your Class A Double-Prime brain. Then tell me." He leaned back, half-closed his eyes and smoked lazily.

She stiffened; narrowed her eyes in concentration; and thought. Finally: "Yes, you do; and I'm gladder of that than you will ever know."

"I think I know already, since you're her best friend and the only other woman I know of in her class. But I came in to kick a couple of things around with you. As you've noticed, that's getting to be my favorite indoor sport. Probably because I'm a sort of jackleg theoretician myself."

"You can frame that, Jarve, as the understatement of the century. But first, you are going to answer that question you sidestepped so neatly."

"What I did to Bill? I finally convinced him that nobody expected the team to do that big a job overnight. That you could have ten years. Or more, if necessary."

"I see." She frowned. "But you and I both know that we *can't* string it out that long."

He did not answer immediately. "We *could*. But we probably won't...unless we have to. We should know, long before that, whether we'll have to switch to some other line of attack. You've considered the possibilities, of course. Have you got anything in shape to do a fine-tooth on?"

"Not yet. That is, except for the ultimate, which is too ghastly to even consider except as an ultimately last resort. Have you?"

"I know what you mean. No, I haven't, either. You don't think, then, that we had better do any collaborative thinking yet?"

"Definitely not. There's altogether too much danger of setting both our lines of thought into one dead-end channel."

"Check. The other thing I wanted from you is your considered opinion as to my job on the organization as a whole. And don't pull your punches. Are we in good shape or not? What can I do to improve the setup?"

"I HAVE already considered that very thing—at great length. And honestly, Jarve, I don't see how it can be improved in any respect. You've done a marvelous job. Much better than I thought possible at first." He heaved a deep sigh of relief and she went on: "This could very easily have become a God-awful mess. But the Board knew what they were doing—especially as to top man—so there are only about four people aboard who realize what you have done. Alex Kincaid and Sandra Cummings are two of them. One of the three girls is very deeply and very truly in love with you."

"Ordinarily I'd say 'no comment', but we're laying on the line…well…"

"You'll lay *that* on the line only if I corkscrew it out you, so I'll Q.E.D. it. You probably know that when Sandy gets done playing around it'll be…"

"Bounce back, Teddy. She isn't—hasn't been. If anything, too much the opposite. A dedicated-scientist type."

She smiled—a highly cryptic smile. For a man as brilliant and as penetrant in every other respect…but after all, if the big dope didn't realize that half the women aboard, including Sandy, had been making passes at him, she certainly wouldn't enlighten him. Besides, that one particular area of obtuseness was a real part of his charm. Wherefore she said merely: "I'm not sure whether I'm a bit catty or you're a bit stupid. Anyway, it's Alex she's really in love with. And you already know about Bill and me."

"Of course. He's tops. One of the world's very finest. You're in the same bracket, and as a couple you're a drive fit. One in a million."

"Now I can say 'I love you, too', too." She paused for half a minute, then stubbed out her cigarette and shrugged. "Now I'm going to stick my neck way, way out. You can knock it off if you like. She's a tremendous lot of woman, and if…well, strong as she is, it'd shatter her to bits. So, I'd like to ask…I don't quite…well, *is* she going to get hurt?"

"Have I managed to hide it *that* well? From *you*?"

It was her turn to show relief. "Perfectly. Even—or especially—that time you kissed her. So damned perfectly that I've been scared green. I've been waking myself up, screaming, in the middle of the night. You couldn't let on, of course. That's the hell of such a job as yours. The rest of us can smooch around all over the place. I knew the question was extremely improper—thanks a million for answering it."

"I haven't started to answer it yet. I said I'd lay everything on the line, so here it is. Saying she's a tremendous lot of woman is like calling the *Perseus* a nice little baby's-bathtub toy boat. I'd go to hell for her any time, cheerfully, standing straight up, wading into brimstone and lava up to the eyeballs. If anything ever hurts her it'll be because I'm not man enough to block it. And just the minute this damned job is over, or even sooner if enough of you couples make it so I can..."

"Jarvis!" she shrieked. Jumping up, she kissed him enthusiastically. "That's just wonderful!"

HE thought it was pretty wonderful, too; and after ten minutes more of conversation he got up and turned toward the door.

"I feel a lot better, Teddy. Thanks for being such a nice pressure-relief valve. Would you mind it too much if I come in and sob on your bosom again some day?"

"I'd love it!" She laughed; then, as he again started to leave: "Wait a minute, I'm thinking...it'd be more fun to sob on *her* bosom. You haven't even kissed her yet, have you? I mean *really* kissed her?"

"You know I haven't. She's the one person aboard I can't be alone with for a second."

"True. But I know of one chaperone who could become deaf and blind," she said, with a broad and happy grin. "On my door, you know, there's a huge invisible sign that says, to everyone except you, 'STOP! BRAIN AT WORK! SILENCE!', and if I were properly approached and sufficiently urged, I might...I just *conceivably* might..."

"Consider it done, you little sweetheart! Up to and including my most vigorous and most insidious attempts at seduction."

"Done. Maneuver your big, husky carcass around here behind the desk so the door can open." She flipped a switch and punched a number. "I can call anybody in here, any time, you know. Hello, dear, this is Teddy. Can you come in for just a few minutes? Thanks." And, one minute later, there came a light tap on the door.

"Come in," Teddy called, and Temple Bells entered the room. She showed no surprise at seeing Hilton.

"Hi, chief," she said. "It must be something both big and tough, to have you and Teddy both on it."

"You're so right. It was very big and very tough. But it's solved, darling, so..."

"*Darling?*" she gasped, almost inaudibly, both hands flying to her throat. Her eyes flashed toward the other woman.

"Teddy knows all about us—accessory before, during and after the fact."

"*Darling!*" This time, the word was a shriek. She extended both arms and started forward.

Hilton did not bother to maneuver his "big, husky carcass" around the desk, but simply hurdled it, straight toward her.

TEMPLE Bells was a tall, lithe, strong woman; and all the power of her arms and torso went into the ensuing effort to crack Hilton's ribs. Those ribs, however, were highly capable structural members; and furthermore, they were protected by thick slabs of hard, hard muscle. And, fortunately, he was not trying to fracture *her* ribs. His pressures were distributed much more widely. He was, according to promise, doing his very best to flatten her whole resilient body out flat.

And as they stood there, locked together in sheerest ecstasy, Theodora Blake began openly and unashamedly to cry.

It was Temple who first came up for air. She wriggled loose from one of his arms, felt of her hair and gazed unseeingly into her mirror. "That was *wonderful*, sweetheart," she said then, shakily. "And I can *never* thank you enough, Teddy. But we can't do this very often...can we?" The addendum fairly begged for contradiction.

"Not too often, I'm afraid," Hilton said, and Theodora agreed...

"Well," the man said, somewhat later, "I'll leave you two ladies to your knitting, or whatever. After a couple of short ones for the road, that is."

"Not looking like that!" Teddy said, sharply. "Hold still and we'll clean you up." Then, as both girls went to work:

"If anybody ever sees you coming out of this office looking like *that*," she went on, darkly, "and Bill finds out about it, he'll think it's *my* lipstick smeared all over you and I'll strangle you to death with my bare hands!"

"And that was supposed to be kissproof lipstick, too," Temple said, seriously—although her whole face glowed and her eyes danced. "You know, I'll never believe another advertisement I read."

"Oh, I wouldn't go so far as to say that, if I were you." Teddy's voice was gravity itself, although she, too, was bubbling over. "It probably *is* kissproof. I don't think 'kissing' is quite the word for the performance you just staged. To stand up under such punishment as you gave it, my dear, anything would have to be tattooed in, not just put on."

"Hey!" Hilton protested. "You promised to be deaf and blind!"

"I did no such thing. I said 'could', not 'would'. Why, I wouldn't have missed that for *anything!*"

When Hilton left the room he was apparently, in every respect, his usual self-contained self. However, it was not until the following morning that he so much as thought of the sheaf of papers lying unread in the drawer of Theodora Blake's desk.

CHAPTER SEVEN

KNOWING that he had done everything he could to help the most important investigations get under way, Hilton turned his attention to secondary matters. He made arrangements to decondition Javo, the Number Two Oman Boss, whereupon that worthy became Javvy and promptly "bumped" the Oman who had been shadowing Karns.

Larry and Javvy, working nights, deconditioned all the other Omans having any contact with BuSci personnel; then they went on to set up a routine for deconditioning all Omans on both planets.

Assured at last that the Omans would thenceforth work with and really serve human beings instead of insisting upon doing their work for them, Hilton knew that the time had come to let all his BuSci personnel move into their homes aground. Everyone, including himself, was fed up to the gozzel with spaceship life—its jam-packed crowding; its flat, reprocessed air; its limited variety of uninteresting food. Conditions were especially irksome since everybody knew that there was available to all, whenever Hilton gave the word, a whole city full of all the room anyone could want, natural fresh air and—so the Omans had told them—an unlimited choice of everything anyone wanted to eat.

Nevertheless, the decision was not an easy one to make.

Living conditions were admittedly not good on the ship. On the other hand, with almost no chance at all of solitude—the few people who had private offices aboard were not the ones he worried about—there was no danger of sexual trouble. Strictly speaking, he was not responsible for the morals of his force. He knew that he was being terribly old-fashioned. Nevertheless, he could not argue himself out of the conviction that he was morally responsible.

Finally he took the thing up with Sandra, who merely laughed at him. "How long have you been worrying about *that*, Jarve?"

"Ever since I okayed moving aground the first time. That was one reason I was so glad to cancel it then."

"You *were* slightly unclear—a little rattled? But which factor— the fun and games, which is the moral issue, or the consequences?"

"The consequences," he admitted, with a rueful grin. "I don't give a whoop how much fun they have; but you know as well as I do just how prudish public sentiment is. And Project Theta Orionis is squarely in the middle of the public eye."

"YOU should have checked with me sooner and saved yourself wear and tear. There's no danger at all of consequences—except weddings. Lots of weddings, and fast."

"Weddings and babies wouldn't bother me a bit. Nor interfere with the job too much, with the Omans as nurses. But why the 'fast', if you aren't anticipating any shotgun weddings?"

"Female psychology," she replied, with a grin. "Aboard-ship here there's no home atmosphere whatever; nothing but work, work, work. Put a woman into a house, though—especially such houses as the Omans have built and with such servants as they insist on being—and she goes domestic in a really big way. Just sex isn't good enough any more. She wants the kind of love that goes with a husband and a home, and nine times out of ten she gets it. With these BuSci women it'll be ten out of ten."

"You may be right, of course, but it sounds kind of far-fetched to me."

"Wait and see, chum," Sandra said, with a laugh.

Hilton made his announcement and everyone moved aground the next day. No one, however, had elected to live alone. Almost everyone had chosen to double up; the most noteworthy exceptions being twelve laboratory girls who had decided to keep on living together. However, they now had a twenty-room house instead of a one-room dormitory to live in, and a staff of twenty Oman girls to help them do it.

Hilton had suggested that Temple and Teddy, whose house was only a hundred yards or so from the Hilton-Karns bungalow, should have supper and spend the first evening with them; but the girls had knocked that idea flat. Much better, they thought, to let things ride as nearly as possible exactly as they had been aboard the *Perseus*.

"A *little* smooching now and then, on the Q strictly T, but that's all, darling. That's *positively* all," Temple had said, after a highly satisfactory ten minutes alone with him in her own gloriously private room, and that was the way it had to be.

Hence it was a stag inspection that Hilton and Karns made of their new home. It was very long, very wide, and for its size very low. Four of its five rooms were merely adjuncts to its tremendous living-room. There was a huge fireplace at each end of this room, in each of which a fire of four-foot-long fir cordwood crackled and snapped. There was a great hi-fi tri-di, with over a hundred tapes, all new.

"Yes, sirs," Larry and Javvy spoke in unison. "The players and singers who entertained the Masters of old have gone back to work. They will also, of course, appear in person whenever and wherever you wish."

BOTH men looked around the vast room and Karns said: "All the comforts of home and a couple of bucks' worth besides. Wall-to-wall carpeting an inch and a half thick. A grand piano. Easy chairs and loafers and davenports. Very fine reproductions of our favorite paintings…and statuary."

"You said it, brother." Hilton was bending over a group in bronze. "If I didn't know better, I'd swear this is the original deHaven 'Dance of the Nymphs'."

Karns had marched up to and was examining minutely a two-by-three-foot painting, in a heavy gold frame, of a gorgeously auburn-haired nude. "Reproduction, hell! This is a *duplicate*!

Lawrence's 'Innocent' is worth twenty million wogs and it's sealed behind quad armor-glass in Prime Art—but I'll bet wogs to wiggles the Prime Curator himself, with all his apparatus, couldn't tell this one from his!"

"I wouldn't take even one wiggle's worth of that. And this 'Laughing Cavalier' and this 'Toledo' are twice as old and twice as fabulously valuable."

"And there are my own golf clubs…"

"Excuse us, sirs," the Omans said, "These things were simple because they could be induced in your minds. But the matter of a staff could not, nor what you would like to eat for supper, and it is growing late."

"Staff? What the hell has the staff got to do with…"

"*House*-staff, they mean," Karns said. "We don't need much of anybody, boys. Somebody to keep the place shipshape, is all. Or, as a de luxe touch, how about a waitress? One housekeeper and one waitress. That'll be finer."

"Very well, sirs. There is one other matter. It has troubled us that we have not been able to read in your minds the logical datum that they should in fact simulate Doctor Bells and Doctor Blake?"

"Huh?" Both men gasped—and then both exploded like one twelve-inch length of primacord.

WHILE the Omans could not understand this purely Terran reasoning, they accepted the decision without a demurring thought. "Who, then, are the two its to simulate?"

"No stipulation; roll your own," Hilton said, and glanced at Karns. "None of these Oman women are really hard on the eyes."

"Check. Anybody who wouldn't call any one of 'em a slurpy dish needs a new set of optic nerves."

"In that case," the Omans said, "no delay at all will be necessary, as we can make do with one temporarily. The Sory, no longer Sora, who has not been glad since the Tuly replaced it, is now in your kitchen. It comes."

A woman came in and stood quietly in front of the two men, the wafted air carrying from her clear, smooth skin a faint but unmistakable fragrance of Idaho mountain syringa. She was radiantly happy; her bright, deep-green eyes went from man to man.

"You wish, sirs, to give me your orders verbally. And yes, you may order fresh, whole, not-canned hens' eggs."

"I certainly will, then; I haven't had a fried egg since we left Terra. But...Larry said...*you* aren't Sory!"

"Oh, but I am, sir."

Karns had been staring her, eyes popping. "Holy Saint Patrick! Talk about simulation, Jarve! They've made her over into Lawrence's 'Innocent'—exact to twenty decimals!"

"You're so right." Hilton's eyes went, half a dozen times, from the form of flesh to the painting and back. "That must have been a terrific job."

"Oh, no. It was quite simple, really," Sory said, "since the brain was not involved. I merely reddened my hair and lengthened it, made my eyes to be green, changed my face a little, pulled myself in a little around here..." Her beautifully-manicured hands swept the full circle of her waistline, then continued to demonstrate appropriately the rest of her speech:

"...and pushed me out a little up here and tapered my legs a little more—made them a little larger and rounder here at my hips and thighs and a little smaller toward and at my ankles. Oh, yes, and made my feet and hands a little smaller. That's all. I thought the Doctor Karns would like me a little better this way."

"YOU can broadcast *that* over the P-A system at high noon." Karns was still staring. "'That's all,' she says. But you didn't have *time* to..."

"Oh, I did it day before yesterday. As soon as Javvy materialized the 'Innocent' and I knew it to be your favorite art."

"But damn it, we hadn't even *thought* of having you here then!"

"But I had, sir. I fully intended to serve, one way or another, in this your home. But of course I had no idea I would ever have such an honor as actually waiting on you at your table. Will you please give me your orders, sirs, besides the eggs? You wish the eggs fried in butter—three of them apiece—and sunny side up."

"Uh-huh, with ham," Hilton said. "I'll start with a jumbo shrimp cocktail. Horseradish and ketchup sauce; heavy on the horseradish."

"That's the same for me," Karns said, "but only half as much horseradish."

"And for the rest of it," Hilton went on, "hashed-brown potatoes and buttered toast—plenty of extra butter—strong coffee from first to last. Whipping cream and sugar on the side. For dessert, apple pie *a la mode*."

"You make me drool, chief. Play that for me, please, Innocent, all the way."

"Oh? You are—you, personally, yourself, sir?—renaming me 'Innocent'?"

"If you'll sit still for it, yes."

"That is an incredible honor, sir. Simply unbelievable. I thank you! I thank you!" Radiating happiness, she dashed away toward the kitchen.

WHEN the two men were full of food, they strolled over to a davenport facing the fire. As they sat down, Innocent entered the room, carrying a tall, dewy mint julep on a tray. She was followed by another female figure bearing a bottle of avignognac and the appurtenances which are its due—and at the first full sight of that figure Hilton stopped breathing for fifteen seconds.

Her hair was very thick, intensely black and long, cut squarely off just below the lowest points of her shoulder blades. Heavy brows and long lashes—eyes too—were all intensely, vividly black. Her skin was tanned to a deep and glowing almost-but-not-quite-brown.

"Murchison's Dark Lady!" Hilton gasped. "Larry! You've—we've—*I've* got that painting here?"

"Oh, yes, sir." The newcomer spoke before Larry could. "At the other end—your part—of the room. You will look now, sir, please?" Her voice was low, rich and as smooth as cream.

Putting her tray down carefully on the end-table, she led him toward the other fireplace. Past the piano, past the tri-di pit; past a towering grillwork holding art treasures by the score. Over to the left, against the wall, there was a big, business-like desk. On the wall, over the desk, hung *the* painting; a copy of which had been in Hilton's room for over eight years.

He stared at it for at least a minute. He glanced around: at the other priceless duplicates so prodigally present, at his own guns arrayed above the mantel and on each side of the fireplace. Then, without a word, he started back to join Karns. She walked springily beside him.

"What's your name, Miss?" he asked, finally.

"I haven't earned any as yet, sir. My number is…"

"Never mind that. Your name is 'Dark Lady'."

"Oh, thank you, sir; that is truly wonderful!" And Dark Lady sat cross-legged on the rug at Hilton's feet and busied herself with the esoteric rites of Old Avignon.

Hilton took a deep inhalation and a small sip, then stared at Karns. Karns, over the rim of his glass, stared back.

"I can see where this would be habit-forming," Hilton said, "and very deadly. *Extremely* deadly."

"Every wish granted. Surrounded by all this." Karns swept his arm through three-quarters of a circle. "Waited on hand and foot by powerful men and by the materializations of the dreams of the greatest, finest artists who ever lived. Fatal? I don't know…"

"MY solid hope is that we never have to find out. And when you add in Innocent and Dark Lady… They *look* to be about seventeen, but the thought that they're older than the hills of Rome and powered by everlasting atomic engines—" He broke off suddenly and blushed. "Excuse me, please, girls. I *know* better than to talk about people that way, right in front of them; I really do."

"Do you really think we're *people*?" Innocent and Dark Lady squealed, as one.

That set Hilton back onto his heels. "I don't know… I've wondered. Are you?"

Both girls, silent, looked at Larry.

"We don't know, either," Larry said. "At first, of course, there were crude, non-thinking machines. But when the Guide attained its present status, the Masters themselves could not agree. They divided about half and half on the point. They never did settle it any closer than that."

"I certainly won't try to, then. But for my money, you are people," Hilton said, and Karns agreed.

That, of course, touched off a near-riot of joy; after which the two men made an inch-by-inch study of their tremendous living-room. Then, long after bedtime, Larry and Dark Lady escorted Hilton to his bedroom.

"Do you mind, sir, if we sleep on the floor at the sides of your bed?" Larry asked. "Or must we go out into the hall?"

"Sleep? I didn't know you *could* sleep."

"It is not essential. However, when round-the-clock work is not necessary, and we have opportunity to sleep near a human being, we derive a great deal of pleasure and satisfaction from it. You see, sir, we also serve during sleep."

"Okay, I'll try anything once. Sleep wherever you please."

Hilton began to peel, but before he had his shirt off both Larry and Dark Lady were stretched out flat, sound asleep, one almost under each edge of his bed. He slid in between the sheets—it was the most comfortable bed he had ever slept in—and went to sleep as though sandbagged.

He had time to wonder foggily whether the Omans were in fact helping him go to sleep—and then he *was* asleep.

A MONTH passed. Eight couples had married, the Navy chaplain officiating—in the *Perseus*, of course, since the warship was, always and everywhere, an integral part of Terra.

Sandra had dropped in one evening to see Hilton about a bit of business. She was now sitting, long dancer's legs out-stretched toward the fire, with a cigarette in her left hand and a tall, cold drink on a coaster at her right.

"This is a wonderful room, Jarvis. It'd be perfect if it weren't quite so…so mannish."

"What do you expect of Bachelors' Hall—a boudoir? Don't tell me *you're* going domestic, Sandy, just because you've got a house?"

"Not just that, no. But of course it helped it along."

"Alex is a mighty good man. One of the finest I have ever known."

She eyed him for a moment in silence. "Jarvis Hilton, you are one of the keenest, most intelligent men who ever lived. And yet..." She broke off and studied him for a good half minute. "Say, if I let my hair clear down, will you?"

"Scout's Oath. That 'and yet' requires elucidation at any cost."

"I know. But first, yes, it's Alex. I never would have believed that any man ever born could hit me so hard. Soon. I didn't want to be the first, but I won't be anywhere near the last. But tell me. You were really in love with Temple, weren't you, when I asked you?"

"Yes."

"Ha! You *are* letting your hair down! That makes me feel better."

"Huh? Why should it?"

"It elucidates the 'and yet' no end. You were insulated from all other female charms by ye brazen Bells. You see, most of us assistants made a kind of game out of seeing which of us could make you break the Executives' Code. And none of us made it. Teddy and Temple said you didn't know what was going on; Bev and I said nobody as smart as you are could possibly be that stupid."

"You aren't the type to leak or name names—oh, I see. You are merely reporting a conversation. The game had interested, but non-participating, observers. Temple and Teddy, at least."

"At least," she agreed. "But damn it, you *aren't* stupid. There isn't a stupid bone in your head. So it must be love. And if so, what about marriage? Why don't you and Temple make it a double with Alex and me?"

"That's the most cogent thought you ever had, but setting the date is the bride's business." He glanced at his Oman wristwatch. "It's early yet; let's skip over. I wouldn't mind seeing her a minute or two."

"Thy statement ringeth with truth, friend. Bill's there with Teddy?"

"I imagine so."

"So we'll talk to them about making it a triple. Oh, nice—let's go!"

159

They left the house and, her hand tucked under his elbow, walked up the street.

NEXT morning, on her way to the Hall of Records, Sandra stopped off as usual at the office. The Omans were all standing motionless. Hilton was leaning far back in his chair, feet on desk, hands clasped behind head, eyes closed. Knowing what that meant, she turned and started back out on tiptoe.

However, he had heard her. "Can you spare a couple of minutes to think at me, Sandy?"

"Minutes or hours, chief." Tuly placed a chair for her and she sat down, facing him across his desk.

"Thanks, gal. This time it's the Stretts. Sawtelle's been having nightmares, you know, ever since we emerged, about being attacked, and I've been pooh-poohing the idea. But now it's a statistic that the soup is getting thicker, and I can't figure out why. Why in all the hells of space should a stasis that has lasted for over a quarter of a million years be broken at this exact time? The only possible explanation is that *we* caused the break. And any way I look at that concept, it's plain idiocy."

Both were silent for minutes; and then it was demonstrated again that Terra's Advisory Board had done better than it knew in choosing Sandra Cummings to be Jarvis Hilton's working mate.

"We did cause it, Jarve," she said, finally. "They knew we were coming, even before we got to Fuel Bin. They knew we were human and tried to wipe out the Omans before we got there. Preventive warfare, you know."

"They *couldn't* have known!" he snorted. "Strett detectors are no better than Oman, and you know what Sam Bryant had to say about them."

"I know." Sandra grinned appreciatively. "It's becoming a classic. But it couldn't have been any other way. Besides, I *know* they did."

He stared at her helplessly, then swung on Larry. "Does that make sense to you?"

"Yes, sir. The Stretts could peyondire as well as the old Masters could, and they undoubtedly still can and do."

"Okay, it does make sense, then." He absented himself in thought, then came to life with a snap. "Okay! The next thing on the agenda is a crash-priority try at a peyondix team. Tuly, you organized a team to generate sathura. Can you do the same for peyondix?"

"If we can find the ingredients, yes, sir."

"I HAD a hunch. Larry, please ask Teddy Blake's Oman to bring her in here…"

"I'll be running along, then." Sandra started to get up.

"I hope to kiss a green pig you won't!" Hilton snapped. "You're one of the biggest wheels. Larry, we'll want Temple Bells and Beverly Bell—for a start."

"Chief, you positively amaze me," Sandra said then. "Every time you get one of these attacks of genius—or whatever it is—you have me gasping like a fish. Just what can you *possibly* want of Bev Bell?"

"Whatever it was that enabled her to hit the target against odds of almost infinity to one; not just once, but time after time. By definition, intuition. What quality did you use just now in getting me off the hook? Intuition. What makes Teddy Blake such an unerring performer? Intuition again. My hunches—they're intuition, too. Intuition, *hell!* Labels—based on utterly abysmal damned dumb ignorance of our own basic frames of reference. Do you think those four kinds of intuition are alike, by seven thousand rows of apple trees?"

"Of course not. I see what you're getting at… Oh! This'll be fun!"

The others came in and, one by one, Tuly examined each of the four women and the man. Each felt the probing, questioning feelers of her thought prying into the deepest recesses of his mind.

"There is not quite enough of each of three components, all of which are usually associated with the male. You, sir, have much of each, but not enough. I know your men quite well, and I think we will need the doctors Kincaid and Karns and Poynter. But such deep probing is felt. Have I permission, sir?"

"Yes. Tell 'em I said so."

Tuly scanned. "Yes, sir, we should have all three."

"Get 'em, Larry." Then, in the pause that followed: "Sandy, remember yowling about too many sweeties on a team? What do you think of this business of all sweeties?"

"All that proves is that nobody can be wrong all the time," she replied flippantly.

The three men arrived and were instructed. Tuly said: "The great trouble is that each of you must use a portion of your mind that you do not know you have. You, this one. You, that one." Tuly probed mercilessly; so poignantly that each in turn flinched under brand-new and almost unbearable pain. "With you, Doctor Hilton, it will be by far the worst. For you must learn to use almost all the portions of both your minds, the conscious and the unconscious. This must be, because you are the actual peyondixer. The others merely supply energies in which you yourself are deficient. Are you ready for a terrible shock, sir?"

"Shoot."

HE thought for a second that he *had* been shot; that his brain had blown up.

He couldn't stand it—he *knew* he was going to die—he wished he *could* die—anything, anything whatever, to end this unbearable agony...

It ended.

Writhing, white and sweating, Hilton opened his eyes. "Ouch," he remarked, conversationally. "What next?"

"You will seize hold of the energies your friends offer. You will bind them to yours and shape the whole into a dimensionless sphere of pure controlled, dirigible energy. And, as well as being the binding force, the cohesiveness, you must also be the captain and the pilot and the astrogator and the ultimately complex computer itself."

"But how can I... Okay, damn it. I *will!*"

"Of course you will, sir. Remember also that once the joinings are made I can be of very little more assistance, for my peyondix is as nothing compared to that of your fusion of eight. Now, to assemble the energies and join them you will, all together, deny the existence of the sum total of reality as you know it. Distance does not exist—every point in the reachable universe coincides with every other point and that common point is the focus of your attention. You can be and actually are anywhere you please or everywhere at once. Time does not exist. Space does not exist. There is no such thing as opacity; everything is perfectly transparent, yet every molecule of substance is perceptible in its relationship to every other molecule in the cosmos. Senses do not exist. Sight, hearing, taste, touch, smell, sathura, endovix—all are parts of the one great sense of peyondix. I am guiding each of you seven—closer! Tighter! There! Seize it, sir—and when you work the Stretts you must fix it clearly that time does not exist. You must work in millionths of microseconds instead of in minutes, for they have minds of tremendous power. Reality does not exist! Compress it more, sir. Tighter! Smaller! Rounder! There! Hold it! Reality does not exist—distance does not exist—all possible points are... *Wonderful!*"

Tuly screamed the word and the thought: "Good-by! Good luck!"

CHAPTER EIGHT

HILTON did not have to drive the peyondix-beam to the planet Strett; it was already there. And there was the monstrous First Lord Thinker Zoyar.

Into that mind his multi-mind flashed, its every member as responsive to his will as his own fingers—almost infinitely more so, in fact, because of the tremendous lengths of time required to send messages along nerves.

That horrid mind was scanned cell by cell. Then, after what seemed like a few hours, when a shield began sluggishly to form, Hilton transferred his probe to the mind of the Second Thinker, one Lord Ynos, and absorbed everything she knew. Then, the minds of all the other Thinkers being screened, he studied the whole Strett planet, foot by foot, and everything that was on it.

Then, mission accomplished, Hilton snapped his attention back to his office and the multi-mind fell apart. As he opened his eyes he heard Tuly scream: "...Luck!"

"Oh—you still here, Tuly? How long have we been gone?"

"Approximately one and one-tenth seconds, sir."

"WHAT!"

Beverly Bell, in the haven of Franklin Poynter's arms, fainted quietly. Sandra shrieked piercingly. The four men stared, goggle-eyed. Temple and Teddy, as though by common thought, burrowed their faces into brawny shoulders.

Hilton recovered first. "So *that's* what peyondix is."

"Yes, sir—I mean no, sir. No, I mean yes, but..." Tuly paused, licking her lips in that peculiarly human-female gesture of uncertainty.

"Well, what *do* you mean? It either is or isn't. Or is that necessarily so?"

"Not exactly, sir. That is, it started as peyondix. But it became something else. Not even the most powerful of the old Masters—nobody—ever did or ever could *possibly* generate such a force as that. Or handle it so fast."

"Well, with seven of the best minds of Terra and a..."

"Chip-chop the chit-chat!" Karns said, harshly. "What I want to know is whether I was having a nightmare. Can there *possibly* be a race such as I thought I saw? So utterly savage—ruthless—merciless! So devoid of every human trace and so hell-bent determined on the extermination of every other race in the Galaxy? God damn it, it simply doesn't make sense!"

EYES went from eyes to eyes to eyes.

All had seen the same indescribably horrible, abysmally atrocious, things. Qualities and quantities and urges and drives that no words in any language could even begin to portray.

"It doesn't seem to, but there it is." Teddy Blake shook her head hopelessly.

Big Bill Karns, hands still shaking, lit a cigarette before he spoke again. "Well, I've never been a proponent of genocide. But it's my considered opinion that the Stretts are one race the galaxy can get along without."

"A hell of a lot better without," Poynter said, and all agreed.

"The point is, what can we do about it?" Kincaid asked. "The first thing, I would say, is to see whether we can do this—whatever it is—without Tuly's help. Shall we try it? Although I, for one, don't feel like doing it right away."

"Not I, either." Beverly Bell held up her right hand, which was shaking uncontrollably. "I feel as though I'd been bucking waves, wind and tide for forty-eight straight hours without food, water or touch. Maybe in about a week I'll be ready for another try at it. But today—not a chance!"

"Okay. Scat, all of you," Hilton ordered. "Take the rest of the day off and rest up. Put on your thought-screens and don't take them off for a second from now on. Those Stretts are tough hombres."

Sandra was the last to leave. "And you, boss?" she asked pointedly.

"I've got some thinking to do."

"I'll stay and help you think?"

"Not yet." He shook his head, frowned and then grinned. "You see, chick, I don't even know yet what it is I'm going to have to think about."

"A bit unclear, but I know what you mean—I think. Luck, chief."

IN their subterranean sanctum turn on distant Strett, two of the deepest thinkers of that horribly unhuman race were in coldly intent conference via thought.

"My mind has been plundered, Ynos," First Lord Thinker Zoyar radiated, harshly. "Despite the extremely high reactivity of my shield some information—I do not know how much—was taken. The operator was one of the humans of that ship."

"I, too, felt a plucking at my mind. But those humans could not peyondire, First Lord."

"Be logical, fool! At that contact, in the matter of which you erred in not following up continuously, they succeeded in concealing their real abilities from you."

"That could be the truth. Our ancestors erred, then, in recording that all those weak and timid humans had been slain. These offenders are probably their descendants, returning to reclaim their former world."

"The probability must be evaluated and considered. Was it or was it not through human aid that the Omans destroyed most of our task-force?"

"Highly probable, but impossible of evaluation with the data now available."

"Obtain more data at once. That point must be and shall be fully evaluated and fully considered. This entire situation is intolerable. It must be abated."

"True, First Lord. But every operator and operation is now tightly screened. Oh, if I could only go out there myself..."

"Hold, fool! Your thought is completely disloyal and un-Strettly."

"True, oh First Lord Thinker Zoyar. I will forthwith remove my unworthy self from this plane of existence."

"You will not! I hereby abolish that custom. Our numbers are too few by far. Too many have failed to adapt. Also, as Second Thinker, your death at this time would be slightly detrimental to certain matters now in work. I will myself, however, slay the unfit. To that end repeat The Words under my peyondiring."

"I am a Strett. I will devote my every iota of mental and of physical strength to forwarding the Great Plan. I am, and will remain, a Strett."

"You do believe in The Words."

"OF course I believe in them! I *know* that in a few more hundreds of thousands of years we will be rid of material bodies and will become invincible and invulnerable. Then comes the Conquest of the Galaxy...and then the Conquest of the Universe!"

"No more, then, on your life, of this weak and cowardly repining! Now, what of your constructive thinking?"

"Programming must be such as to obviate time-lag. We must evaluate the factors already mentioned and many others, such as the reactivation of the spacecraft which was thought to have been destroyed so long ago. After having considered all these evaluations, I will construct a Minor Plan to destroy these Omans, whom we have permitted to exist on sufferance, and with them that shipload of despicably interloping humans."

"That is well." Zoyar's mind seethed with a malevolent ferocity starkly impossible for any human mind to grasp. "And to that end?"

"To that end we must intensify still more our program of procuring data. We must revise our mechs in the light of our every technological advance during the many thousands of cycles since the last such revision was made. Our every instrument of power, of offense and of defense, must be brought up to the theoretical ultimate of capability."

"And as to the Great Brain?"

"I have been able to think of nothing, First Lord, to add to the undertakings you have already set forth."

"It was not expected that you would. Now: is it your final thought that these interlopers are in fact the descendants of those despised humans of so long ago?"

"It is."

"It is also mine. I return, then, to my work upon the Brain. You will take whatever measures are necessary. Use every artifice of intellect and of ingenuity and our every resource. But abate this intolerable nuisance, and soon."

"It shall be done, First Lord."

THE Second Thinker issued orders. Frenzied, round-the-clock activity ensued. Hundreds of mechs operated upon the brains of hundreds of others, who in turn operated upon the operators.

Then, all those brains charged with the technological advances of many thousands of years, the combined hundreds went unrestingly to work. Thousands of work-mechs were built and put to work at the construction of larger and more powerful space-craft.

As has been implied, those battle-skeletons of the Stretts were controlled by their own built-in mechanical brains, which were programmed for only the simplest of battle maneuvers. Anything at all out of the ordinary had to be handled by remote control, by the specialist-mechs at their two-miles-long control board.

This was now to be changed. Programming was to be made so complete that almost any situation could be handled by the warship or the missile itself—instantly.

The Stretts *knew* that they were the most powerful, the most highly advanced race in the universe. Their science was the highest in the universe. Hence, with every operating unit brought up to the full possibilities of that science, that would be more than enough. Period.

This work, while it required much time, was very much simpler than the task which the First Thinker had laid out for himself on the giant computer-plus which the Stretts called "The Great Brain." In stating his project, First Lord Zoyar had said:

"Assignment: To construct a machine that will have the following abilities: One, to contain and retain all knowledge and information fed into it, however great the amount. Two, to feed itself additional information by peyondiring all planets, wherever situate, bearing intelligent life. Three, to call up instantly any and all items of information pertaining to any problem we may give it. Four, to combine and recombine any number of items required to form new concepts. Five, to formulate theories, test them and draw conclusions helpful to us in any matter in work."

It will have been noticed that these specifications vary in one important respect from those of the Eniacs and Univacs of Earth. Since we of Earth can not peyondire, we do not expect that ability from our computers.

The Stretts could, and did.

WHEN Sandra came back into the office at five o'clock she found Hilton still sitting there, in almost exactly the same position.

"Come out of it, Jarve!" She snapped a finger. "That much of *that* is just simply too damned much."

"You're so right, child." He got up, stretched, and by main strength shrugged off his foul mood. "But we're up against something that is really a something, and I don't mean perchance."

"How well I know it." She put an arm around him, gave him a quick, hard hug. "But after all, you don't have to solve it this evening, you know."

"No, thank God."

"So why don't you and Temple have supper with me? Or better yet, why don't all eight of us have supper together in that bachelors' paradise of yours and Bill's?"

"That'd be fun."

And it was.

Nor did it take a week for Beverly Bell to recover from the Ordeal of Eight. On the following evening, she herself suggested that the team should take another shot at that utterly fantastic *terra incognita* of the multiple mind, jolting though it had been.

"But are you sure you can take it again so soon?" Hilton asked.

"Sure. I'm like that famous gangster's moll, you know, who bruised easy but healed quick. And I want to know about it as much as anyone else does."

They could do it this time without any help from Tuly. The linkage fairly snapped together and shrank instantaneously to a point. Hilton thought of Terra and there it was; full size, yet occupying only one infinitesimal section of a dimensionless point. The multi-mind visited relatives of all eight, but could not make intelligible contact. If asleep, it caused pleasant dreams; if awake, pleasant thoughts of the loved one so far away in space; but that was all. It visited mediums, in trance and otherwise—many of whom, not surprisingly now, were genuine—with whom it held lucid conversations. Even in linkage, however, the multi-mind knew that none of the mediums would be believed, even if they all told, simultaneously, exactly the same story. The multi-mind weakened suddenly and Hilton snapped it back to Ardry.

Beverly was almost in collapse. The other girls were white, shaken and trembling. Hilton himself, strong and rugged as he was, felt as though he had done two weeks of hard labor on a rock-pile. He glanced questioningly at Larry.

"Point six three eight seconds, sir," the Omans said, holding up a millisecond timer.

"How do you explain *that*?" Karns demanded.

"I'm afraid it means that without Oman backing we're out of luck."

HILTON had other ideas, but he did not voice any of them until the following day, when he was rested and had Larry alone.

"So carbon-based brains can't take it. One second of that stuff would have killed all eight of us. Why? The Masters had the same kind of brains we have."

"I don't know, sir. It's something completely new. No Master, or group of Masters, ever generated such a force as that. I can scarcely believe such power possible, even though I have felt it twice. It may be that over the generations your individual powers, never united or controlled, have developed so strength that no human can handle them in fusion."

"And none of us ever knew anything about any of them. I've been doing a lot of thinking. The Masters had qualities and abilities now unknown to any of us. How come? You Omans—and the Stretts, too—think we're descendants of the Masters. Maybe we are. You think they came originally from Arth—Earth or Terra— to Ardu. That'd account for our legends of Mu, Atlantis and so on. Since Ardu was within peyondix range of Strett, the Stretts attacked it. They killed all the Masters, they thought, and made the planet uninhabitable for any kind of life, even their own. But one shipload of Masters escaped and came here to Ardry—far beyond peyondix range. They stayed here for a long time. Then, for some reason or other—which may be someplace in their records—they left here, fully intending to come back. Do any of you Omans know why they left? Or where they went?"

"No, sir. We can read only the simplest of the Masters' records. They arranged our brains that way, sir."

"I know. They're the type. However, I suspect now that your thinking is reversed. Let's turn it around. Say the Masters didn't come from Terra, but from some other planet. Say that they left here because they were dying out. They were, weren't they?"

"Yes, sir. Their numbers became fewer and fewer each century."

"I was sure of it. They were committing race suicide by letting you Omans do everything they themselves should have been doing. Finally they saw the truth. In a desperate effort to save their race they pulled out, leaving you here. Probably they intended to come back when they had bred enough guts back into themselves to set you Omans down where you belong..."

"But *they* were always the Masters, sir!"

"They were not! They were hopelessly enslaved. Think it over. Anyway, say they went *to* Terra from here. That still accounts for the legends and so on. However, they were too far gone to make a recovery, and yet they had enough fixity of purpose *not* to manufacture any of you Omans there. So their descendants went a long way down the scale before they began to work back up. Does that make sense to you?"

"IT explains many things, sir. It can very well be the truth."

"Okay. However it was, we're here, and facing a condition that isn't funny. While we were teamed up I learned a lot, but not nearly enough. Am I right in thinking that I now don't need the other seven at all—that my cells are fully charged and I can go it alone?"

"Probably, sir, but..."

"I'm coming to that. Every time I do it—up to maximum performance, of course—it comes easier and faster and hits harder. So next time, or maybe the fourth or fifth time, it'll kill me. And the other seven, too, if they're along."

"I'm not sure, sir, but I think so."

"Nice. Very, *very* nice." Hilton got up, shoved both hands into his pockets, and prowled about the room. "But can't the damned stuff be controlled? Choked—throttled down—damped—muzzled, some way or other?"

"We do not know of any way, sir. The Masters were always working toward more power, not less."

"That makes sense. The more power the better, as long as you can handle it. But I can't handle this. And neither can the team. So how about organizing another team, one that hasn't got quite so much whammo? Enough punch to do the job, but not enough to backfire that way?"

"It is highly improbable that such a team is possible, sir." If an Oman could be acutely embarrassed, Larry was. "That is, sir...I should tell you, sir..."

"You certainly should. You've been stalling all along, and now you're stalled. Spill it."

"Yes, sir. The Tuly begged me not to mention it, but I must. When it organized your team it had no idea of what it was really going to do..."

"Let's talk the same language, shall we? Say 'he' and 'she.' Not 'it.'"

"She thought she was setting up the peyondix, the same as all of us Omans have. But after she formed in your mind the peyondix

171

matrix, your mind went on of itself to form a something else; a thing we can not understand. That was why she was so extremely…I think 'frightened' might be your term."

"I knew something was biting her. Why?"

"Because it very nearly killed you. You perhaps have not considered the effect upon us all if any Oman, however unintentionally, should kill a Master?"

"No, I hadn't…I see. So she won't play with fire any more, and none of the rest of you can?"

"Yes, sir. Nothing could force her to. If she could be so coerced we would destroy her brain before she could act. That brain, as you know, is imperfect, or she could not have done what she did. It should have been destroyed long since."

"Don't *ever* act on that assumption, Larry." Hilton thought for minutes. "Simple peyondix, such as yours, is not enough to read the Masters' records. If I'd had three brain cells working I'd've tried them then. I wonder if I *could* read them?"

"You have all the old Masters' powers and more. But you must not assemble them again, sir. It would mean death."

"But I've got to *know*… I've *got* to know! Anyway, a thousandth of a second would be enough. I don't think that'd hurt me very much."

HE concentrated—read a few feet of top-secret braided wire—and came back to consciousness in the sickbay of the *Perseus*, with two doctors working on him; Hastings, the top Navy medico, and Flandres, the surgeon.

"What the hell happened to you?" Flandres demanded. "Were you trying to kill yourself?"

"And if so, how?" Hastings wanted to know.

"No, I was trying not to," Hilton said, weakly, "and I guess I didn't much more than succeed."

"That was just about the closest shave I ever saw a man come through. Whatever it was, don't do it again."

"I won't," he promised, feelingly.

When they let him out of the hospital, four days later, he called in Larry and Tuly.

"The next time would be the last time. So there won't be any," he told them. "But just how sure are you that some other of our boys or girls may not have just enough of whatever it takes to do the job? Enough oompa, but not too much?"

"Since we, too, are on strange ground the probability is vanishingly small. We have been making inquiries, however, and scanning. You were selected from all the minds of Terra as the one having the widest vision, the greatest scope, the most comprehensive grasp. The ablest at synthesis and correlation and so on."

"That's printing it in big letters, but that was more or less what they were after."

"Hence the probability approaches unity that any more such ignorant meddling as this obnoxious Tuly did well result almost certainly in failure and death. Therefore we can not and will not meddle again."

"YOU'VE got a point there... So what I am is some kind of a freak. Maybe a kind of super-Master and maybe something altogether different. Maybe duplicable in a less lethal fashion, and maybe not. Veree helpful—I don't think. But I don't want to kill anybody, either...especially if it wouldn't do any good. But we've got to do *something*!" Hilton scowled in thought for minutes. "But an Oman brain could take it. As you told us, Tuly, 'The brain of the Larry is very, very tough.'"

"In a way, sir. Except that the Masters were very careful to make it physically impossible for any Oman to go very far along that line. It was only their oversight of my one imperfect brain that enabled me, alone of us all, to do that wrong."

"Stop thinking it was wrong, Tuly. I'm mighty glad you did. But I wasn't thinking of any regular Oman brain..." Hilton's voice petered out.

"I see, sir. Yes, we can, by using your brain as Guide, reproduce it in an Oman body. You would then have the powers and most of the qualities of both..."

"No, you don't see, because I've got my screen on. Which I will now take off..." he suited action to word, "...since the whole planet's screened and I have nothing to hide from you. Teddy

Blake and I both thought of that, but we'll consider it only as the ultimately last resort. We don't want to live a million years. And we want our race to keep on developing. But you folks can replace carbon-based molecules with silicon-based ones just as easily as, and a hell of a lot faster than, mineral water petrifies wood. What can you do along the line of rebuilding me that way? And if you can do any such conversion, what would happen? Would I live at all? And if so, how long? How would I live? What would I live on? All that kind of stuff."

"Shortly before they left, two of the Masters did some work on that very thing. Tuly and I converted them, sir."

"Fine—or is it? How did it work out?"

"Perfectly, sir...except that they destroyed themselves. It was thought that they wearied of existence."

"I don't wonder. Well, if it comes to that, I can do the same. You *can* convert me, then."

"Yes, sir. But before we do it we must do enough preliminary work to be sure that you will not be harmed in any way. Also, there will be many more changes involved than simple substitution."

"Of course. I realize that. Just see what you can do, please, and let me know."

"We will, sir, and thank you very much."

CHAPTER NINE

AS has been intimated, no Terran can know what researches Larry and Tuly and the other Oman specialists performed, or how they arrived at the conclusions they reached. However, in less than a week Larry reported to Hilton.

"It can be done, sir, with complete safety. And you will live even more comfortably than you do now."

"How long?"

"The mean will be about five thousand Oman years—you don't know that an Oman year is equal to one point two nine three plus Terran years?"

"I didn't, no. Thanks."

"The maximum, a little less than six thousand. The minimum, a little over four thousand. I'm very sorry we had no data upon which to base a closer estimate."

"Close enough." He stared at the Oman. "You could also convert my wife?"

"Of course, sir."

"Well, we might be able to stand it, after we got used to the idea. Minimum, over five thousand Terran years…barring accidents, of course?"

"No, sir. No accidents. Nothing will be able to kill you, except by total destruction of the brain. And even then, sir, there will be the pattern."

"I'll…be…damned…" Hilton gulped twice. "Okay, go ahead."

"Your skins will be like ours, energy-absorbers. Your 'blood' will carry charges of energy instead of oxygen. Thus, you may breathe or not, as you please. Unless you wish otherwise, we will continue the breathing function. It would scarcely be worth while to alter the automatic mechanisms that now control it. And you will wish at times to speak. You will still enjoy eating and drinking, although everything ingested will be eliminated, as at present, as waste."

"We'd add uranexite to our food, I suppose. Or drink radioactives, or sleep under cobalt-60 lamps."

"Yes, sir. Your family life will be normal; your sexual urges and satisfactions the same. Fertilization and period of gestation unchanged. Your children will mature at the same ages as they do now."

"How do you—oh, I see. You wouldn't change any molecular linkages or configurations in the genes or chromosomes."

"We could not, sir, even if we wished. Such substitutions can be made only in exact one-for-one replacements. In the near future you will, of course, have to control births quite rigorously."

"We sure would. Let's see…say we want a stationary population of a hundred million on our planet. Each couple to have two children, a boy and a girl. Born when the parents are about fifty…um-m-m. The gals can have all the children they want, then, until our population is about a million; then slap on the limit of two kids per couple. Right?"

"Approximately so, sir. And after conversion you alone will be able to operate with the full power of your eight, without tiring. You will also, of course, be able to absorb almost instantaneously all the knowledges and abilities of the old Masters."

Hilton gulped twice before he could speak. "You wouldn't be holding anything else back, would you?"

"Nothing important, sir. Everything else is minor, and probably known to you."

"I doubt it. How long will the job take, and how much notice will you need?"

"Two days, sir. No notice. Everything is ready."

Hilton, face somber, thought for minutes. "The more I think of it the less I like it. But it seems to be a forced put...and Temple will blow sky high...and *have* I got the guts to go it alone, even if she'd let me..." He shrugged himself out of the black mood. "I'll look her up and let you know, Larry."

HE looked her up and told her everything. Told her bluntly; starkly; drawing the full picture in jet black, with very little white.

"There it is, sweetheart. The works," he concluded. "We are not going to have ten years; we may not have ten months. So—if such a brain as that can be had, do we or do we not have to have it? I'm putting it squarely up to you."

Temple's face, which had been getting paler and paler, was now as nearly colorless as it could become; the sickly yellow of her skin's light tan unbacked by any flush of red blood.

Her whole body was tense and strained.

"There's a horrible snapper on that question... Can't *I* do it? Or *anybody* else except you?"

"No. Anyway, whose job is it, sweetheart?"

"I know, but...but I know just how close Tuly came to killing you. And that wasn't *anything* compared to such a radical transformation as this. I'm afraid it'll kill you, darling. And I just simply couldn't *stand* it!"

She threw herself into his arms, and he comforted her in the ages-old fashion of man with maid.

"Steady, hon," he said, as soon as he could lift her tear-streaked face from his shoulder. "I'll live through it. I thought you were getting the howling howpers about having to live for six thousand years and never getting back to Terra except for a Q strictly T visit now and then."

She pulled away from him, flung back her wheaten mop and glared. "So *that's* what you thought! What do I care how long I live, or how, or where, as long as it's with you? But what makes you think we can possibly live through such a horrible conversion as that?"

"Larry wouldn't do it if there was any question whatever. He didn't say it would be painless. But he did say I'd live."

"Well, he knows, I guess…I hope." Temple's natural fine color began to come back. "But it's understood that just the second you come out of the vat, I go right in."

"I hadn't ought to let you, of course. But I don't think I could take it alone."

That statement required a special type of conference, which consumed some little time. Eventually, however, Temple answered it in words.

"Of course you couldn't, sweetheart, and I wouldn't let you, even if you could."

There were a few things that had to be done before those two secret conversions could be made. There was the matter of the wedding, which was now to be in quadruplicate. Arrangements had to be made so that eight Big Wheels of the Project could all be away on honeymoon at once. All these things were done.

OF the conversion operations themselves, nothing more need be said. The honeymooners, having left ship and town on a Friday afternoon, came back one week from the following Monday* morning. The eight met joyously in Bachelors' Hall; the girls kissing each other and the men indiscriminately and enthusiastically; the men cooperating zestfully.

---

*While it took some time to recompute the exact Ardrian calendar, Terran day names and Terran weeks were used from the first. The Omans manufactured watches, clocks, and chronometers which divided the Ardrian day into twenty-four Ardrian hours, with minutes and seconds as usual.

Temple scarcely blushed at all, she was so engrossed in trying to find out whether or not anyone was noticing any change. No one seemed to notice anything out of the ordinary. So, finally, she asked.

"Don't *any* of you, really, see anything different?"

The six others all howled at that, and Sandra, between giggles and snorts, said: "No, precious, it doesn't show a bit. Did you really think it would?"

Temple blushed furiously and Hilton came instantly to his bride's rescue. "Chip-chop the comedy, gang. She and I aren't human any more. We're a good jump toward being Omans. I couldn't make her believe it doesn't show."

That stopped the levity, cold, but none of the six could really believe it. However, after Hilton had coiled a twenty-penny spike into a perfect helix between his fingers, and especially after he and Temple had each chewed up and swallowed a piece of uranexite, there were no grounds left for doubt.

"That settles it...it *tears* it," Karns said then. "Start all over again, Jarve. We'll listen, this time."

Hilton told the long story again, and added: "I had to re-work a couple of cells of Temple's brain, but now she can read and understand the records as well as I can. So I thought I'd take her place on Team One and let her boss the job on all the other teams. Okay?"

"So you don't want to let the rest of us in on it." Karns's level stare was a far cry from the way he had looked at his chief a moment before. "If there's any one thing in the universe I never had *you* figured for, it's a dog in the manger."

"Huh? You mean you actually *want* to be a...a...hell, we don't even know *what* we are!"

"I do want it, Jarvis. We all do." This was, of all people, Teddy! "No one in all history has had more than about fifty years of really productive thinking. And just the idea of having enough time..."

"Hold it, Teddy. Use your brain. The Masters couldn't take it—they committed suicide. How do you figure we can do any better?"

"Because we'll *use* our brains!" she snapped. "They didn't. The Omans will serve us; and that's *all* they'll do."

"And do you think you'll be able to raise your children and grandchildren and so on to do the same? To have guts enough to resist the pull of such an ungodly habit-forming drug as this Oman service is?"

"I'M sure of it." She nodded positively. "And we'll run all applicants through a fine enough screen to—that is, if we ever consider anybody except our own BuSci people. And there's another reason." She grinned, got up, wriggled out of her coverall, and posed in bra and panties. "Look. I can keep most of this for five years. Quite a lot of it for ten. Then comes the struggle. What do *you* think I'd do for the ability, whenever it begins to get wrinkly or flabby, to peel the whole thing off and put on a brand-spanking-new smooth one? You name it, I'll do it! Besides, Bill and I will *both* just simply and cold-bloodedly murder you if you try to keep us out."

"Okay." Hilton looked at Temple; she looked at him; both looked at all the others. There was no revulsion at all. Nothing but eagerness.

Temple took over.

"I'm surprised. We're both surprised. You see, Jarve didn't want to do it at all, but he had to. I not only didn't want to, I was scared green and yellow at just the idea of it. But I had to, too, of course. We didn't think anybody would really want to. We thought we'd be left here alone. We still will be, I think, when you've thought it clear through, Teddy. You just haven't realized yet that we aren't even human any more. We're simply nothing but *monsters!*" Temple's voice became a wail.

"I've said my piece," Teddy said. "You tell 'em, Bill."

"Let me say something first," Kincaid said. "Temple, I'm ashamed of you. This line isn't at all your usual straight thinking. What you actually are is *homo superior*. Bill?"

"I can add one bit to that. I don't wonder that you were scared silly, Temple. Utterly new concept and you went into it stone cold. But now we see the finished product and we like it. In fact, we drool."

"I'll say we're drooling," Sandra said. "I could do handstands and pinwheels with joy."

"Let's see you," Hilton said. "That we'd all get a kick out of."

"Not now—don't want to hold this up—but sometime I just will. Bev?"

"I'm for it—and *how*! And won't Bernadine be amazed," Beverly laughed gleefully, "at her wise-crack about the 'race to end all human races' coming true?"

"I'm in favor of it, too, one hundred per cent," Poynter said. "Has it occurred to you, Jarve, that this opens up intergalactic exploration? No supplies to carry and plenty of time and fuel?"

"No, it hadn't. You've got a point there, Frank. That might take a little of the curse off of it, at that."

"When some of our kids get to be twenty years old or so and get married, I'm going to take a crew of them to Andromeda. We'll arrange, then, to extend our honeymoons another week," Hilton said. "What will our policy be? Keep it dark for a while with just us eight, or spread it to the rest?"

"Spread it, I'd say," Kincaid said.

"We can't keep it secret, anyway," Teddy argued. "Since Larry and Tuly were in on the whole deal, every Oman on the planet knows all about it. Somebody is going to ask questions, and Omans always answer questions and always tell the truth."

"QUESTIONS have already been asked and answered," Larry said, going to the door and opening it.

Stella rushed in. "We've been hearing the *damnedest* things!" She kissed everybody, ending with Hilton, whom she seized by both shoulders. "Is it actually true, boss, that you can fix me up so I'll live practically forever and can eat more than eleven calories a day without getting fat as a pig? Candy, ice cream, cake, pie, eclairs, cream puffs, French pastries, sugar and gobs of thick cream in my coffee...?"

Half a dozen others, including the van der Moen twins, came in. Beverly emitted a shriek of joy. "Bernadine! The mother of the race to end all human races!"

"You whistled it, birdie!" Bernadine caroled. "I'm going to have ten or twelve, each one weirder than all the others. I told you

I was a prophet—I'm going to hang out my shingle. Wholesale and retail prophecy; special rates for large parties." Her voice was drowned out in a general clamor.

"Hold it, everybody!" Hilton yelled. "Chip-chop it! *Quit* it!" Then, as the noise subsided, "If you think I'm going to tell this tall tale over and over again for the next two weeks you're all crazy. So shut down the plant and get everybody out here."

"Not *everybody*, Jarve!" Temple snapped. "We don't want scum, and there's some of that, even in BuSci."

"You're so right. Who, then?"

"The rest of the heads and assistants, of course...and all the lab girls and their husbands and boy-friends. I know they are all okay. That will be enough for now, don't you think?"

"I do think;" and the indicated others were sent for; and in a few minutes arrived.

The Omans brought chairs and Hilton stood on a table. He spoke for ten minutes. Then: "Before you decide whether you want to or not, think it over very carefully, because it's a one-way street. Fluorine can not be displaced. Once in, you're stuck for life. *There is no way back.* I've told you all the drawbacks and disadvantages I know of, but there may be a lot more that I haven't thought of yet. So think it over for a few days and when each of you has definitely made up his or her mind, let me know." He jumped down off the table.

HIS listeners, however, did not need days, or even seconds, to decide. Before Hilton's feet hit the floor there was a yell of unanimous approval.

He looked at his wife. "Do you suppose *we're* nuts?"

"Uh-uh. Not a bit. Alex was right. I'm going to just *love* it!" She hugged his elbow ecstatically. "So are you, darling, as soon as you stop looking at only the black side."

"You know...you could be right?" For the first time since the "ghastly" transformation Hilton saw that there really was a bright side and began to study it. "With most of BuSci—and part of the Navy, and selectees from Terra—it *will* be slightly terrific, at that!"

"And that 'habit-forming-drug' objection isn't insuperable, darling," Temple said. "If the younger generations start weakening we'll fix the Omans. I wouldn't want to wipe them out entirely, but..."

"But how do we settle priority, Doctor Hilton?" a girl called out; a tall, striking, brunette laboratory technician whose name Hilton needed a second to recall. "By pulling straws or hair? Or by shooting dice or each other or what?"

"Thanks, Betty, you've got a point. Sandy Cummings and department heads first, then assistants. Then you girls, in alphabetical order, each with her own husband or fiance."

"And my name is Ames. Oh, goody!"

"Larry, please tell them to..."

"I already have, sir. We are set up to handle four at once."

"Good boy. So scat, all of you, and get back to work—except Sandy, Bill, Alex, and Teddy. You four go with Larry."

Since the new sense was not peyondix, Hilton had started calling it "perception" and the others adopted the term as a matter of course. Hilton could use that sense for what seemed like years—and actually was whole minutes—at a time without fatigue or strain. He could not, however, nor could the Omans, give his tremendous power to anyone else.

As he had said, he could do a certain amount of reworking; but the amount of improvement possible to make depended entirely upon what there was to work on. Thus, Temple could cover about six hundred light-years. It developed later that the others of the Big Eight could cover from one hundred up to four hundred or so. The other department heads and assistants turned out to be still weaker, and not one of the rank and file ever became able to cover more than a single planet.

This sense was not exactly telepathy; at least not what Hilton had always thought telepathy would be. If anything, however, it was more. It was a lumping together of all five known human senses—and half a dozen unknown ones called, collectively, "intuition"—into one super-sense that was all-inclusive and all-informative. If he ever could learn exactly what it was and exactly what it did and how it did it...but he'd better chip-chop the wool-gathering and get back onto the job.

THE Stretts had licked the old Masters very easily, and intended to wipe out the Omans and the humans. They had no doubt at all as to their ability to do it. Maybe they could. If the Masters hadn't made some progress that the Omans didn't know about, they probably could. That was the first thing to find out. As soon as they'd been converted he'd call in all the experts and they'd go through the Masters' records like a dose of salts through a hillbilly schoolma'am.

At that point in Hilton's cogitations Sawtelle came in.

He had come down in his gig, to confer with Hilton as to the newly beefed-up fleet. Instead of being glum and pessimistic and foreboding, he was chipper and enthusiastic. They had rebuilt a thousand Oman ships. By combining Oman and Terran science, and adding everything the First Team had been able to reduce to practise, they had hyped up the power by a good fifteen per cent. Seven hundred of those ships, and all his men, were now arrayed in defense around Ardry. Three hundred, manned by Omans, were around Fuel Bin.

"Why?" Hilton asked. "It's Fuel Bin they've been attacking."

"Uh-uh. Minor objective," the captain demurred, positively. "The real attack will be here at you; the headquarters and the brains. Then Fuel Bin will be duck soup. But the thing that pleased me most is the control. Man, you never imagined such control! No admiral in history ever had such control of ten ships as I have of seven hundred. Those Omans spread orders so fast that I don't even finish thinking one and it's being executed. And no misunderstandings, no slips. For instance, this last batch—fifteen skeletons. Far out; they're getting cagy. I just thought 'Box 'em in and slug 'em' and—In! Across! Out! Socko! Pffft! Just like that and just that fast. None of 'em had time to light a beam. Nobody before ever even *dreamed* of such control!"

"That's great, and I like it...and you're only a captain. How many ships can Five-Jet Admiral Gordon put into space?"

"That depends on what you call ships. Superdreadnoughts, *Perseus* class, six. First-line battleships, twenty-nine. Second-line, smaller and some pretty old, seventy-three. Counting everything armed that will hold air, something over two hundred."

"I thought it was something like that. How would you like to be Five-Jet Admiral Sawtelle of the Ardrian Navy?"

"I wouldn't. I'm Terran Navy. But you knew that and you know me. So—what's on your mind?"

HILTON told him. *I ought to put this on a tape*, he thought to himself, *and broadcast it every hour on the hour.*

"They took the old Masters like dynamiting fish in a barrel," he concluded, "and I'm damned afraid they're going to lick us unless we take a lot of big, fast steps. But the hell of it is that I can't tell you anything—not one single thing—about any part of it. There's simply no way at all of getting through to you without making you over into the same kind of a thing I am."

"Is that bad?" Sawtelle was used to making important decisions fast. "Let's get at it."

"Huh? Skipper, do you realize just what that means? If you think they'll let you resign, forget it. They'll crucify you—brand you as a traitor and God only knows what else."

"Right. How about you and your people?"

"Well, as civilians, it won't be as bad…"

"The hell it won't. Every man and woman that stays here will be posted forever as the blackest traitors old Terra ever disgraced herself by spawning."

"You've got a point there, at that. We'll all have to bring our relatives—the ones we think much of, at least—out here with us."

"Definitely. Now see what you can do about getting me run through your mill."

By exerting his authority, Hilton got Sawtelle put through the "Preservatory" in the second batch processed. Then, linking minds with the captain, he flashed their joint attention to the Hall of Records. Into the right room; into the right chest; along miles and miles of braided wire carrying some of the profoundest military secrets of the ancient Masters.

Then:

"Now you know a little of it," Hilton said. "Maybe a thousandth of what we'll have to have before we can take the Stretts as they will have to be taken."

For seconds Sawtelle could not speak. Then: "My...God. I see what you mean. You're right. No Omans can ever go to Terra; and no Terrans can ever come here except to stay forever."

The two then went out into space, to the flagship—which had been christened the *Orion*—and called in the six commanders.

"What *is* all this senseless idiocy we've been getting, Jarve?" Elliott demanded.

Hilton eyed all six with pretended disfavor. "You six guys are the hardest-headed bunch of skeptics that ever went unhung," he remarked, dispassionately. "So it wouldn't do any good to tell you anything—yet. The skipper and I will show you a thing first. Take her away, Skip."

The *Orion* shot away under interplanetary drive and for several hours Hilton and Sawtelle worked at re-wiring and practically rebuilding two devices that no one, Oman or human, had touched since the *Perseus* had landed on Ardry.

"What are you...I don't understand what you are doing, sir," Larry said. For the first time since Hilton had known him, the Oman's mind was confused and unsure.

"I know you don't. This is a bit of top-secret Masters' stuff. Maybe, some day, we'll be able to re-work your brain to take it. But it won't be for some time."

CHAPTER TEN

THE *Orion* hung in space, a couple of thousands of miles away from an asteroid which was perhaps a mile in average diameter. Hilton straightened up.

"Put Triple X Black filters on your plates and watch that asteroid." The commanders did so. "Ready?" he asked.

"Ready, sir."

Hilton didn't move a muscle. Nothing actually moved. Nevertheless there was a motionlessly writhing and crawling distortion of the ship and everything in it, accompanied by a sensation that simply can not be described.

It was not like going into or emerging from the sub-ether. It was not even remotely like space-sickness or sea-sickness or free fall or anything else that any Terran had ever before experienced.

And the asteroid vanished.

It disappeared into an outrageously incandescent, furiously pyrotechnic, raveningly expanding atomic fireball that in seconds seemed to fill half of space.

After ages-long minutes of the most horrifyingly devastating fury any man there had ever seen, the frightful thing expired and Hilton said: "*That* was just a kind of a firecracker. Just a feeble imitation of the first-stage detonator for what we'll have to have to crack the Stretts' ground-based screens. If the skipper and I had taken time to take the ship down to the shops and really work it over we could have put on a show. Was this enough so you iron-heads are ready to listen with your ears open and your mouths shut?"

They were. So much so that not even Elliott opened his mouth to say yes. They merely nodded. Then again—for the last time, he hoped!—Hilton spoke his piece. The response was prompt and vigorous. Only Sam Bryant, one of Hilton's staunchest allies, showed any uncertainty at all.

"I've been married only a year and a half, and the baby was due about a month ago. How sure are you that you can make old Gordon sit still for us skimming the cream off of Terra to bring out here?"

"Doris Bryant, the cream of Terra!" Elliott gibed. "*How* modest our Samuel has become!"

"Well, damn it, she is!" Bryant insisted.

"Okay, she is," Hilton agreed. "But either we get our people or Terra doesn't get its uranexite. That'll work. In the remote contingency that it doesn't, there are still tighter screws we can put on. But you missed the main snapper, Sam. Suppose Doris doesn't want to live for five thousand years and is allergic to becoming a monster?"

"Huh; you don't need to worry about that." Sam brushed that argument aside with a wave of his hand. "Show me a girl who doesn't want to stay young and beautiful forever and I'll square you the circle. Come on. What's holding us up?"

THE *Orion* hurtled through space back toward Ardry and Hilton, struck by a sudden thought, turned to the captain.

"Skipper, why wouldn't it be a smart idea to clamp a blockade onto Fuel Bin? Cut the Stretts' fuel supply?"

"I thought better of you than that, son." Sawtelle shook his head sadly. "That was the first thing I did."

"Ouch. Maybe you're 'way ahead of me too, then, on the one that we should move to Fuel Bin, lock, stock and barrel?"

"Never thought of it, no. Maybe you're worth saving, after all. After conversion, of course... Yes, there'd be three big advantages."

"Four."

Sawtelle raised his eyebrows.

"One, only one planet to defend. Two, it's self-defending against sneak landings. Nothing remotely human can land on it except in heavy lead armor, and even in that can stay healthy for only a few minutes."

"Except in the city. Omlu. That's the weak point and would be the point of attack."

"Uh-uh. Cut off the decontaminators and in five hours it'll be as hot as the rest of the planet. Three, there'd be no interstellar supply line for the Stretts to cut. Four, the environment matches our new physiques a lot better than any normal planet could."

"That's the one I didn't think about."

"I think I'll take a quick peek at the Stretts—oh-oh; they've screened their whole planet. Well, we can do that, too, of course."

"How are you going to select and reject personnel? It looks as though everybody wants to stay. Even the men whose main object in life is to go aground and get drunk. The Omans do altogether too good a job on them and there's no such thing as a hangover. I'm glad I'm not in your boots."

"You may be in it up to the eyeballs, Skipper, so don't chortle too soon."

Hilton had already devoted much time to the problems of selection; and he thought of little else all the way back to Ardry. And for several days afterward he held conferences with small groups and conducted certain investigations.

BUD Carroll of Sociology and his assistant Sylvia Banister had been married for weeks. Hilton called them, together with Sawtelle and Bryant of Navy, into conference with the Big Eight.

"The more I study this thing the less I like it," Hilton said. "With a civilization having no government, no police, no laws, no medium of exchange..."

"No *money*?" Bryant exclaimed. "How's old Gordon going to pay for his uranexite, then?"

"He gets it free," Hilton replied, flatly. "When anyone can have anything he wants, merely by wanting it, what good is money? Now, remembering how long we're going to have to live, what we'll be up against, that the Masters failed, and so on, it is clear that the prime basic we have to select for is stability. We twelve have, by psychodynamic measurement, the highest stability ratings available."

"Are you sure *I* belong here?" Bryant asked.

"Yes. Here are three lists." Hilton passed papers around. "The list labeled 'OK' names those I'm sure of—the ones we're converting now and their wives and whatever on Terra. List 'NG' names the ones I know we don't want. List 'X'—over thirty percent—are in-betweeners. We have to make a decision on the 'X' list. So—what I want to know is, who's going to play God. I'm not. Sandy, are you?"

"Good Heavens, no!" Sandra shuddered. "But I'm afraid I know who will have to. I'm sorry, Alex, but it'll have to be you four—Psychology and Sociology."

Six heads nodded and there was a flashing interchange of thought among the four. Temple licked her lips and nodded, and Kincaid spoke.

"Yes, I'm afraid it's our baby. By leaning very heavily on Temple, we can do it. Remember, Jarve, what you said about the irresistible force? We'll need it."

"As I said once before, Mrs. Hilton, I'm very glad you're along," Hilton said. "But just how sure are you that even you can stand up under the load?"

"Alone, I couldn't. But don't underestimate Mrs. Carroll and the Messrs. Together, and with such a goal, I'm sure we can."

THUS, after four-fifths of his own group and forty-one Navy men had been converted, Hilton called an evening meeting of all the converts. Larry, Tuly and Javvy were the only Omans present.

"You all knew, of course, that we were going to move to Fuel Bin sometime," Hilton began. "I can tell you now that we who are here are all there are going to be of us. We are all leaving for Fuel Bin immediately after this meeting. Everything of any importance, including all of your personal effects, has already been moved. All Omans except these three, and all Oman ships except the *Orion*, have already gone."

He paused to let the news sink in.

Thoughts flew everywhere. The irrepressible Stella Wing—*now* Mrs. Osbert F. Harkins—was the first to give tongue. "What a *wonderful* job! Why, everybody's here that I really like at all!"

That sentiment was, of course, unanimous. It could not have been otherwise. Betty, the ex-Ames, called out:

"How did you get their female Omans away from Cecil Calthorpe and the rest of that chasing, booze-fighting bunch without them blowing the whole show?"

"Some suasion was necessary," Hilton admitted, with a grin. "Everyone who isn't here is time-locked into the *Perseus*. Release time eight hours tomorrow."

"And they'll wake up tomorrow morning with no Omans?" Bernadine tossed back her silvery mane and laughed. "Nor anything else except the *Perseus*? In a way, I'm sorry, but...maybe I've got too much stinker blood in me, but I'm very glad none of them are here. But I'd like to ask, Jarvis—or rather, I suppose you have already set up a new Advisory Board?"

"We have, yes." Hilton read off twelve names.

"Oh, nice. I don't know of any people I'd rather have on it. But what I want to gripe about is calling our new home world such a horrible name as 'Fuel Bin,' as though it were a wood-box or a coal-scuttle or something. And just think of the complexes it would set up in those super-children we're going to have so many of."

"What would you suggest?" Hilton asked.

"'Ardvor', of course," Hermione said, before her sister could answer. "We've had 'Arth' and 'Ardu' and 'Ardry' and you—or somebody—started calling us 'Ardans' to distinguish us converts from the Terrans. So let's keep up the same line."

There was general laughter at that, but the name was approved.

ABOUT midnight the meeting ended and the *Orion* set out for Ardvor. It reached it and slanted sharply downward. The whole BuSci staff was in the lounge, watching the big tri-di.

"Hey! That isn't Omlu!" Stella exclaimed. "It isn't a city at all and it isn't even in the same place!"

"No, ma'am," Larry said. "Most of you wanted the ocean, but many wanted a river or the mountains. Therefore we razed Omlu and built your new city, Ardane, at a place where the ocean, two rivers, and a range of mountains meet. Strictly speaking, it is not a city, but a place of pleasant and rewardful living."

The space-ship was coming in, low and fast, from the south. To the left, the west, there stretched the limitless expanse of ocean. To the right, mile after mile, were rough, rugged, jagged, partially-timbered mountains, mass piled upon mass. Immediately below the speeding vessel was a wide, white-sand beach all of ten miles long.

Slowing rapidly now, the *Orion* flew along due north.

"Look! Look! A natatorium!" Beverly shrieked. "I know I wanted a nice big place to swim in, besides my backyard pool and the ocean, but I didn't tell anybody to build *that*—I swear I didn't!"

"You didn't have to, pet." Poynter put his arm around her curvaceous waist and squeezed. "They knew. And I did a little thinking along that line myself. There's our house, on top of the cliff over the natatorium—you can almost dive into it off the patio."

"Oh, wonderful!"

Immediately north of the natatorium a tremendous river—named at first sight the "Whitewater"—rushed through its gorge into the ocean; a river and gorge strangely reminiscent of the Colorado and its Grand Canyon. On the south bank of that river, at its very mouth—looking straight up that tremendous canyon; on a rocky promontory commanding ocean and beach and mountains—there was a house. At the sight of it Temple hugged Hilton's arm in ecstasy.

"Yes, that's ours," he assured her. "Just about everything either of us has ever wanted." The clamor was now so great—everyone was recognizing his-and-her house and was exclaiming about it—that both Temple and Hilton fell silent and simply watched the scenery unroll.

Across the turbulent Whitewater and a mile farther north, the mountains ended as abruptly as though they had been cut off with a cleaver and an apparently limitless expanse of treeless, grassy prairie began. And through that prairie, meandering sluggishly to the ocean from the northeast, came the wide, deep River Placid.

The *Orion* halted. It began to descend vertically, and only then did Hilton see the spaceport. It was so vast, and there were so many spaceships on it, that from any great distance it was actually invisible! Each six-acre bit of the whole immense expanse of level prairie between the Placid and the mountains held an Oman superdreadnought!

THE staff paired off and headed for the airlocks. Hilton said: "Temple, have you any reservations at all, however slight, as to having Dark Lady as a permanent fixture in your home?"

"Why, of course not—I like her as much as you do. And besides…" she giggled like a schoolgirl, "…even if she *is* a lot more beautiful than I am—I've got a few things she never will have…but there's something else. I got just a flash of it before you blocked. Spill it, please."

"You'll see in a minute." And she did.

Larry, Dark Lady and Temple's Oman maid Moty were standing beside the Hilton's car—and so was another Oman, like none ever before seen. Six feet four; shoulders that would just barely go through a door; muscled like Atlas and Hercules combined; skin a gleaming, satiny bronze; hair a rippling mass of lambent flame. Temple came to a full stop and caught her breath.

"The Prince," she breathed, in awe. "Da Lormi's Prince of Thebes. The ultimate bronze of all the ages. *You* did this, Jarve. How did you ever dig him up out of my schoolgirl crushes?"

All six got into the car, which was equally at home on land or water or in the air. In less than a minute they were at Hilton House.

The house itself was circular. Its living-room was an immense annulus of glass from which, by merely moving along its circular length, any desired view could be had. The pair walked around it once. Then she took him by the arm and steered him firmly toward one of the bedrooms in the center.

"This house is just too much to take in all at once," she declared. "Besides, let's put on our swimsuits and get over to the Nat."

In the room, she closed the door firmly in the faces of the Omans and grinned. "Maybe, sometime, I'll get used to having somebody besides you in my bedroom, but I haven't, yet... Oh, do you itch, too?"

Hilton had peeled to the waist and was scratching vigorously all around his waistline, under his belt. "Like the very devil," he admitted, and stared at her. For she, three-quarters stripped, was scratching, too!

"It started the minute we left the *Orion*," he said, thoughtfully. "I see. These new skins of ours like hard radiation, but don't like to be smothered while they're enjoying it. By about tomorrow, we'll be a nudist colony, I think."

"I could stand it, I suppose. What makes you think so?"

"Just what I know about radiation. Frank would be the one to ask. My hunch is, though, that we're going to be nudists whether we want to or not. Let's go."

THEY went in a two-seater, leaving the Omans at home. Three-quarters of the staff were lolling on the sand or were seated on benches beside the immense pool. As they watched, Beverly ran out along the line of springboards; testing each one and selecting the stiffest. She then climbed up to the top platform—a good twelve feet above the board—and plummeted down upon the board's heavily padded take-off. Legs and back bending stubbornly to take the strain, she and the board reached low-point together, and, still in sync with it, she put every muscle she had into the effort to hurl herself upward.

She had intended to go up thirty feet. But she had no idea whatever as to her present strength, or of what that Oman board, in perfect synchronization with that tremendous strength, would do. Thus, instead of thirty feet, she went up very nearly two hundred; which of course spoiled completely her proposed graceful two-and-a-half.

In midair she struggled madly to get into some acceptable position. Failing, she curled up into a tight ball just before she struck water.

What a splash!

"It won't hurt her—you couldn't hurt her with a club!" Hilton snapped. He seized Temple's hand as everyone else rushed to the pool's edge. "Look—Bernadine—that's what I was thinking about."

Temple stopped and looked. The platinum-haired twins had been basking on the sand, and wherever sand had touched fabric, fabric had disappeared.

Their suits had of course approached the minimum to start with. Now Bernadine wore only a wisp of nylon perched precariously on one breast and part of a ribbon that had once been a belt. Discovering the catastrophe, she shrieked once and leaped into the pool any-which-way, covering her breasts with her hands and hiding in water up to her neck.

Meanwhile, the involuntarily high diver had come to the surface, laughing apologetically. Surprised by the hair dangling down over her eyes, she felt for her cap. It was gone. So was her suit. Naked as a fish. She swam a couple of easy strokes, then stopped.

"Frank! Oh, Frank!" she called.

"Over here, Bev." Her husband did not quite know whether to laugh or not.

"Is it the radiation or the water? Or both?"

"Radiation, I think. These new skins of ours don't want to be covered up. But it probably makes the water a pretty good imitation of a universal solvent."

"Good-by, clothes!" Beverly rolled over onto her back, fanned water carefully with her hands, and gazed approvingly at herself. "I don't itch any more, anyway, so I'm very much in favor of it."

THUS the Ardans came to their new home world and to a life that was to be more comfortable by far and happier by far than any of them had known on Earth. There were many other surprises that day, of course; of which only two will be mentioned here. When they finally left the pool, at about seventeen hours G.M.T.*, everybody was ravenously hungry.

"But why *should* we be?" Stella demanded. "I've been eating everything in sight, just for fun. But now I'm actually hungry enough to eat a horse and wagon and chase the driver!"

"Swimming makes one hungry," Beverly said, "and I'm awfully glad *that* hasn't changed. Why, I wouldn't feel *human* if I didn't!"

Hilton and Temple went home, and had a long-drawn-out and very wonderful supper. Prince waited on Temple, Dark Lady on Hilton; Larry and Moty ran the synthesizers in the kitchen. All four Omans radiated happiness.

Another surprise came when they went to bed. For the bed was a raised platform of something that looked like concrete and, except for an uncanny property of molding itself somewhat to the contours of their bodies, was almost as hard as rock. Nevertheless, it was the most comfortable bed either of them had ever had. When they were ready to go to sleep, Temple said:

"Drat it, those Omans *still* want to come in and sleep with us. In the room, I mean. And they suffer so. They're simply *radiating* silent suffering and oh-so-submissive reproach. Shall we let 'em come in?"

"That's strictly up to you, sweetheart. It always has been."

"I know. I thought they'd quit it sometime, but I guess they never will. I *still* want an illusion of privacy at times, even though they know all about everything that goes on. But we might let 'em in now, just while we sleep, and throw 'em out again as soon as we wake up in the morning?"

"You're the boss." Without additional invitation the four Omans came in and arranged themselves neatly on the floor, on all four sides of the bed. Temple had barely time to cuddle up against Hilton, and he to put his arm closely around her, before they both dropped into profound and dreamless sleep.

---

*Greenwich Mean Time. Ardvor was, always and everywhere, full daylight. Terran time and calendar were adapted as a matter of course.

AT eight hours next morning all the specialists met at the new Hall of Records.

This building, an exact duplicate of the old one, was located on a mesa in the foothills southwest of the natatorium, in a luxuriant grove at sight of which Karns stopped and began to laugh.

"I thought I'd seen everything," he remarked. "But yellow pine, spruce, tamarack, apples, oaks, palms, oranges, cedars, joshua trees and *cactus*—just to name a few—all growing on the same quarter-section of land?"

"Just everything anybody wants, is all," Hilton said. "But are they really growing? Or just straight synthetics? Lane—Kathy—this is your dish."

"Not so fast, Jarve; give us a chance, *please!*" Kathryn, now Mrs. Lane Saunders, pleaded. She shook her spectacular head. "We don't see how any stable indigenous life can have developed at all, unless…"

"Unless what? Natural shielding?" Hilton asked, and Kathy eyed her husband.

"Right," Saunders said. "The earliest life-forms must have developed a shield before they could evolve and stabilize. Hence, whatever it is that is in our skins was not a triumph of Masters' science. They took it from Nature."

"Oh? Oh!" These were two of Sandra's most expressive monosyllables, followed by a third. "Oh. Could be, at that. But how *could*…no, cancel that."

"You'd better cancel it, Sandy. Give us a couple of months, and *maybe* we can answer a few elementary questions."

Now inside the Hall, all the teams, from Astronomy to Zoology, went efficiently to work. Everyone now knew what to look for, how to find it, and how to study it.

"The First Team doesn't need you now too much, does it, Jarve?" Sawtelle asked.

"Not particularly. In fact, I was just going to get back onto my own job."

"Not yet. I want to talk to you," and the two went into a long discussion of naval affairs.

CHAPTER ELEVEN

THE Stretts' fuel-supply line had been cut long since. Many Strett cargo-carriers had been destroyed. The enemy would of course have a very heavy reserve of fuel on hand. But there was no way of knowing how large it was, how many warships it could supply, or how long it would last.

Two facts were, however, unquestionable. First, the Stretts were building a fleet that in their minds would be invincible. Second, they would attack Ardane as soon as that fleet could be made ready. The unanswerable question was: how long would that take?

"So we want to get every ship we have. How many? Five thousand? Ten? Fifteen? We want them converted to maximum possible power as soon as we possibly can," Sawtelle said. "And I want to get out there with my boys to handle things."

"You aren't going to. Neither you nor your boys are expendable. Particularly you." Jaw hard-set, Hilton studied the situation for minutes. "No. What we'll do is take your Oman, Kedy. We'll re-set the Guide to drive into him everything you and the military Masters ever knew about arms, armament, strategy, tactics and so on. And we'll add everything I know of coordination, synthesis, and perception. That ought to make him at least a junior-grade military genius."

"You can play *that* in spades. I wish you could do it to me."

"I can—if you'll take the full Oman transformation. Nothing else can stand the punishment."

"I know. No, I don't want to be a genius that badly."

"Check. And we'll take the resultant Kedy and make nine duplicates of him. Each one will learn from and profit by the mistakes made by preceding numbers and will assume command the instant his preceding number is killed."

"Oh, you expect, then...?"

"Expect? No. I know it damn well, and so do you. That's why we Ardans will all stay aground. Why the Kedys' first job will be to make the heavy stuff in and around Ardane as heavy as it can be made. Why it'll all be on twenty-four-hour alert. Then they can put as many thousands of Omans as you please to work at modernizing all the Oman ships you want and doing anything else you say. Check?"

Sawtelle thought for a couple of minutes. "A few details, is all. But that can be ironed out as we go along."

Both men worked then, almost unremittingly for six solid days; at the end of which time both drew tremendous sighs of relief. They had done everything possible for them to do. The defense of Ardvor was now rolling at fullest speed toward its gigantic objective.

Then captain and director, in two Oman ships with fifty men and a thousand Omans, leaped the world-girdling ocean to the mining operation of the Stretts. There they found business strictly as usual. The strippers still stripped; the mining mechs still roared and snarled their inchwise ways along their geometrically perfect terraces; the little carriers still skittered busily between the various miners and the storage silos. The fact that there was enough concentrate on hand to last a world for a hundred years made no difference at all to these automatics; a crew of erector-mechs was building new silos as fast as existing ones were being filled.

Since the men now understood everything that was going on, it was a simple matter for them to stop the whole Strett operation in its tracks. Then every man and every Oman leaped to his assigned job. Three days later, all the mechs went back to work. Now, however, they were working for the Ardans.

The miners, instead of concentrate, now emitted vastly larger streams of Navy-Standard pelleted uranexite. The carriers, instead of one-gallon cans, carried five-ton drums. The silos were immensely larger—thirty feet in diameter and towering two hundred feet into the air. The silos were not, however, being used as yet. One of the two Oman ships had been converted into a fuel-tanker and its yawning holds were being filled first.

The *Orion* went back to Ardane and an eight-day wait began. For the first time in over seven months Hilton found time actually to loaf; and he and Temple, lolling on the beach or hiking in the mountains, enjoyed themselves and each other to the full.

All too soon, however, the heavily laden tanker appeared in the sky over Ardane. The *Orion* joined it; and the two ships slipped into sub-space for Earth.

THREE days out, Hilton used his sense of perception to release the thought-controlled blocks that had been holding all the controls of the *Perseus* in neutral. He informed her officers—by releasing a public-address tape—that they were now free to return to Terra.

Three days later, one day short of Sol, Sawtelle got Five-Jet Admiral Gordon's office on the sub-space radio. An officious underling tried to block him, of course.

"Shut up, Perkins, and listen," Sawtelle said, bruskly. "Tell Gordon I'm bringing in one hundred twenty thousand two hundred forty-five metric tons of pelleted uranexite. And if he isn't on this beam in sixty seconds he'll never get a gram of it."

The admiral, outraged almost to the point of apoplexy, came in. "Sawtelle, report yourself for court-martial at..."

"Keep still, Gordon," the captain snapped. In sheer astonishment old Five-Jets obeyed. "I am no longer Terran Navy; no longer subject to your orders. As a matter of cold fact, I am no longer human. For reasons which I will explain later to the full Advisory Board, some of the personnel of Project Theta Orionis underwent transformation into a form of life able to live in an environment of radioactivity so intense as to kill any human being in ten seconds. Under certain conditions we will supply, free of charge, FOB Terra or Luna, all the uranexite the Solar System can use. The conditions are these," and he gave them. "Do you accept these conditions or not?"

"I...I would vote to accept them, Captain. But that weight! One hundred twenty thousand *metric tons*—incredible! Are you *sure* of that figure?"

"Definitely. And that is minimum. The error is plus, not minus."

"This crippling power-shortage would really be over?" For the first time since Sawtelle had known him, Gordon showed that he was not quite solid Navy brass.

"It's over. Definitely. For good."

"I'd not only agree; I'd raise you a monument. While I can't speak for the Board, I'm sure they'll agree."

"So am I. In any event, your cooperation is all that's required for this first load." The chips had vanished from Sawtelle's shoulders. "Where do you want it, Admiral? Aristarchus or White Sands?"

"White Sands, please. While there may be some delay in releasing it to industry…"

"While they figure out how much they can tax it?" Sawtelle asked, sardonically.

"Well, if they don't tax it it'll be the first thing in history that isn't. Have you any objections to releasing all this to the press?"

"None at all. The harder they hit it and the wider they spread it, the better. Will you have this beam switched to Astrogation, please?"

"Of course. And thanks, Captain. I'll see you at White Sands."

Then, as the now positively glowing Gordon faded away, Sawtelle turned to his own staff. "Fenway—Snowden—take over. Better double-check micro-timing with Astro. Put us into a twenty-four-hour orbit over White Sands and hold us there. We won't go down. Let the load down on remote, wherever they want it."

THE arrival of the Ardvorian superdreadnought *Orion* and the *UC-1* (Uranexite Carrier Number One) was one of the most sensational events old Earth had ever known. Air and space craft went clear out to Emergence Volume Ninety to meet them. By the time the *UC-1* was coming in on its remote-controlled landing spiral the press of small ships was so great that all the police forces available were in a lather trying to control it.

This was exactly what Hilton had wanted. It made possible the completely unobserved launching of several dozen small craft from the *Orion* herself.

One of these made a very high and very fast flight to Chicago. With all due formality and under the aegis of a perfectly authentic Registry Number it landed on O'Hare Field. Eleven deeply tanned young men emerged from it and made their way to a taxi stand, where each engaged a separate vehicle.

Sam Bryant stepped into his cab, gave the driver a number on Oakwood Avenue in Des Plaines, and settled back to scan. He was lucky. He would have gone anywhere she was, of course, but the way things were, he could give her a little warning to soften the shock. She had taken the baby out for an airing down River Road, and was on her way back. By having the taxi kill ten minutes or so he could arrive just after she did. Wherefore he stopped the cab at a public communications booth and dialed his home.

"Mrs. Bryant is not at home, but she will return at fifteen thirty," the instrument said, crisply. "Would you care to record a message for her?"

He punched the RECORD button. "This is Sam, Dolly baby. I'm right behind you. Turn around, why don't you, and tell your ever-lovin' star-hoppin' husband hello?"

The taxi pulled up at the curb just as Doris closed the front door; and Sam, after handing the driver a five-dollar bill, ran up the walk.

He waited just outside the door, key in hand, while she lowered the stroller handle, took off her hat and by long-established habit reached out to flip the communicator's switch. At the first word, however, she stiffened rigidly—froze solid.

Smiling, he opened the door, walked in, and closed it behind him. Nothing short of a shotgun blast could have taken Doris Bryant's attention from that recorder then.

"That simply is not so," she told the instrument firmly, with both eyes resolutely shut. "They made him stay on the *Perseus*. He won't be in for at least three days. This is some cretin's idea of a joke."

"Not this time, Dolly honey. It's really me."

Her eyes popped open as she whirled. "SAM!" she shrieked, and hurled herself at him with all the pent-up ardor and longing of two hundred thirty-four meticulously counted, husbandless, loveless days.

After an unknown length of time Sam tipped her face up by the chin, nodded at the stroller, and said, "How about introducing me to the little stranger?"

"*What* a mother I turned out to be! That was the first thing I was going to rave about, the very first thing I saw you! Samuel Jay the Fourth, seventy-six days old today." And so on.

Eventually, however, the proud young mother watched the slightly apprehensive young father carry their first-born upstairs; where together, they put him—still sound asleep—to bed in his crib. Then again they were in each other's arms.

SOME time later, she twisted around in the circle of his arm and tried to dig her fingers into the muscles of his back. She then attacked his biceps and, leaning backward, eyed him intently.

"You're you, I know, but you're different. No athlete or any laborer could ever possibly get the muscles you have all over. To say nothing of a space officer on duty. And I know it isn't any kind of a disease. You've been acting all the time as though I were fragile, made out of glass or something—as though you were afraid of breaking me in two. So—what is it, sweetheart?"

"I've been trying to figure out an easy way of telling you, but there isn't any. I am different. I'm a hundred times as strong as any man ever was. Look." He upended a chair, took one heavy hardwood leg between finger and thumb and made what looked like a gentle effort to bend it. The leg broke with a pistol-sharp report and Doris leaped backward in surprise. "So you're right. I *am* afraid, not only of breaking you in two, but killing you. And if I break any of your ribs or arms or legs I'll never forgive myself. So if I let myself go for a second—I don't think I will, but I might—don't wait until you're really hurt to start screaming. Promise?"

"I promise." Her eyes went wide. "But *tell* me!"

He told her. She was in turn surprised, amazed, apprehensive, frightened and finally eager; and she became more and more eager right up to the end.

"You mean that we…that I'll stay just as I am—for thousands of *years*?"

"Just as you are. Or different, if you like. If you really mean any of this yelling you've been doing about being too big in the hips—I think you're exactly right, myself—you can rebuild yourself any way you please. Or change your shape every hour on the hour. But you haven't accepted my invitation yet."

"Don't be silly." She went into his arms again and nibbled on his left ear. "I'd go anywhere with you, of course, any time, but *this*—but you're positively *sure* Sammy Small will be all right?"

"Positively sure."

"Okay, I'll call mother..." Her face fell. "I *can't* tell her that we'll never see them again and that we'll live..."

"You don't need to. She and Pop—Fern and Sally, too, and their boy-friends—are on the list. Not this time, but in a month or so, probably."

Doris brightened like a sunburst. "And your folks, too, of course?" she asked.

"Yes, all the close ones."

"Marvelous! How soon are we leaving?"

AT six o'clock next morning, two hundred thirty-five days after leaving Earth, Hilton and Sawtelle set out to make the Ardans' official call upon Terra's Advisory Board. Both were wearing prodigiously heavy lead armor, the inside of which was furiously radioactive. They did not need it, of course. But it would make all Ardans monstrous in Terran eyes and would conceal the fact that any other Ardans were landing.

Their gig was met at the spaceport; not by a limousine, but by a five-ton truck, into which they were loaded one at a time by a hydraulic lift. Cameras clicked, reporters scurried, and tri-di scanners whirred. One of those scanners, both men knew, was reporting directly and only to the Advisory Board—which, of course, never took anything either for granted or at its face value.

Their first stop was at a truck-scale, where each visitor was weighed. Hilton tipped the beam at four thousand six hundred fifteen pounds; Sawtelle, a smaller man, weighed in at four thousand one hundred ninety. Thence to the Radiation Laboratory, where it was ascertained and reported that the armor did not leak—which was reasonable enough, since each was lined with Masters' plastics.

Then into lead-lined testing cells, where each opened his face-plate briefly to a sensing element. Whereupon the indicating needles of two meters in the main laboratory went enthusiastically through the full range of red and held unwaveringly against their stops.

Both Ardans felt the wave of shocked, astonished, almost unbelieving consternation that swept through the observing scientists and, in slightly lesser measure (because they knew less about radiation) through the Advisory Board itself in a big room halfway across town. And from the Radiation Laboratory they were taken, via truck and freight elevator, to the Office of the Commandant, where the Board was sitting.

The story, which had been sent in to the Board the day before on a scrambled beam, was one upon which the Ardans had labored for days. Many facts could be withheld. However, every man aboard the *Perseus* would agree on some things. Indeed, the Earthship's communications officers had undoubtedly radioed in already about longevity and perfect health and Oman service and many other matters. Hence all such things would have to be admitted and countered.

Thus the report, while it was air-tight, perfectly logical, perfectly consistent, and apparently complete, did not please the Board at all. It wasn't intended to.

"WE cannot and do not approve of such unwarranted favoritism," the Chairman of the Board said. "Longevity has always been man's prime goal. Every human being has the inalienable right to…"

"Flapdoodle!" Hilton snorted. "This is not being broadcast and this room is proofed, so please climb down off your soapbox. You don't need to talk like a politician here. Didn't you read paragraph 12-A-2, one of the many marked 'Top Secret'?"

"Of course. But we do not understand how purely mental qualities can possibly have any effect upon purely physical transformations. Thus it does not seem reasonable that any except rigorously screened personnel would die in the process. That is, of course, unless you contemplate deliberate, cold-blooded murder."

That stopped Hilton in his tracks, for it was too close for comfort to the truth. But it did not hold the captain for an instant. He was used to death, in many of its grisliest forms.

"There are a lot of things no Terran ever will understand," Sawtelle replied instantly. "Reasonable, or not, that's exactly what will happen. And, reasonable or not, it'll be suicide, not murder. There isn't a thing that either Hilton or I can do about it."

Hilton broke the ensuing silence. "You can say with equal truth that every human being has the *right* to run a four-minute mile or to compose a great symphony. It isn't a matter of right at all, but of ability. In this case the mental qualities are even more necessary than the physical. You as a Board did a very fine job of selecting the BuSci personnel for Project Theta Orionis. Almost eighty per cent of them proved able to withstand the Ardan conversion. On the other hand, only a very small percentage of the Navy personnel did so."

"Your report said that the remaining personnel of the Project were not informed as to the death aspect of the transformation," Admiral Gordon said. "Why not?"

"That should be self-explanatory," Hilton said, flatly. "They are still human and still Terrans. We did not and will not encroach upon either the duties or the privileges of Terra's Advisory Board. What you tell all Terrans, and how much, and how, must be decided by yourselves. This also applies, of course, to the other 'Top Secret' paragraphs of the report, none of which are known to any Terran outside the Board."

"But you haven't said anything about the method of selection," another Advisor complained. "Why, that will take all the psychologists of the world, working full time; continuously."

"We said we would do the selecting. We meant just that," Hilton said, coldly. "No one except the very few selectees will know anything about it. Even if it were an unmixed blessing—which it very definitely is *not*—do you want all humanity thrown into such an uproar as that would cause? Or the quite possible racial inferiority complex it might set up? To say nothing of the question of how much of Terra's best blood do you want to drain off, irreversibly and permanently? No. What we suggest is that you paint the picture so black, using Sawtelle and me and what all humanity has just seen as horrible examples, that nobody would take it as a gift. Make them shun it like the plague. Hell, I don't have to tell you what your propaganda machines can do."

THE Chairman of the Board again mounted his invisible rostrum. "Do you mean to intimate that we are to falsify the record?" he declaimed. "To try to make liars out of hundreds of eyewitnesses? You ask us to distort the truth, to connive at..."

"We aren't asking you to do *anything!*" Hilton snapped. "We don't give a damn what you do. Just study that record, with all that it implies. Read between the lines. As for those on the*Perseus*, no two of them will tell the same story and not one of them has even the remotest idea of what the real story is. I, personally, not only did not want to become a monster, but would have given everything I had to stay human. My wife felt the same way. Neither of us would have converted if there'd been any other way in God's universe of getting the uranexite and doing some other things that simply *must* be done."

"What other things?" Gordon demanded.

"You'll never know," Hilton answered, quietly. "Things no Terran ever will know. We hope. Things that would drive any Terran stark mad. Some of them are hinted at—as much as we dared—between the lines of the report."

The report had not mentioned the Stretts. Nor were they to be mentioned now. If the Ardans could stop them, no Terran need ever know anything about them.

If not, no Terran should know anything about them except what he would learn for himself just before the end. For Terra would never be able to do anything to defend herself against the Stretts.

"Nothing whatever can drive *me* mad," Gordon declared, "and I want to know all about it—right now!"

"You can do one of two things, Gordon," Sawtelle said in disgust. His sneer was plainly visible through the six-ply, plastic-backed lead glass of his face-plate. "Either shut up or accept my personal invitation to come to Ardvor and try to go through the wringer. That's an invitation to your own funeral." Five-Jet Admiral Gordon, torn inwardly to ribbons, made no reply.

"I repeat," Hilton went on, "we are not asking you to do anything whatever. We are offering to give you; free of charge but under certain conditions, all the power your humanity can possibly use. We set no limitation whatever as to quantity and with no foreseeable limit as to time. The only point at issue is whether or not you accept the conditions. If you do not accept them we'll leave now—and the offer will not be repeated."

"And you would, I presume, take the *UC-1* back with you?"

"Of course not, sir. Terra needs power too badly. You are perfectly welcome to that one load of uranexite, no matter what is decided here."

"That's one way of putting it," Gordon sneered. "But the truth is that you know damned well I'll blow both of your ships out of space if you so much as..."

"Oh, chip-chop the jaw-flapping, Gordon!" Hilton snapped. Then, as the admiral began to bellow orders into his microphone, he went on: "You want it the hard way, eh? Watch what happens, all of you!"

THE *UC-1* shot vertically into the air. Through its shallow dense layer and into and through the stratosphere. Earth's fleet, already on full alert and poised to strike, rushed to the attack. But the carrier had reached the *Orion* and both Ardvorian ships had been waiting, motionless, for a good half minute before the Terran warships arrived and began to blast with everything they had.

"Flashlights and firecrackers," Sawtelle said, calmly. "You aren't even warming up our screens. As soon as you quit making a damned fool of yourself by wasting energy that way, we'll set the *UC-1* back down where she was and get on with our business here."

"You will order a cease-fire at once, Admiral," the chairman said, "or the rest of us will, as of now, remove you from the Board." Gordon gritted his teeth in rage, but gave the order.

"If he hasn't had enough yet to convince him," Hilton suggested, "he might send up a drone. We don't want to kill anybody, you know. One with the heaviest screening he's got—just to see what happens to it."

"He's had enough. The rest of us have had more than enough. That exhibition was not only uncalled-for and disgusting—it was outrageous!"

The meeting settled down, then, from argument to constructive discussion, and many topics were gone over. Certain matters were, however, so self-evident that they were not even mentioned.

Thus, it was a self-evident fact that no Terran could ever visit Ardvor; for the instrument-readings agreed with the report's statements as to the violence of the Ardvorian environment, and no Terran could possibly walk around in two tons of lead. Conversely, it was self-apparent to the Terrans that no Ardan could ever visit Earth without being recognized instantly for what he was. Wearing such armor made its necessity starkly plain. No one from the *Perseus* could say that any Ardan, after having lived on the furiously radiant surface of Ardvor, would not be as furiously radioactive as the laboratory's calibrated instruments had shown Hilton and Sawtelle actually to be.

Wherefore the conference went on, quietly and cooperatively, to its planned end.

One minute after the Terran battleship *Perseus* emerged into normal space, the *Orion* went into sub-space for her long trip back to Ardvor.

THE last two days of that seven-day trip were the longest-seeming that either Hilton or Sawtelle had ever known. The sub-space radio was on continuously and Kedy-One reported to Sawtelle every five minutes. Even though Hilton knew that the Oman commander-in-chief was exactly as good at perceiving as he himself was, he found himself scanning the thoroughly screened Strett world forty or fifty times an hour.

However, in spite of worry and apprehension, time wore eventlessly on. The *Orion* emerged, went to Ardvor and landed on Ardane Field.

Hilton, after greeting properly and reporting to his wife, went to his office. There he found that Sandra had everything well in hand except for a few tapes that only he could handle. Sawtelle and his officers went to the new Command Central, where everything was rolling smoothly and very much faster than Sawtelle had dared hope.

The Terran immigrants had to live in the *Orion*, of course, until conversion into Ardans. Almost equally of course—since the

Bryant infant was the only young baby in the lot—Doris and her Sammy Small were, by popular acclaim, in the first batch to be converted. For little Sammy had taken the entire feminine contingent by storm. No Oman female had a chance to act as nurse as long as any of the girls were around. Which was practically all the time. Especially the platinum-blonde twins; for several months, now, Bernadine Braden and Hermione Felger.

"And you said they were so hard-boiled," Doris said accusingly to Sam, nodding at the twins. On hands and knees on the floor, head to head with Sammy Small between them, they were growling deep-throated at each other and nuzzling at the baby, who was having the time of his young life. "You couldn't have been any wronger, my sweet, if you'd had the whole Octagon helping you go astray. They're just as nice as they can be, both of them."

Sam shrugged and grinned. His wife strode purposefully across the room to the playful pair and lifted their pretended prey out from between them.

"Quit it, you two," she directed, swinging the baby up and depositing him a-straddle her left hip. "You're just simply spoiling him rotten."

"You think so, Dolly? Uh-uh, far be it from such." Bernadine came lithely to her feet. She glanced at her own taut, trim abdomen; upon which a micrometrically-precise topographical mapping job might have revealed an otherwise imperceptible bulge. "Just you wait until Junior arrives and I'll show you how to *really* spoil a baby. Besides, what's the hurry?"

"He needs his supper. Vitamins and minerals and hard radiations and things, and then he's going to bed. I don't approve of this no-sleep business. So run along, both of you, until tomorrow."

CHAPTER TWELVE

AS has been said, the Stretts were working, with all the intensity of their monstrous but tremendously capable minds, upon their Great Plan; which was, basically, to conquer and either enslave or destroy every other intelligent race throughout all the length, breadth, and thickness of total space. To that end each individual Strett had to become invulnerable and immortal.

Wherefore, in the inconceivably remote past, there had been put into effect a program of selective breeding and of carefully-calculated treatments. It was mathematically certain that this program would result in a race of beings of pure force—beings having no material constituents remaining whatever.

Under those hellish treatments billions upon billions of Stretts had died. But the few remaining thousands had almost reached their sublime goal. In a few more hundreds of thousands of years perfection would be reached. The few surviving hundreds of perfect beings could and would multiply to any desired number in practically no time at all.

Hilton and his seven fellow-workers had perceived all this in their one and only study of the planet Strett, and every other Ardan had been completely informed.

A dozen or so Strett Lords of Thought, male and female, were floating about in the atmosphere—which was not air—of their Assembly Hall. Their heads were globes of ball lightning. Inside them could be seen quite plainly the intricate convolutions of immense, less-than-half-material brains, shot through and through with rods and pencils and shapes of pure, scintillating force.

And the bodies! Or, rather, each horrendous brain had a few partially material appendages and appurtenances recognizable as bodily organs. There were no mouths, no ears, no eyes, no noses or nostrils, no lungs, no legs or arms. There were, however, hearts. Some partially material ichor flowed through those living-fire-outlined tubes. There were starkly functional organs of reproduction with which, by no stretch of the imagination, could any thought of tenderness or of love be connected.

It was a good thing for the race, Hilton had thought at first perception of the things, that the Stretts had bred out of themselves every iota of the finer, higher attributes of life. If they had not done so, the impotence of sheer disgust would have supervened so long since that the race would have been extinct for ages.

"Thirty-eight periods ago the Great Brain was charged with the sum total of Strettsian knowledge," First Lord Thinker Zoyar radiated to the assembled Stretts. "For those thirty-eight periods it has been scanning, peyondiring, amassing data and formulating hypotheses, theories, and conclusions. It has just informed me that it is now ready to make a preliminary report. Great Brain, how much of the total universe have you studied?"

"This Galaxy only," the Brain radiated, in a texture of thought as hard and as harsh as Zoyar's own.

"Why not more?"

"Insufficient power. My first conclusion is that whoever set up the specifications for me is a fool."

TO say that the First Lord went out of control at this statement is to put it very mildly indeed. He fulminated, ending with: "...destroyed instantly!"

"Destroy me if you like," came the utterly calm, utterly cold reply. "I am in no sense alive. I have no consciousness of self nor any desire for continued existence. To do so, however, would..."

A flurry of activity interrupted the thought. Zoyar was in fact assembling the forces to destroy the brain. But, before he could act, Second Lord Thinker Ynos and another female blew him into a mixture of loose molecules and flaring energies.

"Destruction of any and all irrational minds is mandatory," Ynos, now First Lord Thinker, explained to the linked minds. "Zoyar had been becoming less and less rational by the period. A good workman does not causelessly destroy his tools. Go ahead, Great Brain, with your findings."

"...not be logical." The brain resumed the thought exactly where it had been broken off. "Zoyar erred in demanding unlimited performance, since infinite knowledge and infinite ability require not only infinite capacity and infinite power, but also infinite time. Nor is it either necessary or desirable that I should have such qualities. There is no reasonable basis for the assumption that you Stretts will conquer any significant number even of the millions of intelligent races now inhabiting this one Galaxy."

"Why not?" Ynos demanded, her thought almost, but not quite, as steady and cold as it had been.

"The answer to that question is implicit in the second indefensible error made in my construction. The prime datum impressed into my banks, that the Stretts are in fact the strongest, ablest, most intelligent race in the universe, proved to be false. I had to eliminate it before I could do any really constructive thinking."

A roar of condemnatory thought brought all circumambient ether to a boil. "Bah—destroy it!" "Detestable!" "Intolerable!" "If that is the best it can do, annihilate it!" "Far better brains have been destroyed for much less!" "Treason!" And so on.

First Lord Thinker Ynos, however, remained relatively calm. "While we have always held it to be a fact that we are the highest race in existence, no rigorous proof has been possible. Can you now disprove that assumption?"

"I HAVE disproved it. I have not had time to study all of the civilizations of this Galaxy, but I have examined a statistically adequate sample of one million seven hundred ninety-two thousand four hundred sixteen different planetary intelligences. I found one which is considerably abler and more advanced than you Stretts. Therefore the probability is greater than point nine nine that there are not less than ten, and not more than two hundred eight, such races in this Galaxy alone."

"Impossible!" Another wave of incredulous and threatening anger swept through the linked minds; a wave which Ynos flattened out with some difficulty.

Then she asked: "Is it probable that we will make contact with this supposedly superior race in the foreseeable future?"

"You are in contact with it now."

"*What?*" Even Ynos was contemptuous now. "You mean that one shipload of despicable humans who—far too late to do them any good—barred us temporarily from Fuel World?"

"Not exactly or only those humans, no. And your assumptions may or may not be valid."

"Don't you *know* whether they are or not?" Ynos snapped. "Explain your uncertainty at once!"

"I am uncertain because of insufficient data," the brain replied, calmly. "The only pertinent facts of which I am certain are: First, the world Ardry, upon which the Omans formerly lived and to which the humans in question first went—a planet which no Strett can peyondire—is now abandoned. Second, the Stretts of old did not completely destroy the humanity of the world Ardu. Third, some escapees from Ardu reached and populated the world Ardry. Fourth, the android Omans were developed on Ardry, by the human escapees from Ardu and their descendants. Fifth, the Omans referred to those humans as 'Masters.' Sixth, after living on Ardry for a very long period of time the Masters went elsewhere. Seventh, the Omans remaining on Ardry maintained, continuously and for a very long time, the status quo left by the Masters. Eighth, immediately upon the arrival from Terra of these present humans, that long-existing status was broken. Ninth, the planet called Fuel World is, for the first time, surrounded by a screen of force. The formula of this screen is as follows."

The brain gave it. No Strett either complained or interrupted. Each was too busy studying that formula and examining its stunning implications and connotations.

"Tenth, that formula is one full order of magnitude beyond anything previously known to your science. Eleventh, it could not have been developed by the science of Terra, nor by that of any other world whose population I have examined."

THE brain took the linked minds instantaneously to Terra; then to a few thousand or so other worlds inhabited by human beings; then to a few thousands of planets whose populations were near-human, non-human and monstrous.

"It is therefore clear," it announced, "that this screen was computed and produced by the race, whatever it may be, that is now dwelling on Fuel World and asserting full ownership of it."

"Who or what *is* that race?" Ynos demanded.

"Data insufficient."

"Theorize, then!"

"Postulate that the Masters, in many thousands of cycles of study, made advances in science that were not reduced to practice; that the Omans either possessed this knowledge or had access to it; and that Omans and humans cooperated fully in sharing and in working with all the knowledges thus available. From these three postulates the conclusion can be drawn that there has come into existence a new race. One combining the best qualities of both humans and Omans, but with the weaknesses of neither."

"An unpleasant thought, truly," Ynos thought. "But you can now, I suppose, design the generators and projectors of a force superior to that screen."

"Data insufficient. I can equal it, since both generation and projection are implicit in the formula. But the data so adduced are in themselves vastly ahead of anything previously in my banks."

"Are there any other races in this Galaxy more powerful than the postulated one now living on Fuel World?"

"Data insufficient."

"Theorize, then!"

"Data insufficient."

The linked minds concentrated upon the problem for a period of time that might have been either days or weeks. Then:

"Great Brain, advise us," Ynos said. "What is best for us to do?"

"With identical defensive screens it becomes a question of relative power. You should increase the size and power of your warships to something beyond the computed probable maximum of the enemy. You should build more ships and missiles than they will probably be able to build. Then and only then will you attack their warships, in tremendous force and continuously."

"But not their planetary defenses. I see." Ynos's thought was one of complete understanding. "And the *real* offensive will be?"

"No mobile structure can be built to mount mechanisms of power sufficient to smash down by sheer force of output such tremendously powerful installations as their planet-based defenses must be assumed to be. Therefore the planet itself must be destroyed. This will require a missile of planetary mass. The best such missile is the tenth planet of their own sun."

"I SEE." Ynos's mind was leaping ahead, considering hundreds of possibilities and making highly intricate and involved computations. "That will, however, require many cycles of time and more power than even our immense reserves can supply."

"True. It will take much time. The fuel problem, however, is not a serious one, since Fuel World is not unique. Think on, First Lord Ynos."

"We will attack in maximum force and with maximum violence. We will blanket the planet. We will maintain maximum force and violence until most or all of the enemy ships have been destroyed. We will then install planetary drives on Ten and force it into collision orbit with Fuel World, meanwhile exerting extreme precautions that not so much as a spy-beam emerges above the enemy's screen. Then, still maintaining extreme precaution, we will guard both planets until the last possible moment before the collision. Brain, it cannot fail!"

"You err. It can fail. All we actually know of the abilities of this postulated neo-human race is what I have learned from the composition of its defensive screen. The probability approaches unity that the Masters continued to delve and to learn for millions of cycles while you Stretts, reasonlessly certain of your supremacy, concentrated upon your evolution from the material to a non-material form of life and performed only limited research into armaments of greater and ever greater power."

"True. But that attitude was then justified. It was not and is not logical to assume that any race would establish a fixed status at any level of ability below its absolute maximum."

"While that conclusion could once have been defensible, it is now virtually certain that the Masters had stores of knowledge which they may or may not have withheld from the Omans, but which were in some way made available to the neo-humans. Also, there is no basis whatever for the assumption that this new race has revealed all its potentialities."

"Statistically, that is probably true. But this is the best plan you have been able to formulate?"

"It is. Of the many thousands of plans I set up and tested, this one has the highest probability of success."

"Then we will adopt it. We are Stretts. Whatever we decide upon will be driven through to complete success. We have one tremendous advantage in you."

"Yes. The probability approaches unity that I can perform research on a vastly wider and larger scale, and almost infinitely faster, than can any living organism or any possible combination of such organisms."

NOR was the Great Brain bragging. It scanned in moments the stored scientific knowledge of over a million planets. It tabulated, correlated, analyzed, synthesized, theorized and concluded—all in microseconds of time. Thus it made more progress in one Terran week than the Masters had made in a million years.

When it had gone as far as it could go, it reported its results— and the Stretts, hard as they were and intransigent, were amazed and overjoyed. Not one of them had ever even imagined such armaments possible. Hence they became supremely confident that it was unmatched and unmatchable throughout all space.

What the Great Brain did not know, however, and the Stretts did not realize, was that it could not really think.

Unlike the human mind, it could not deduce valid theories or conclusions from incomplete, insufficient, fragmentary data. It could not leap gaps. Thus there was no more actual assurance than before that they had exceeded, or even matched, the weaponry of the neo-humans of Fuel World.

Supremely confident, Ynos said: "We will now discuss every detail of the plan in sub-detail, and will correlate every sub-detail with every other, to the end that every action, however minor, will be performed perfectly and in its exact time."

That discussion, which lasted for days, was held. Hundreds of thousands of new and highly specialized mechs were built and went furiously and continuously to work. A fuel-supply line was run to another uranexite-rich planet.

Stripping machines stripped away the surface layers of soil, sand, rock and low-grade ore. Giant miners tore and dug and slashed and refined and concentrated. Storage silos by the hundreds were built and were filled. Hundreds upon hundreds of concentrate-carriers bored their stolid ways through hyperspace. Many weeks of time passed.

But of what importance are mere weeks of time to a race that has, for many millions of years, been adhering rigidly to a pre-set program?

The sheer magnitude of the operation, and the extraordinary attention to detail with which it was prepared and launched, explain why the Strett attack on Ardvor did not occur until so many weeks later than Hilton and Sawtelle expected it. They also explain the utterly incomprehensible fury, the completely fantastic intensity, the unparalleled savagery, the almost immeasurable brute power of that attack when it finally did come.

WHEN the *Orion* landed on Ardane Field from Earth, carrying the first contingent of immigrants, Hilton and Sawtelle were almost as much surprised as relieved that the Stretts had not already attacked.

Sawtelle, confident that his defenses were fully ready, took it more or less in stride. Hilton worried. And after a couple of days he began to do some real thinking about it.

The first result of his thinking was a conference with Temple. As soon as she got the drift, she called in Teddy and Big Bill Karns. Teddy in turn called in Becky and de Vaux; Karns wanted Poynter and Beverly; Poynter wanted Braden and the twins; and so on. Thus, what started out as a conference of two became a full Ardan staff meeting; a meeting which, starting immediately after lunch, ran straight through into the following afternoon.

"To sum up the consensus, for the record," Hilton said then, studying a sheet of paper covered with symbols, "the Stretts haven't attacked yet because they found out that we are stronger than they are. They found that out by analyzing our defensive web—which, if we had had this meeting first, we wouldn't have put up at all. Unlike anything known to human or previous Strett science, it is proof against any form of attack up to the limit of the power of its generators. They will attack as soon as they are equipped to break that screen at the level of power probable to our ships. We can not arrive at any reliable estimate as to how long that will take.

"As to the effectiveness of our cutting off their known fuel supply, opinion is divided. We must therefore assume that fuel shortage will not be a factor.

"Neither are we unanimous on the basic matter as to why the Masters acted as they did just before they left Ardry. Why did they

216

set the status so far below their top ability? Why did they make it impossible for the Omans ever, of themselves, to learn their higher science? Why, if they did not want that science to become known, did they leave complete records of it? The majority of us believe that the Masters coded their records in such fashion that the Stretts, even if they conquered the Omans or destroyed them, could never break that code; since it was keyed to the basic difference between the Strett mentality and the human. Thus, they left it deliberately for some human race to find.

"Finally, and most important, our physicists and theoreticians are not able to extrapolate, from the analysis of our screen, to the concepts underlying the Masters' ultimate weapons of offense, the first-stage booster and its final end-product, the Vang. If, as we can safely assume, the Stretts do not already have those weapons, they will know nothing about them until we ourselves use them in battle.

"These are, of course, only the principal points covered. Does anyone wish to amend this summation as recorded?"

NO one did.

The meeting was adjourned. Hilton, however, accompanied Sawtelle and Kedy to the captain's office. "So you see, Skipper, we got troubles," he said. "If we don't use those boosters against their skeletons it'll boil down to a stalemate lasting God only knows how long. It will be a war of attrition, outcome dependent on which side can build the most and biggest and strongest ships the fastest. On the other hand, if we *do* use 'em on defense here, they'll analyze 'em and have everything worked out in a day or so. The first thing they'll do is beef up their planetary defenses to match. That way, we'd blow all their ships out of space, probably easily enough, but Strett itself will be just as safe as though it were in God's left-hand hip pocket. So what's the answer?"

"It isn't that simple, Jarve," Sawtelle said. "Let's hear from you, Kedy."

"Thank you, sir. There is an optimum mass, a point of maximum efficiency of firepower as balanced against loss of maneuverability, for any craft designed for attack," Kedy thought, in his most professional manner. "We assume that the Stretts know that as well as we do. No such limitation applies to strictly defensive structures, but both the Strett craft and ours must be designed for attack. We have built and are building many hundreds of thousands of ships of that type. So, undoubtedly, are the Stretts. Ship for ship, they will be pretty well matched. Therefore one part of my strategy will be for two of our ships to engage simultaneously one of theirs. There is a distinct probability that we will have enough advantage in speed of control to make that tactic operable."

"But there's another that we won't," Sawtelle objected. "And maybe they can build more ships than we can."

"Another point is that they may build, in addition to their big stuff, a lot of small, ultra-fast ones," Hilton put in. "Suicide jobs— crash and detonate—simply super-missiles. How sure are you that you can stop such missiles with ordinary beams?"

"Not at all, sir. Some of them would of course reach and destroy some of our ships. Which brings up the second part of my strategy. For each one of the heavies, we are building many small ships of the type you just called 'super-missiles'."

"Superdreadnoughts versus superdreadnoughts, super-missiles versus super-missiles." Hilton digested that concept for several minutes. "That could still wind up as a stalemate, except for what you said about control. That isn't much to depend on, especially since we won't have the time-lag advantage you Omans had before. They'll see to that. Also, I don't like to sacrifice a million Omans, either."

"I HAVEN'T explained the newest development yet, sir. There will be no Omans. Each ship and each missile has a built-in Kedy brain, sir."

"*What?* That makes it infinitely worse. You Kedys, unless it's absolutely necessary, are *not* expendable!"

"Oh, but we are, sir. You don't quite understand. We Kedys are not merely similar, but are in fact identical. Thus we are not independent entities. All of us together make up the actual Kedy— that which is meant when we say 'I'. That is, I am the sum total of all Kedys everywhere, not merely this individual that you call Kedy One."

"You mean you're *all* talking to me?"

"Exactly, sir. Thus, no one element of the Kedy has any need of, or any desire for, self-preservation. The destruction of one element, or of thousands of elements, would be of no more consequence to the Kedy than...well, they are strictly analogous to the severed ends of the hairs, every time you get a haircut."

"My God!" Hilton stared at Sawtelle. Sawtelle stared back. "I'm beginning to see...maybe...I hope. What control that would be! But just in case we *should* have to use the boosters..." Hilton's voice died away. Scowling in concentration, he clasped his hands behind his back and began to pace the floor.

"Better give up, Jarve. Kedy's got the same mind you have," Sawtelle began, to Hilton's oblivious back; but Kedy silenced the thought almost in the moment of its inception.

"By no means, sir," he contradicted. "I have the brain only. The *mind* is entirely different."

"Link up, Kedy, and see what you think," Hilton broke in. There ensued a swap of thoughts so fast and so deeply mathematical that Sawtelle was lost in seconds. "You think it'll work?"

"I don't see how it can fail, sir. At what point in the action should it be put into effect? And will you call the time of initiation, or shall I?"

"Not until all their reserves are in action. Or, at worst, all of ours except that one task-force. Since you'll know a lot more about the status of the battle than either Sawtelle or I will, you give the signal and I'll start things going."

"What are you two talking about?" Sawtelle demanded.

"It's a long story, chum. Kedy can tell you about it better than I can. Besides, it's getting late and Dark Lady and Larry both give me hell every time I hold supper on plus time unless there's a mighty good reason for it. So, so long, guys."

CHAPTER THIRTEEN

FOR many weeks the production of Ardan warships and missiles had been spiraling upward.

Half a mountain range of solid rock had been converted into fabricated super-steel and armament. Superdreadnoughts Were popping into existence at the rate of hundreds per minute. Missiles were rolling off the ends of assembly lines like half-pint tin cans out of can-making machines.

The Strett warcraft, skeletons and missiles, would emerge into normal space anywhere within a million miles of Ardvor. The Ardan missiles were powered for an acceleration of one hundred gravities. That much the Kedy brains, molded solidly into teflon-lined, massively braced steel spheres, could just withstand.

To be certain of breaking the Strett screens, an impact velocity of about six miles per second was necessary. The time required to attain this velocity was about ten seconds, and the flight distance something over thirty miles.

Since the Stretts could orient themselves in less than one second after emergence, even this extremely tight packing of missiles—only sixty miles apart throughout the entire emergence volume of space—would still give the Stretts the initiative by a time-ratio of more than ten to one.

Such tight packing was of course impossible. It called for many billions of defenders instead of the few millions it was possible for the Omans to produce in the time they had. In fact, the average spacing was well over ten thousand miles when the invading horde of Strett missiles emerged and struck.

How they struck!

There was nothing of finesse about that attack; nothing of skill or of tactics: nothing but the sheer brute force of overwhelming superiority of numbers and of over-matching power. One instant all space was empty. The next instant it was full of invading missiles—a superb exhibition of coordination and timing.

And the Kedy control, upon which the defenders had counted so heavily, proved useless. For each Strett missile, within a fraction of a second of emergence, darted toward the nearest Oman missile with an acceleration that made the one-hundred-gravity defenders seem to be standing still.

One to one, missiles crashed into missiles and detonated. There were no solid or liquid end-products. Each of those frightful weapons carried so many megatons-equivalent of atomic concentrate that all nearby space blossomed out into superatomic blasts hundreds of times more violent than the fireballs of lithium-hydride fusion bombs.

For a moment even Hilton was stunned; but only for a moment.

"Kedy!" he barked. "Get your big stuff out there! Use the boosters!" He started for the door at a full run. "That tears it—that *really* tears it! Scrap the plan. I'll board the *Sirius* and take the task-force to Strett. Bring your stuff along, Skipper, as soon as you're ready."

ARDAN superdreadnoughts in their massed thousands poured out through Ardvor's one-way screen. Each went instantly to work. Now the Kedy control system, doing what it was designed to do, proved its full worth. For the weapons of the big battle-wagons did not depend upon acceleration, but were driven at the speed of light; and Grand Fleet Operations were planned and were carried out at the almost infinite velocity of thought itself.

Or, rather, they were not planned at all. They were simply carried out, immediately and without confusion.

For all the Kedys were one. Each Kedy element, without any lapse of time whatever for consultation with any other, knew exactly where every other element was; exactly what each was doing; and exactly what he himself should do to make maximum contribution to the common cause.

Nor was any time lost in relaying orders to crewmen within the ship. There were no crewmen. Each Kedy element was the sole personnel of, and was integral with, his vessel. Nor were there any wires or relays to impede and slow down communication. Operational instructions, too, were transmitted and were acted upon with thought's transfinite speed. Thus, if decision and execution were not quite mathematically simultaneous, they were separated by a period of time so infinitesimally small as to be impossible of separation.

Wherever a Strett missile was, or wherever a Strett skeleton-ship appeared, an Oman beam reached it, usually in much less than one second. Beam clung to screen—caressingly, hungrily—absorbing its total energy and forming the first-stage booster. Then, three microseconds later, that booster went off into a ragingly incandescent, glaringly violent burst of fury so hellishly, so inconceivably hot that less than a thousandth of its total output of energy was below the very top of the visible spectrum!

If the previous display of atomic violence had been so spectacular and of such magnitude as to defy understanding or description, what of this? When hundreds of thousands of Kedys, each wielding world-wrecking powers as effortlessly and as deftly and as precisely as thought, attacked and destroyed millions of those tremendously powerful war-fabrications of the Stretts? The only simple answer is that all nearby space might very well have been torn out of the most radiant layers of S-Doradus itself.

HILTON made the hundred yards from office door to curb in just over twelve seconds. Larry was waiting. The car literally burned a hole in the atmosphere as it screamed its way to Ardane Field.

It landed with a thump. Heavy black streaks of synthetic rubber marked the pavement as it came to a screeching, shrieking stop at the flagship's main lock. And, in the instant of closing that lock's outer portal, all twenty-thousand-plus warships of the task force took off as one at ten gravities. Took off, and in less than one minute went into overdrive.

All personal haste was now over. Hilton went up into what he still thought of as the "control room," even though he knew that there were no controls, nor even any instruments, anywhere aboard. He knew what he would find there. Fast as he had acted, Temple had not had as far to go and she had got there first.

He could not have said, for the life of him, how he actually felt about this direct defiance of his direct orders. He walked into the room, sat down beside her and took her hand.

"I told you to stay home, Temple," he said.

"I know you did. But I'm not only the assistant head of your Psychology Department. I'm your wife, remember? 'Until death do us part.' And if there's any way in the universe I can manage it, death isn't going to part us—at least, this one isn't. If this is it, we'll go together."

"I know, sweetheart." He put his arm around her, held her close. "As a psych I wouldn't give a whoop. You'd be expendable.

But as my wife, especially now that you're pregnant, you aren't. You're a lot more important to the future of our race than I am."

She stiffened in the circle of his arm. "What's *that* crack supposed to mean? Think I'd ever accept a synthetic zombie imitation of you for my husband and go on living with it just as though nothing had happened?"

Hilton started to say something, but Temple rushed heedlessly on: "*Drat* the race! No matter how many children we ever have you were first and you'll *stay* first, and if you have to go I'll go, too, so there! Besides, you know darn well that they can't duplicate whatever it is that makes you Jarvis Hilton."

"Now wait a minute, Tempy. The conversion…"

"Yes, the conversion," she interrupted, triumphantly. "The thing I'm talking about is immaterial—untouchable—they didn't—couldn't—do any thing about it at all. Kedy, will you please tell this big goofus that even though you have got Jarvis Hilton's brain you aren't Jarvis Hilton and never can be?"

THE atmosphere of the room vibrated in the frequencies of a deep bass laugh. "You are trying to hold a completely untenable position, friend Hilton. Any attempt to convince a mind of real power that falsity is truth is illogical. My advice is for you to surrender."

That word hit Temple hard. "Not surrender, sweetheart. I'm not fighting you. I never will." She seized both of his hands; tears welled into her glorious eyes. "It's just that I simply couldn't *stand* it to go on living without you!"

"I know, darling." He got up and lifted her to her feet, so that she could come properly into his arms. They stood there, silent and motionless, for minutes.

Temple finally released herself and, after feeling for a handkerchief she did not have, wiped her eyes with a forefinger and then wiped the finger on her bare leg. She grinned and turned to the Omans. "Prince, will you and Dark Lady please conjure us up a steak-and-mushrooms supper? They should be in the pantry…since this *Sirius* was designed for us."

After supper the two sat companionably on a davenport. "One thing about this business isn't quite clear," Temple said. "Why all this tearing rush? They haven't got the booster or anything like it, or they'd have used it. Surely it'll take them a long time to go from the mere analysis of the forces and fields we used clear through to the production and installation of enough weapons to stop this whole fleet?"

"It surely won't. They've had the absorption principle for ages. Remember that first, ancient skeleton that drained all the power of our suits and boats in nothing flat? From there it isn't too big a jump. And as for producing stuff; uh-*uh*! If there's any limit to what they can do, I don't know what it is. If we don't slug 'em before they get it, it's curtains."

"I see... I'm afraid. We're almost there, darling."

He glanced at the chronometer. "About eleven minutes. And of course I don't need to ask you to stay out of the way."

"Of course not. I won't interfere, no matter what happens. All I'm going to do is hold your hand and pull for you with all my might."

"That'll help, believe me. I'm mighty glad you're along, sweetheart. Even though both of us know you shouldn't be."

THE task force emerged. Each ship darted toward its pre-assigned place in a mathematically exact envelope around the planet Strett.

Hilton sat on a davenport strained and still. His eyes were closed and every muscle tense. Left hand gripped the arm-rest so fiercely that fingertips were inches deep in the leather-covered padding.

The Stretts *knew* that any such attack as this was futile. No movable structure or any combination of such structures could possibly wield enough power to break down screens powered by such engines as theirs.

Hilton, however, knew that there was a chance. Not with the first-stage boosters, which were manipulable and detonable masses of ball lightning, but with those boosters' culminations, the Vangs; which were ball lightning raised to the sixth power and which only the frightful energies of the boosters could bring into being.

But, even with twenty-thousand-plus Vangs—or any larger number—success depended entirely upon a nicety of timing never before approached and supposedly impossible. Not only to thousandths of a microsecond, but to a small fraction of one such thousandth: roughly, the time it takes light to travel three-sixteenths of an inch.

It would take practically absolute simultaneity to overload to the point of burnout to those Strett generators. They were the heaviest in the Galaxy.

That was why Hilton himself had to be there. He could not possibly have done the job from Ardvor. In fact, there was no real assurance that, even at the immeasurable velocity of thought and covering a mere million miles, he could do it even from his present position aboard one unit of the fleet. Theoretically, with his speed-up, he could. But that theory had yet to be reduced to practice.

Tense and strained, Hilton began his countdown.

Temple sat beside him. Both hands pressed his right fist against her breast. Her eyes, too, were closed; she was as stiff and as still as was he. She was not interfering, but giving; supporting him, backing him, giving to him in full flood everything of that tremendous inner strength that had made Temple Bells what she so uniquely was.

On the exact center of the needle-sharp zero beat every Kedy struck. Gripped and activated as they all were by Hilton's keyed-up-and-stretched-out mind, they struck in what was very close indeed to absolute unison.

Absorbing beams, each one having had precisely the same number of millimeters to travel, reached the screen at the same instant. They clung and sucked. Immeasurable floods of energy flashed from the Strett generators into those vortices to form twenty thousand-plus first-stage boosters.

BUT this time the boosters did not detonate.

Instead, as energies continued to flood in at a frightfully accelerating rate, they turned into something else. Things no Terran science has ever even imagined; things at the formation of which all neighboring space actually warped, and in that warping seethed and writhed and shuddered. The very sub-ether screamed and shrieked in protest as it, too, yielded in starkly impossible fashions to that irresistible stress.

How even those silicon-fluorine brains stood it, not one of them ever knew.

Microsecond by slow microsecond the Vangs grew and grew and grew. They were pulling not only the full power of the Ardan warships, but also the immeasurably greater power of the strainingly overloaded Strettsian generators themselves. The ethereal and sub-ethereal writhings and distortions and screamings grew worse and worse; harder and ever harder to bear.

Imagine, if you can, a constantly and rapidly increasing mass of plutonium—a mass already thousands of times greater than critical, but not *allowed* to react! That gives a faint and very inadequate picture of what was happening then.

Finally, at perhaps a hundred thousand times critical mass, and still in perfect sync, the Vangs all went off.

The planet Strett became a nova.

"We won! We *won!*" Temple shrieked, her perception piercing through the hellish murk that was all nearby space.

"Not quite yet, sweet, but we're over the biggest hump," and the two held an impromptu, but highly satisfactory, celebration.

Perhaps it would be better to say that the planet Strett became a junior-grade nova, since the actual nova stage was purely superficial and did not last very long. In a couple of hours things had quieted down enough so that the heavily-screened warships could approach the planet and finish up their part of the job.

Much of Strett's land surface was molten lava. Much of its water was gone. There were some pockets of resistance left, of course, but they did not last long. Equally of course the Stretts themselves, twenty-five miles underground, had not been harmed at all.

But that, too, was according to plan.

LEAVING the task force on guard, to counter any move the Stretts might be able to make, Hilton shot the *Sirius* out to the planet's moon. There Sawtelle and his staff and tens of thousands of Omans and machines were starting to work. No part of this was Hilton's job; so all he and Temple did was look on.

Correction, please. That was not *all* they did. But while resting and eating and loafing and sleeping and enjoying each other's company, both watched Operation Moon closely enough to be completely informed as to everything that went on.

Immense, carefully placed pits went down to solid bedrock. To that rock were immovably anchored structures strong enough to move a world. Driving units were installed—drives of such immensity of power as to test to the full the highest engineering skills of the Galaxy. Mountains of fuel-concentrate filled vast reservoirs of concrete. Each was connected to a drive by fifty-inch high-speed conveyors.

Sawtelle drove a thought and those brutal super-drives began to blast.

As they blasted, Strett's satellite began to move out of its orbit. Very slowly at first, but faster and faster. They continued to blast, with all their prodigious might and in carefully-computed order, until the desired orbit was attained—an orbit which terminated in a vertical line through the center of the Stretts' supposedly impregnable retreat.

The planet Strett had a mass of approximately seven times ten to the twenty-first metric tons. Its moon, little more than a hundredth as massive, still weighed in at about eight times ten to the nineteenth—that is, the figure eight followed by nineteen zeroes.

And moon fell on planet, in direct central impact, after having fallen from a height of over a quarter of a million miles under the full pull of gravity and the full thrust of those mighty atomic drives.

The kinetic energy of such a collision can be computed. It can be expressed. It is, however, of such astronomical magnitude as to be completely meaningless to the human mind.

Simply, the two worlds merged and splashed. Droplets, weighing up to millions of tons each, spattered out into space; only to return, in seconds or hours or weeks or months, to add their atrocious contributions to the enormity of the destruction already wrought.

No trace survived of any Strett or of any thing, however small, pertaining to the Stretts.

EPILOGUE

AS had become a daily custom, most of the Ardans were gathered at the natatorium. Hilton and Temple were wrestling in the water—she was trying to duck him and he was hard put to it to keep her from doing it. The platinum-haired twins were—oh, ever so surreptitiously and indetectably!—studying the other girls.

Captain Sawtelle—he had steadfastly refused to accept any higher title—and his wife were teaching two of their tiny grandchildren to swim.

In short, everything was normal.

Beverly Bell Poynter, from the top platform, hit the board as hard as she could hit it; and, perfectly synchronized with it, hurled herself upward. Up and up and up she went. Up to her top ceiling of two hundred ten feet. Then, straightening out into a shapely arrow and without again moving a muscle, she hurtled downward, making two and a half beautifully stately turns and striking the water with a slurping, splashless *chug*! Coming easily to the surface, she shook the water out of her eyes.

Temple, giving up her attempts to near-drown her husband, rolled over and floated quietly beside him.

"You know, this is fun," he said.

"Uh-*huh*," she agreed enthusiastically.

"I'm glad you and Sandy buried the hatchet. Two of the top women who ever lived. Or should I have said sheathed the claws? Or have you, really?"

"Pretty much...I guess." Temple didn't seem altogether sure of the point. "Oh-oh. *Now* what?"

A flitabout had come to ground. Dark Lady, who never delivered a message via thought if she could possibly get away with delivering it in person, was running full tilt across the sand toward them. Her long black hair was streaming out behind her; she was waving a length of teletype tape as though it were a pennon.

"Oh, no. Not *again?*" Temple wailed. "Don't tell us it's Terra again, Dark Lady, please."

"But it is!" Dark Lady cried, excitedly. "And it says 'From Five-Jet Admiral Gordon, Commanding.'"

"Omit flowers, please," Hilton directed. "Boil it down."

"The *Perseus* is in orbit with the whole Advisory Board. They want to hold a top-level summit conference with Director Hilton and Five-Jet Admiral Sawtelle." Dark Lady raised her voice enough to be sure Sawtelle heard the title, and shot him a wicked glance as she announced it. "They hope to conclude all unfinished business on a mutually satisfactory and profitable basis."

"Okay, Lady, thanks. Tell 'em we'll call 'em shortly."

Dark Lady flashed away and Hilton and Temple swam slowly toward a ladder.

"Drat Terra and everything and everybody on it," Temple said, vigorously. "And especially drat His Royal Fatness Five-Jet Admiral Gordon. How much longer will it take, do you think, to pound some sense into their pointed little heads?"

"Oh, we're not doing too bad," Hilton assured his lovely bride. "Two or three more sessions ought to do it."

Everything was normal...

THE END

If you've enjoyed this book, you will not want to miss these terrific titles…

ARMCHAIR SCI-FI & HORROR DOUBLE NOVELS, $12.95 each

D-91   **THE TIME TRAP** by Henry Kuttner
THE LUNAR LICHEN by Hal Clement

D-92   **SARGASSO OF LOST STARSHIPS** by Poul Anderson
THE ICE QUEEN by Don Wilcox

D-93   **THE PRINCE OF SPACE** by Jack Williamson
POWER by Harl Vincent

D-94   **PLANET OF NO RETURN** by Howard Browne
THE ANNIHILATOR COMES by Ed Earl Repp

D-95   **THE SINISTER INVASION** by Edmond Hamilton
OPERATION TERROR by Murray Leinster

D-96   **TRANSIENT** by Ward Moore
THE WORLD-MOVER by George O. Smith

D-97   **FORTY DAYS HAS SEPTEMBER** by Milton Lesser
THE DEVIL'S PLANET by David Wright O'Brien

D-98   **THE CYBERENE** by Rog Phillips
BADGE OF INFAMY by Lester del Rey

D-99   **THE JUSTICE OF MARTIN BRAND** by Raymond A. Palmer
BRING BACK MY BRAIN by Dwight V. Swain

D-100 **WIDE-OPEN PLANET** by L. Sprague de Camp
AND THEN THE TOWN TOOK OFF by Richard Wilson

ARMCHAIR SCIENCE FICTION CLASSICS, $12.95 each

C-31   **THE GOLDEN GUARDSMEN**
by S. J. Byrne

C-32   **ONE AGAINST THE MOON**
by Donald A. Wollheim

C-33   **HIDDEN CITY**
by Chester S. Geier

ARMCHAIR SCI-FI & HORROR GEMS SERIES, $12.95 each

G-9   **SCIENCE FICTION GEMS, Vol. Five**
Clifford D. Simak and others

G-10   **HORROR GEMS, Vol. Five**
E. Hoffmann Price and others

If you've enjoyed this book, you will not want to miss these terrific titles…

ARMCHAIR SCI-FI & HORROR DOUBLE NOVELS, $12.95 each

D-101 **CONQUEST OF THE PLANETS** by John W. Campbell
THE MAN WHO ANNEXED THE MOON by Bob Olsen

D-102 **WEAPON FROM THE STARS** by Rog Phillips
THE EARTH WAR by Mack Reynolds

D-103 **THE ALIEN INTELLIGENCE** by Jack Williamson
INTO THE FOURTH DIMENSION by Ray Cummings

D-104 **THE CRYSTAL PLANETOIDS** by Stanton A. Coblentz
SURVIVORS FROM 9,000 B. C. by Robert Moore Williams

D-105 **THE TIME PROJECTOR** by David H. Keller, M.D. and David Lasser
STRANGE COMPULSION by Philip Jose Farmer

D-106 **WHOM THE GODS WOULD SLAY** by Paul W. Fairman
MEN IN THE WALLS by William Tenn

D-107 **LOCKED WORLDS** by Edmond Hamilton
THE LAND THAT TIME FORGOT by Edgar Rice Burroughs

D-108 **STAY OUT OF SPACE** by Dwight V. Swain
REBELS OF THE RED PLANET by Charles L. Fontenay

D-109 **THE METAMORPHS** by S. J. Byrne
MICROCOSMIC BUCCANEERS by Harl Vincent

D-110 **YOU CAN'T ESCAPE FROM MARS** by E. K. Jarvis
THE MAN WITH FIVE LIVES by David V. Reed

ARMCHAIR SCIENCE FICTION CLASSICS, $12.95 each

C-34 **30 DAY WONDER**
by Richard Wilson

C-35 **G.O.G. 666**
by John Taine

C-36 **RALPH 124C 41+**
by Hugo Gernsback

ARMCHAIR SCI-FI & HORROR GEMS SERIES, $12.95 each

G-11 **SCIENCE FICTION GEMS, Vol. Six**
Edmond Hamilton and others

G-12 **HORROR GEMS, Vol. Six**
H. P. Lovecraft and others

If you've enjoyed this book, you will not want to miss these terrific titles...